# WILCOX PLACE

*"Wilcox Place"* is a memoir and reflects the author's recollections and experiences over time. All names resembling likeness to a person have been changed in good conscience. Other individuals are composites drawn from multiple people and no character should be assumed to represent any real person. Events, dialogue, time, settings have been altered, changed, or dramatized for publication.

Paperback ISBN: 9798994197400

First edition, January 2026.

# Dedication:

This book was written as a love story at heart. Dedicated to all those who dream of an unforgettable love, a love that can be turned into a story.

It is not just a love story between two people, but a love story between me and the city of Los Angeles. I dedicate the following pages to the community and those affected by the Palisades and Eaton fires. My heart goes out to all that was lost. I love Los Angeles with all my heart and while my time spent in the city was not perfect, I loved the life I experienced in the city of angels. The great state of California gets a bad reputation, as does my home state of Florida. What I have come to understand from my time in the state is we are more alike than we are different.

To the powerful women in my life who have guided me to where I needed to be today. My Aunts, my cousins, my junior year English teacher, my sister, and my mother who without a doubt has been the driving force behind my life, this was all for you.

And to my queer community in Orlando and those affected by the Pulse tragedy, love is love is love is love is love is love is love is love is love is love is love is love. This was for you. May the memory of the 49+1 and those lost after never fade.

And lastly, to my dear friends in Los Angeles, the three girls I spent my last days as an Angeleno with - there are not enough words to dedicate my adoration for you all. I doubt my mental state would have survived if it were not for you three. Thank you is not enough.

This is dedicated to those who try

# WILCOX PLACE

## G.P. Anthony

gpanthony.substack.com

## *January 2025*

The night that I left, the city was on fire, and so was the life we had built. By the end of the weekend all that remained were ashes, burnt to the ground like those houses in the Palisades or Altadena. Only the bare bones of structures remained.

I've tried desperately to cling to the memories from the past year with Gartner. His vibrant blue eyes flash in my mind, and I begin to weep for the life I once had. Since I began my drive from the city two nights ago, I've been unable to calm my mind and stifle the tears within me.

The Santa Ana winds were still howling as I crossed over the harrowing mountains into Palm Springs via Interstate 10.

I was alone, aside from my two cats, my dog, and less boxes of clothes and belongings than I originally came with on the tenured journey when Gartner had moved me across the country. Florida is flat, in fact, the flattest state in the continental United States. I had yet to get used to driving through mountainous terrain. My hands gripped the wheel tightly, my knuckles turning white.

The city lights twinkle below as dust ripples across my windshield, the slope evening out at a mild decline as it snakes through the valley in my final descent into Coachella Valley. A tumbleweed the size of my XL SUV hood smashes into the vehicle so ferociously from the winds that it embeds itself in the grill of the rental car. I left it there as I drove across the United States, from desert to grasslands to swamp.

Once I crossed over the state line to Arizona, I pulled over at the nearest gas station and park the car, crawling into the back seat with my dog Ghost and the kitties. I put the Sex and the City movie on my iPad and tried to fall asleep.

When I arrive in Texas, I aim to make it as far as I can through the state. I needed to sleep in a proper bed tonight. I was able to book a hotel through the points I saved up from the summer I went to Europe and booked all the accommodation under my account. I had, however, forgotten to check if it was a pet friendly hotel. I was in no position to pay a pet fee regardless. My bank account had $300 in it. I had taken two weeks off from work - Christmas, New Years, and Gartner's birthday - all before he sent me on a one-way trip back to Florida.

I wasn't just fleeing the life I had grown with Gartner in Los Angeles or a natural disaster. The entire central and southeastern United States was facing an unprecedented freeze.

The cold was piercing, and I had to sneak my animals in through a side door and up five flights of stairs at three in the morning. After sleeping in my rental, the night before I hardly had an hour of REM sleep under my belt.

## One Year Prior

I was ready to leave, I wanted out. Out of the state of Florida, out of the city of Orlando, out of my nonexistent life. I wanted adventure. I was born an adrenaline junkie, always left wanting more. I had to see it. I understood Ethel Cain when she said, "You fell in love with America when you were twelve years old, and when you were seventeen you knew you had to see it all," and I sure tried. It wasn't intentional, no preconceived notion or malicious intent. It was honest and innocent, my yearning, my drive, my intensity.

After a yearlong tumultuous job market, I hoped for change. I began to doubt myself, there had to be more to life than what I currently had. I longed for change. The air in California was fresh and the sun was reviving. I knew I could make it if I tried.

To be frank, I cannot recall how I managed to buy the original flight myself. I remember the ticket being cheap, and my friend Bondi offering up her spare room for me to crash in for a week escape from Florida. I had recently visited her in October, and had a visceral reaction to leaving the city, sobbing awkwardly in the stranger's car on the ride to LAX. In the handful of times, I had visited Los Angeles I never thought about living there. Then one day, suddenly, it became my deepest desire, like my soul had sensed something within the city I could not pick up naturally myself. After attending Coachella in 2023, something had changed within me. I felt a magnetic pull to the west coast. Long gone were the days of gold mining, but perhaps the gold had transformed California into something new. Maybe the city of Los Angeles had become gold itself.

After LA has pissed you off, after you've scratched the surface, you strike the realities of its core that defines a city and makes it a home.

I scratched the surface, and then I dove, crashing into the water and creating a notable splash in my wake. I sought out the hard-kept secrets of the city with some help from Bondi and Princess, who had lived in Los Angeles for a handful of years.

***

I swiped right on Gartner a week before I flew out to the city to visit Bondi, my friend Kash tagged along the trip with me. Kash was an easy travel partner. He was nonchalant and care-free. Our friendship had been forged through the Twitter-sphere, where a bulk of my friendships blossomed. I admired our friendship for many reasons, but mainly our ability to recognize that we both enjoyed solo activities during group vacations. I was able to discretely split off from Kash and Bondi on my own separate outing.

Gartner would tell those who asked that I was adamantly pursuing a first date together while I was visiting. I wanted to see the city from a local's point of view. I was excited when he initially asked me out on a date. What could he show me that I had not seen before? I craved the excitement, the rush and thrill of something different. I was ready for the western moonlight to kiss my skin.

Gartner picked me up outside of Pink's apartment, another friend from the Twitter-verse who moved from south Florida to LA that I'd frequently visit. I remember his outfit entirely. Dressed in dark pants that sagged a bit, black leather boots, and a black shirt with a pullover jacket.

My first thought of Gartner was: "I'm not gonna like this guy." He was not what I would consider my type. His face was beautiful, his eyebrows so perfectly shaped he was often asked if he manicured them himself. I went on the date anyway by chance. Maybe I would change my mind. Maybe I will have fun, I told myself.

I craved a new experience. I was in search of a feeling that resembled comfortability in a familiar space. I was nervous but tried to play it off, over boosting my self-confidence to get through my initial awkwardness. I scanned the inside of his vehicle from my side across to the driver's side, and my second observation of Gartner was the cleanliness of his vehicle. After spending time riding in Bondi and Pink's notoriously messy cars, I was impressed enough by the upkeep and cleanliness inside his vehicle.

I talked while Gartner listened intently as we drove to his apartment on Wilcox Place. A few months later, Gartner would confess that I stood out to him because of how much I talked, because I kept a conversation flowing between us. We parked the car in his designated spot and walked north up the few blocks to the Billiards spot he had told me about in one of our prior conversations.

The Billiards bar is located upstairs above a shopping plaza, with plenty of tables to line the room. The windows in the main pool room stretch from floor to ceiling, exposing the outside street and cars that rumble past on Cahuenga Boulevard.

"I like to come here and pretend this is what New York would look like, with how close the building is to the road and how you can overlook everything," Gartner said thoughtfully as we stared out over the view.

"I guess this resembles New York. The last time I was there was ten years ago, but I have a wedding to attend there in May. I'm excited to finally visit as a legal adult," I said.
"I would love to go with you one day," was his response.

After a few beers and rounds of billiards, Gartner escorted me to Mama Shelter, a rooftop bar, where we continued the date. I later read in the news that it closed a month or so after we had broken up. It felt symbolic of the end of us in a way that made me feel sick to my stomach. The universe can be cruel.

At least two hours into the date, I knew I liked Gartner. He was nerdy and a little awkward, but had these stunning blue eyes, and a kindness that could not be matched. He possessed a genuineness that was lost to many. He was extremely independent, relying on himself to live in Los Angeles with no roommates - one of the qualities he possessed that I truly admired. He was able to support himself as a successful hairdresser, he established himself with no socials at a barbershop at the crosshairs Fairfax and Melrose.

The rooftop we went to overlooks Hollywood and gives a partial view of downtown Los Angeles in the distance, beyond the skyscrapers of Mid-City.

Large lounge beds were sprawled across the terrace as a shoddy-DJ attempted to corral a dancefloor in the far right corner. In hindsight, I can understand why it closed.

We shared another drink between us and an intimate moment on one of the couches. For once I was tolerating a higher consumption of alcohol, and I didn't mind. We decided to let ourselves into one of the bathrooms and began to kiss feverishly. We ran our hands over each other's bodies, exploring each other in a more intimate way than conversation allows for. I slipped my hand under his waist belt and found that he wasn't wearing underwear, which I found hot. I felt my pulse quicken. He was becoming intensely attractive to me with each moment we touched. His skin was soft, he wore a slight dad bod, with faint abs showing underneath a layer of healthy fat. His tattoos complimented him nicely, too. I was hooked.

This felt new for me, but refreshing. I was quickly hurling towards a fiery love. I could tell he felt the same, his eyes intensely focused on my own when he spoke.

"I almost gave up on dating, who knew the man I needed to date was in Florida?" he stared into my eyes passionately before he sealed his statement with a kiss.

Once we finished our third round of drinks at Mama Shelter, we returned to the apartment on Wilcox Place and fell asleep in his bed. I had no intention to stay over but it was easy for me to feel comfortable enough to fall asleep soundly. His apartment was comfy, hearty-green plants draped across his open windows as an ornamental string of white lights weaved around them and the curtain rod holding them up. Gartner began burning a piece of Palo Santo, cleansing the room while its pungent aroma allowed my mind to feel at peace.

In the morning my eyes fluttered open without sleepy hesitation. It was the first time I had felt well-rested in months.

Next to me Gartner was awake already, his phone propped up in his hand as he scrolled morning news headlines. His cat, Jude, was opposite of us sprawled across the window ledge. The large windows stretched across the entirety of the apartment, letting natural light flood the wooden floors and tan walls.

"You think we could get married?" I said with extreme comfortability, then registering in my sleep-fogged mind how insane that sounded. We had just met last night. But deep down, I knew I meant it. Gartner not only felt exhilarating to be around, but he calmed me all the same. I had just slept soundly and peacefully for the first time in months. I felt like he must have been good for me.

"You're crazy and I like that - we can fall in love first," Gartner said to me with such conviction that matched my own. Two halves of crazy finding each other. Eventually we pushed ourselves out of bed, but only after lazily cuddling with each other to avoid the wet, cold morning that waited for us outside.

"Last night felt like a dream," Gartner said sweetly, holding my eye contact in the close quarters of his apartment. "Your kisses felt warm, and you were so peaceful while you slept. I stayed up for a bit after you fell asleep to clean up. That's why I let you have the bed to yourself."

The thought of him watching over me while I slept brought a shy smile to my face. I slept peacefully because I subconsciously knew I was protected. I could make him fall in love with me, somehow, I just knew - we were meant to be.

Gartner drove me back to Bondi's apartment, driving Wilcox Avenue up north till he cut east on Franklin, towards Silver Lake.

The air was crisp. The dead of winter had struck the desert. It felt dry and fresh outside, less harmful than in the damning summertime. We turned onto Russell Avenue where Gartner put his car into park outside of Bondi's apartment. We shared a brief, soft kiss. It was strange, already feeling that leaving him was so hard to do. Maybe it was the change in scenery, I was far away from my life in Florida and somehow, I felt at home with Gartner here in Los Angeles at the moment.

On the horizon were days of exploration for us to conquer together as one. The first was the distance while we called opposite sides of the country home.

"When do you fly home to Florida?" he asked once I pulled away from his embrace.

"I leave Monday morning."

"Man, that is so soon, can I see you tonight? I have a client scheduled this evening, but I can meet after."

"I'm going out tonight with some friends after dinner, but maybe we can meet there and then go to another club together?" I suggested.

"That sounds great man," he replied, beaming.

Later in the evening, Kash and I visited our friend Rafo for dinner, who insisted on cooking for us; he insisted on preparing a dish that included a special ant sourced from Mexico. After we favored our pallets, we headed out to an afterparty in the warehouse sector of the city. It was located downtown just on the outskirts of the tall brick and metal skyscrapers.

The venue was a beautiful industrial warehouse, with its bare bones and concrete walls supporting the now turned pop-up venue for Los Angeles' constantly changing facets and exchanges. The first room after the entrance door houses a small art shop, and behind that lies a separate small room with a DJ booth against a wall. Two small, single stall bathrooms sit tucked away opposite of two bar stands. That night the room was full of partygoers dressed in all black, decked out in leather, chains, and chunky boots. I love the culture and performance of dance music. The dry cold of the night penetrated the concrete and steel structure of the club, while cooling the warming bodies on the dancefloor. The room was densely packed, and yet the flow of movement was effortless. The collective group of partygoers appeared as though they had achieved a tranquil consciousness amongst each other, a powerful force unable to be seen.

Rafo, Kash, and I blended seamlessly into the crowd, our color palette matched the aesthetic of the others in the room, for we knew how to dress for the occasion. We bumped into a friend of Rafo's and began dancing with each other in the back right of the room.

Once Gartner arrived outside of the venue, I realized that I did not want to leave. The funky beats made the dancing infectious. The environment was sustaining a higher frequency than my daily life, and I wanted to inject it straight into my blood stream. I dipped outside the venue to meet Gartner, hoping I could convince him to come dance with me.

Outside the sky was gray and overcast, with the city lights shining through the misty air, and the skyscrapers reaching high into the gloomy clouds that shrouded the city. I spotted Gartner across the street at the end of the block. He was leaning against his car, scrolling on his cellphone. He looked up and caught my eye, smirking. I was overcome with feeling, an unexpected feeling for this man I had just made the day before. I ran in his direction with all my might, pleased to see him brace himself for impact. Gartner caught my embrace, hoisting me up in the air. He must have felt it, too. I kicked my legs up and kissed him on the lips without a second thought. He set me back down on the ground gently. He was stronger than I would have thought.

It was easy to convince Gartner to join me inside the warehouse. It seemed he, too, was happy just being together. I pulled him inside by the hand, and we quickly became intertwined with each other, dancing with the flow of partygoers around us. We remained at the warehouse for an hour. Bumps were passed around our friend group across the dance floor, heightening the adrenaline already coursing through my veins.

"Will you be my Valentine next month?" he asked me, in between moments of saliva swapping, "I will buy your flight back."

I felt my heart skip several beats, the butterflies swarming the inside of my stomach. Was it the drugs? Or was it the mere fact that this incredible man was picking me, and wanting me to choose him in return? I didn't care.

I was transported to a time where my innocence had yet to wane, and love was the oxygen that could cure the asphyxiation in my lungs. Maybe I would get what I wanted in the end. I thought maybe this was exactly the type of love I deserve.

We left Rafo at the warehouse as Kash, Gartner, and I bar hopped to the next stop on our roster, stopping to pick up Bondi and Pink along the way. We headed to Jumbo's Clown Room; a burlesque styled bar located in Hollywood.

Jumbos is small enough to be classified as a spacious studio apartment in New York City. One small stage tucked into the corner with roughly twenty seats wrapped around it. It has mirrored floors and ceilings, with a single pole in the middle of the stage.

My friends and I love strip clubs. The dancers always love us because they can show off and show out once they have recognized that we are not diabolical creep-azoids, like the men who go there to harass them.

Pleaser-branded heels clacked and banged against the mirrored dancefloor as the dancers twist and glide around the dancefloor, using the pole to their advantage. Some of the dancers could even flip their bodies upward, using inertia to smack themselves back down into a split on the ground floor.

Once the night started to inch closer to daylight, Gartner drove us home to Bondi's apartment on Russell Avenue. Gartner worked the following morning, and I would be on a flight back to Orlando. He lent me his black O'Neil hoodie to take with me back to Florida until I see him again.

The next morning, I was the first to wake out of the four inside Bondi's apartment. I stirred Kash and Bondi awake. We strolled through Los Feliz while Bondi cosplayed as a tour guide around the neighborhood she's lived in for eight years. We had breakfast at the Mustard Seed cafe and afterwards stopped into a local bookstore, continuing our walking tour around the area. Bondi pointed out the Vista theater at the crosshairs of Sunset and Hollywood Boulevard, a historic theater recognized as a symbol of the Los Feliz neighborhood.

We walked in a loop around the community back towards her apartment.

After we got back to Bondi's she quickly changed her outfit and left for her work shift. Kash and I finished packing up our belongings into suitcases. Afterwards, Bondi's boyfriend, Chad, drove us a few blocks south to El Condor where Bondi was bartending for the evening.

Bondi crafted me a beverage based with mezcal and Kash and I ordered chips and salsa. After the hour is up Kash and I hail our Uber. As Bondi and I hugged goodbye, I began to cry. I let myself out quickly, for I did not want Bondi to see me upset. I cried silently in the Uber next to Kash, thankful he was content with riding in silence for once.

Once I returned to Orlando, Gartner and I developed a routine, FaceTiming each other nightly. We talked about mundane subjects that held no significance while lazily watching one of our favorite shows, Dragula, together. In the following mornings when I roused myself from sleep, I'd discover a good morning text from him and swoon. This was something special. We continued our nightly ritual until I flew back to Los Angeles later in February.

As we continued this familial rhythm, my feelings only intensified with each night I laid my head to rest. One morning I woke up to find that Gartner had drawn a picture of me, sleeping peacefully, with my head on my pillow. The drawing was comparable to a middle-school passion project, and yet my heart fluttered. A gleaming sense of pride was displayed across Gartner's face as he presented the drawing to me.

I found myself daydreaming of a life I previously thought unattainable, and for once it seemed possible. A glimmer of hope was on the horizon. I had been slipping away from myself the past year, and I needed a change. I expected Gartner to ignore me, to have blocked my number while I flew the five-hour flight home, but it had been the opposite. I wasn't shocked, I was besotted.

He confided in me about his relationship with his family, as it had been a few years since he had spoken to them.

His relationship with his family was strained beyond conceivable repair. He told me he wanted to change his name, and that he had gone through the name-change process once before and was now ready to complete the process. I felt honored that he felt so comfortable telling me all of this and letting me in.

Every night I fell asleep, he stayed on FaceTime with me over a thousand miles away. He adored me just as much as I did him. The fire between us began to burn bright as we continued to fall rapidly in love with one another. In those weeks after I returned home I kept him as a secret to myself, only choosing to gush about him to Bondi, Pink or Kash. I was too scared to jinx myself if I mentioned him to my friends or family in Florida. For the first time in a long time, I felt myself fearing the thought of losing someone to heartbreak.

The first night we facetimed Gartner said to me: "I never thought you would call me, I thought for sure you were going to ghost me after you landed back in Orlando. You would never have to come back to LA if you did not want to" And I thought it was funny, because I was worried that I would surely be the one ghosted.

I knew we both felt each other's intensity when one night Gartner told me over FaceTime about the poem his mother read him before bed when he was a child:
"I love you deeper than the Ocean,
Higher than the Sky
Bigger than the Universe,
And so much more"

I let the poem fill my heart with adoration. There was vulnerability in the recital from him. I knew he loved me. We were meant for each other.
"And so much more," I said back, fully meaning it.

## Down on Santa Monica

I was due back in Southern California for Rissa's bachelorette party, another twitter-sphere friend turned life-long soul sister. The bachelorette party would take place a week after Valentine's Day, and because I was still fun-employed, Gartner offered to purchase my flight back to Los Angeles. An extremely generous offer, and one I couldn't afford to turn down. Plus, I was giddy with the thought of seeing him again. After deplaning I found my way to the ground floor of the airport to get picked up. I found Gartner waiting for me with a dozen long stemmed roses. His smile was infectious as I saw it reflected through his window. I felt my mood lift and my heart flutter. I breathed in the beautiful Southern California day. It was a cloudless day, and I let the western sunshine warm my skin through the sharp winter air.

Bondi met us at Gartner's apartment on Wilcox Place. From there we left to meet Pink at Hugo's Diner in West Hollywood. The diner offered a variety of dairy-free alternatives that I could rarely self-indulge in back home, so I enjoyed my meal thoroughly. After I had stuffed my face with a dairy free waffle, we walked around West Hollywood until Bondi needed to leave to ready herself for work. Pink, Gartner, and I agreed to meet at Bondi's bar in Silverlake later that night, so I went back to the apartment on Wilcox to take a nap with Gartner.

I was exhausted from the morning and was prepared to nap. When I typically fall asleep during a nap, I knock out. My nap turns into an intermittent REM cycle comparable to a full six hours of sleep. It has been this way since I was a kid. I would go down for a nap and be out for the remainder of the day.

My mom eventually realized as I got older that a nap for me in the day meant I would remain asleep until the following morning.

I fell asleep in Gartner's arms around three in the afternoon. When I woke again it was after nine pm, the dark of night greeting me as my eyes adjusted from slumber. I remained in bed with the a-typical nausea that unfortunately greeted me whenever I first woke up, morning or not. Around ten, I was able to push myself out of Gartner's bed and get dressed for the night out. I grabbed one of Gartner's jackets from his closet. Denim gray with a tear in the shoulder. I liked it so I pulled it on over me. It was a chilly night in LA, but not terrible.

Gartner came up behind me; we examined each other in the mirror. We looked good together. I am not tall. My height is five ft seven, and Gartner is an inch or so taller than me. He has blonde hair, blue eyes, and an infectious smile. He was devilishly handsome, a California boy with sandy-blonde hair that would fall perfectly after a dip in the ocean. His tattoos compliment every facet of his personality: a delicately faint rose running down the side of his neck, an anime character on his forearm and bicep, an owl to match his wisdom, and a wolf. Sometimes I fantasized about licking the rose on his neck - indulging in the taste of his salty skin on my tongue. His look was complete with diamond stud piercings in both ears.

His eyebrows are perfectly fine threaded. A natural feature that helps to shape and frame his face. Gartner is gorgeous, truly a pretty man.

Then I stared at myself more intently, taking note of my own appearance. Brown unkept hair that usually I style with a hat or bandana if I don't take the time to shape it with putty. Hazel eyes that are striking in the winter, more of an icy green than any other color. I unfortunately must maintain my bushy eyebrows, but I do have a slit in my right eyebrow that follows a diagonal line that meets my nose ring and follows the two piercings in my left ear. My button nose forms the center of focus of my face.

Hidden vaguely underneath my beard at the left corner of my face is a small mole, and around my neck hangs two necklaces- a gold chain with a gold Elephant charm and a black twine choker with a Labradorite pendant hanging delicately from the sturdy thread.

In a way, we were complete opposites of each other. Gartner was raised by the crashing waves and coastal cliffsides of Northern California along the Pacific Ocean. Whereas I was raised by the rivers and swampy lakes that met the Atlantic and Gulf of Mexico. And yet even with our polar opposite upbringings, we found each other. It was as if magnetics drew us together from our respective homes and laid out the plan for us both to meet, both oceans working in tandem with one another to seal our fate. Our opposing aesthetics meshed together like a river meeting an ocean.

Bondi was working at Shim Sham, a local bar bordering Silverlake and Korea town. In the distance the skyscrapers of downtown reached up towards the stars. A fog creeped into the night over the city, blanketing itself over the downtown skyline. So long to the beautiful day and hello to the hazy night.

Once inside we found Pinky, along with friends from my high school graduating class, Princess, Ali, and Joseph; all of whom had moved to LA within a few years of each other. Bondi was the first to make the move.

I found Bondi behind the bar, in her typical workspace. When she noticed Gartner and I among the crowded bar her face beamed. She quickly ran around to where we stood, slamming into my body first with a warm embrace.

"Do you want a Mezcal drink?" she asked after she released us from the dual embrace, she pulled Gartner into. "Yeah, why not!" I responded.

I was born with Hereditary sphero-cytosis, a blood disorder that has a direct correlation to my body's tolerance of altering substances. Basically, I can hardly endure any alcohol. A single drink is enough to buzz me up. Some would say I am a cheap date. Due to my alcohol intolerance and the negative effect, it has on my body, I seldom find myself drinking to excess. I learned over time what I can manage and which type of alcohol I can ingest, along with which ones make me more nauseous than others. Oddly enough, Mezcal is tolerable.

After a few inhibiting drinks and copious amounts of photobooth photos, Gartner and I execute an Irish goodbye around one in the morning. My eyes were heavy and I couldn't continue gabbing with patrons around the bar. I was far too tired to give a proper goodbye to Bondi or our other friends spread out around Shim Sham. The party was beginning to stale, with the sunrise only a few hours away. The night had passed and I was ready to go.

When we arrived back at the apartment on Wilcox Place, Gartner asked me to sleep naked. Initially a simple request, but I eventually grew to understand its complexity.

His response confirmed my suspicions:

"I dislike it when my boyfriends sleep with underwear on. Not when they're in the same bed as me."

I fell asleep before I was able to fully think it through.

When I awoke the following morning, I glanced through the open window to find the sun shrouded behind dull fog. I guess the city didn't want to greet me with gorgeous weather, instead deciding I would suffer beneath clouds of gray.

Gartner remained sleeping peacefully beside me, facing away in the opposite direction. We must have drifted apart while we slept during the night. I assumed it had been too hot, and I subconsciously pushed him away from me.

Gartner continued to sleep for a half hour longer. I scrolled through Twitter and Instagram. I texted my mom good morning, catching up with the East Coast that is three hours ahead, teeming with life that continues to transpire every second.

"Do you want some breakfast? I can make it for you," Gartner said once he was awake, rubbing the sleep out of his eyes.

"Potatoes, for sure," I replied.

Gartner got out of bed, pulling on a pair of gray sweatpants from his dresser before heading to the kitchen area.

He took out a pack of Trader Joe's potato medley and heated up a skillet on the stove.

"Have any of your previous boyfriends ever made you breakfast in bed before?" he asked me over his shoulder.

I had to think about it before I responded, "no, actually."

I continued, "no one ever has, but I'm usually the cook myself, you know."

There was a pause in the conversation. Then: "Has anyone ever bought you anything like I have?" He followed up.

"What do you mean?" I asked back, thinking it was a generally odd question to ask, but Gartner always seemed to ask odd questions. I found Gartner to be a tad quirkier than me, which is saying something. I passed no judgement, as we've all got our quirks, and a lot can be overlooked. People are not all they are summed up to be, and I believed we could actively remove some of the facets that reflect poor nature. I found it silly to let them negatively affect me. Plus, I tended to find everything he said charming or endearing.

"Has anyone ever bought you a flight somewhere? Or bought you roses as they picked you up from the airport? Or made you breakfast in bed?" he asked knowingly, firing off one question after the next.

And for the first time in my life, I was forced to reflect on my past relationships. Specifically, how none of this had happened before. I had received the occasional flowers, but never roses, and certainly not at the airport as I was picked up. I did have one flight bought for me, years ago when an ex had bought me a flight to Montreal while he was actively traveling for his job.

"I've had flowers bought for me before, and one flight to Canada, but that was a long time ago" I told him.
"I am a great boyfriend, you won't find one like me again," he said afterwards.

Maybe this was when I should have started catching onto the signs of a disastrous breakup. Because in a sane and healthy reality, that's not a normal thing to say to a romantic partner.

*\*\**

Gartner's charismatic charm caused me to fall in love easily. I told him I loved him almost instantaneously, the words falling off my tongue and into the world, unable to take them back. My words of affirmation penetrated Gartner's reserves deep within him, to which he would hold onto. He would take the love I so freely gave him and use it for his benefit.

The love I felt grew rapidly despite the subtle red flags he displayed. My vulnerability was played into by Gartner's intense desire to fuel his narcissistic tendencies he carried around with him. And I was oblivious, for an empathic intuitive, I was blind to his true personality. And I wonder why that was? Had I longed to be loved for so long that I was sub-consciously ignoring the signs?

Months later would I understand that when Gartner found me, it was like I had been plucked from the universe for his enjoyment - as if it was a karmic debt I owed back. I was in a narcissistic ideal headspace, ignorant and unknowing because he told me he loved me and I believed it.

The intensity in which Gartner expressed his love caused me to re-evaluate what I originally considered love to be. In the beginning it was flowers. He always gave me roses because they were my favorite other than Hyacinths, which is a hard flower to find in bloom aside from in winter.

Gartner would call me daily, and when I was back in Florida we would FaceTime until I promptly fell asleep. Then there were other gifts. Gartner would buy me my favorite dairy-free chocolates. He always showed that he paid deep attention to me.

He expressed to me what I needed at the moment - and today, I am not so sure if that was intentional or not. When your "ideal love" begins to unravel before your eyes, you start to think everything ever said was a lie.

*** 

The time we spent together was purity in its rarest form, starting with good faith and honest intentions. Yet everything began to rot somewhere in the remainder of the year we were together.

Some nights we spent so entangled with one another, we would forget the outside world beyond the walls of Wilcox. Gartner would ask his Alexa to "play romantic slow songs," and then he'd pull me in close on the vintage hardwood floors of his apartment. There he danced with me slowly, guiding me smoothly around his living room.

After his shift at work one day, Gartner picked me up and drove us to Venice Beach. On the way to the beach as we drove west on Wilshire Boulevard, our vehicle came to a four way stop.

As Gartner approached the stop, we noticed a stopped car in the lane to our left, and a man on a bike circling it. The man on the bike was exchanging heated words with the man in the vehicle. As Gartner pressed the brakes into a complete stop the man on the bicycle whipped around the car to our left and swung towards our vehicle, purposefully knocking his wheel into the edge of Gartner's car.

The man on the bike suddenly flung himself purposefully over the hood of Gartner's Camry. He rolled onto the street and began to thrash around on the ground, acting out in fake pain. The man in the car next to us informed us that the man has been scamming people in the area and yelled at the man to get up and get out of there. Gartner and I locked eyes, and I could tell he was just as stressed as I was within the moment.

Around us people continued walking around the neighborhood, glancing in the direction of the scam artist causing a commotion in the street. In a quick maneuver Gartner steered the car around the man, continuing our drive towards Santa Monica. I glanced in the rearview mirror as we pulled away, watching as the man on the bike pushed himself off the floor and proceeded to dust himself off before climbing back onto his bike to continue his ruse.

Once we arrived at the beach, Gartner handed me a pair of roller skates from the trunk of his car and grabbed his longboard. We spent the afternoon cruising around Santa Monica, the Pier, and Muscle beach.

It was a childlike bucket list item completed for me: a beach date in Santa Monica. My heart was full. In all my years, I would have never guessed this would have been my life at that moment. Despite the chaotic start to the day, things felt perfect with Gartner. Once again, I thought to myself that I deserved this kind of love. The sun eventually started to make its descent on our near-perfect day together. The coastal breeze started to pick up, prompting me to throw on a hoodie.

My perception of that day has now been transformed in my head, not exactly how it was in that moment. Rolling around the concrete soiled with sand blowing onto the pathway, Gartner pretended to crash into me, only to grab me and kiss me, pulling me into him, holding me up so I could avoid slipping and falling in his skates. After my calves had grown too tired to continue, I sat on the back of his car, watching him glide through the parking lot.

Before sunset, Gartner drove us through Venice towards Marina Del Rey, in search of the local Sea Lion that crowd the docks surrounding Burton W. Chace Park. The marina housed a plethora of boats, where dotted among the docks, close to one hundred sea lions danced about the marina.

Hordes of sea lions as far as we could see: some big, some small, some pups, some sleeping, some sunbathing, some antagonizing others that approached their buoy they struck their claim to. It was like the British invading the Caribbean, fully staking claim to the island. The park was calm and peaceful, at least up until a Los Angeles Police Department helicopter sputtered over the water, flying past us overhead. It circled around and back, searchlight primed to scan the streets as it glided over from above. The sun was setting and the sea lions had begun to nest themselves into sleepy, comfortable positions. It was time to go home and ride out the high from our day together.

On the drive back from Marina Del Rey I asked Gartner, "Who would you say was your first love?"

He answered almost immediately. "A dude named Evan, he was the first boyfriend I ever had. I was at the mall with my girlfriend at the time and he was at the mall with his then-girlfriend. I locked eyes with him, and something spoke from deep within me, saying I had to be with him. I was suddenly convinced he had to be my boyfriend. I ended up getting us both to break up with our girlfriends so we could date each other, but then I became obsessed with him. He was a beautiful surfer boy," he finished, but not before I caught a sense of arrogance from his tone.

I remained quiet, taking in all the information he had just given me.

"You know, I am not gay" he said after a moment of silence. "What do you mean?"

"I am demisexual" he shrugged and continued, "I can date anyone, but I always felt like I had to date guys after I first dated Evan"

My first thought was that this was a lot to unpack, and that I could deal with it later. Part of me thought he expected me to give a negative reaction of some sort. I wondered why he would want something like that but also hoped he would know me well enough to understand I don't care what his sexuality is defined as, nor his identification. If he loved me then none of it made any difference. I decided to let it go.

***

The following morning Gartner and I woke up early to make the drive East to Palm Springs. It was time for the bachelorette party I was meant to come to LA for in the first place. Rissa and the rest of her bachelorette party had arrived the night before. Gartner and I agreed to meet them in downtown Palm Springs at a local brunch spot.

After brunch we toured the Trixie Motel, an extremely hyped-up spot that I was initially excited to see, until we all realized that while aesthetically cute, it was a small venue, not offering much other than a gift shop with merchandise that is priced exclusively too high in my opinion.

Gartner left shortly after, dropping me off at the timeshare where the rest of the bachelorette party was staying.

Once Gartner was gone and I found myself wondering if I would feel out of place amongst the others in attendance - at least other than Rissa, her sister, and their few childhood friends I had met once before.

I also wondered if I would feel the same when it came time for the wedding in a few months. My wedding experiences as of late had been hit or miss, often feeling overwhelmed and out of place within the crowd. After years of dealing with massive packs of people, I started to question if my comfortability with them had run its course.

I found that my imagination ran rampant with doubt. Rissa and her friends were happy to have me and yet my anxiety heightened, decentering my focus.

After a few hours laying leisurely around the pool, we all returned to our rooms and readied ourselves for the drag show at Toucans bar. Toucans was a well-known gay bar within Palm Springs; I had been once before with another bachelorette party I attended a few years prior.

I find comfort in knowing it's a west coast tradition to attend a Toucans drag show if you're heading to Palm Springs for a Bachelorette party. I took a moment to acknowledge the realization that I had made the life I always wanted into a reality, content with my current life taking place in California. Then another thought came to me: how I could feel so loved and seen while simultaneously feeling sad. It was strange, finding this new love with Gartner and spending what was meant to be an incredible weekend celebrating a close friend who was soon-to-be married. And yet there I was, stuck in a rut of melancholy. Maybe this is how it would always be for me, balancing an immense sadness with feelings of love and gratitude. I think two things can be true at once.

While we were at Toucans, I realized how good I was at faking it when one of the performers pulled me on stage to participate in the show. I put aside my conflicting thoughts and fed into the lap dance I was receiving.

I thought to myself that I should focus on giving Rissa a positive memory; to know I love her and care for her. I may not always be able to provide my absolute best self, but I'll make sure you know that doesn't mean I love you any less.

Later that night after everyone had gone to bed, I stayed up on my own in the rental living room, staring out at the desert as the night shone on. Even in the silvery light of the moon the desert's natural beauty was radiant, allowing me to make out the silhouettes of palm trees and mountains.

I'd always liked the moments when I can breathe my own air and hear my thoughts fully. This is what nature does to a person. I realized I have felt like this my entire life - I vividly remember times during the sixth grade when I was never allowed by any group to join their table at lunch, even after asking if I could sit. I'd end up finding my own place on the rough concrete. I felt the same sadness then that I felt now in the desert, and I had no reason to feel that way.

It was well into the early morning hours before my brain gave in to rest long enough for me to fall asleep. I was awoken a few short hours later by the group of girls as they began packing up the remaining of their belongings. The bach weekend was already over, and it was time to head home.

Rissa dropped me off at the Metrolink station in Covina. While seated on the train to Union Station, I once again felt the pride in knowing I had cultivated the life on the West Coast that I always dreamed of.

Once I got back to the city, the marine layer had cleared, and the sun was shining over downtown Los Angeles and the Hollywood Hills.

Pink was the one to pick me up this time, outside of Union Station where we battled mid-day traffic as she drove me back to Gartner's apartment.

I was finally back in apartment three at Wilcox Place. I let myself into the apartment with my own personal key - Gartner had made me one before the trip. It seemed like everything was happening quickly but heading in a direction we were both happy with. He would be home from work in a few hours. In the meantime, I climbed into his bed and put Sex and the City on the television. I was overly tired from the lack of sleep I'd had the night before from all my overthinking.

I was able to fall asleep quickly in Gartner's bed. The last thought I had before drifting off was wondering how I could feel so serene in Gartner's space. When I opened my eyes hours later, I found Gartner preparing dinner in the kitchen. Displayed on the coffee table in front of the bed before me was a fresh flower bouquet. I assumed Gartner had picked them up on his way home from work.

I studied him from the bed, careful not to make any sudden movements or noise. He was shirtless, his arm muscles contracting as he moved a pan on the stove. I was enjoying watching this domestic routine. Even from a distance I could tell his skin was smooth and soft, inviting me to pull myself into him and breathe in his scent. He greeted me sweetly, and with a plate of food. I was overcome with emotion, and grateful for the little things he did for me.

After dinner I fell asleep again, still exhausted from the past week. We were sound asleep when we were woken up by loud thuds from the upstairs neighbor. Groggy and still fighting against unconsciousness, the thuds remained consistent. It sounded like there was a loud crash, with items clattering against the hardwood floors above us.

"Well, that is annoying" I said, finally giving up on falling back asleep.

"It's been going on for an hour," Gartner replied, clearly annoyed.

"And it just woke me up? I must be a heavy sleeper..." I said, glancing at the clock on the stove that read five in the morning.

The loud crashing continued for another twenty minutes. Sleep seemed impossible at this point. Gartner decided to go upstairs and ask them to stop making so much noise this early in the morning. Through the thin walls of the apartment, I could hear muffled voices exchanging words.

Upon returning to the apartment, Gartner informed me that they were drunk and thrashing all around the place.
"I will not be able to fall back asleep," I said.

"Me neither," Gartner replied, "Should we do something instead?"
"Give me an option," I suggested.

"Should we go to Six Flags? I know it's the last park you need to check off your box around here" he offered, a small smile on his face.

The spontaneous inclination to take me to the last park I had yet to visit caused me to fall deeper in love with Gartner. The simplest of gestures can change everything for me. This many clearly paid attention to my desires, and even more, wanted to help me fulfill them. I nodded my head in agreement before jumping on him in a thankful embrace. Then Gartner hopped out of bed and turned the coffee pot on.

Thirty minutes later we were seated in Gartner's car heading north to Valencia, trying to beat the rush hour traffic. On the way we stopped by the 7-11 so I could purchase a black coffee, with three Splenda, my standard. I have learned how to survive on the go.

The park was worn down, more so than I thought. A few of the rollercoasters were dormant and inoperable. Nonetheless, we were there. I let the thrill of it all course through me. We wandered the expansive park grounds that carried over hills and I couldn't help but think of the significance of maintaining flat terrain in a theme park - because the constant up and down of hills in this park was exhausting.

My mind was wandering again. I thought about what it must be like to live and die in Los Angeles, to grow up in California.

The individual human experience was so vastly different.

I wondered how it must feel to have your soul recognize rolling hills and mountainous terrain as a customary experience of your everyday geography.

In a way, part of me felt like I already lived there, and from the moment I met Gartner my life had shifted. I had become an honorary California resident in mere seconds.

The state felt like home to me. Since the new year started, I spent more time in California than I had in my home state of Florida. I found that all my dreams were coming true: I was getting out of my hometown, and I was falling in love with someone I could have only dreamed up.

We rode a few of the rollercoasters, although most of the ones I had wanted to ride were inoperable due to the operations decline from COVID-19. Once the inevitable tiredness began to hit us from the lack of sleep, we began the trek back to Gartner's car from the back of the park. We stopped off at a craft stall along the way and found collectibles elephants for purchase. I picked up a white one with a light blue saddle and blue features painted over its white base. Gartner offered to buy me the knick-knack as a commemorative gift of our Six Flags date. Again, he had me swooning with his thoughtfulness.

I rolled the windows down as we drove home to Wilcox Place, letting the crisp winter air nip at my skin. Always prepared to keep me comfortable, I was able to cover myself up with a blanket Gartner kept in the car for that exact reason.

Gartner and I started to talk about our future. I decided to show him the notes app on my phone, where I had jotted down quick blips about my dream wedding. He brought up the potential reality of us marrying.

"If you are serious about getting married, then you have to ask my family for permission- they would appreciate it" I stated to him firmly. It was a strict rule I'd have with any person who wanted to be with me.

"I would do that for you easily," he responded as if it was the simplest request in the world. "Plus, you already showed me your dream wedding itinerary anyway" he said with an air of confidence. His immediacy of making such a big commitment seemed slightly concerning. But then again, we were both crazy about each other.

"We have to be together for a year" I said after a moment, trying to mask my nerves.

"How many requirements do you have before we can get married? At first it was just for me to ask your family for permission, but now it feels like you have more stipulations," he said jokingly. I let out a laugh.

"I have never felt so strongly for a person in all my past relationships. This is different and it makes me nervous, but I just did not expect this," I said, trying to reassure him that it was a possibility I was already thinking of as well.

"I searched for a long time man… I think you are it for me and I am prepared for that," he said firmly, glancing over at me from the driver's seat with a look of intensity. "I will do anything for you. I am a great boyfriend, and soon to be husband."

I let his words seep into my being, trying to believe that what he said was true. Could I really be getting everything I ever wanted, and so easily, so quickly? I let my mind wander as I stared out the passenger window.

"Do you think you could live anywhere else other than Florida?" he asked after a peaceful silence had passed between us.

I let out an audible sigh. One of my biggest personal struggles had been my separation from home. I am not sure if I could leave Florida again if I returned. As many times as I had said goodbye, something always pulled me back to what I was familiar with. On the other hand, California was starting to feel more like a second home. I could certainly try. I was honest with my response to Gartner:

"I would give it a shot for you, if you wanted me to move here - but I should let you know that I did not do well when I moved to Denver, but I think it was because I had left right after a difficult time for myself and Denver is landlocked with a cold climate. I often think I should have moved to Los Angeles instead. But I wanted to be different, and in hindsight it's funny because a large mass of Floridians ended up migrating to Denver around the same time I went there."

I could see the disappointment on his face with my answer. I knew he liked to be a nomad, exploring different states and cities whenever he pleased. He quickly moved past his apparent disappointment though and brought the conversation back to our imagined marriage.

"What kind of ring would you want?" he asked.

I tried not to act off guard, but it did feel forward even at the time. Again, I took my time with my answer, wanting to be as truthful as possible with Gartner about a topic I found so important.

"Something simple and plain, even just a gold band. Then if I added anything, it would be our birth stones" I said.

He seemed to take that as a decent answer, nodding to himself and smiling before turning back up the radio for the rest of the drive home.

*** 

After arriving home from our adventurous day together, we decided to wind down by streaming an episode of Drag Race. A joint is smoked lazily between one another. And once the episode has finished, I crawl into bed with Gartner, and we quickly begin to intertwine our bodies with each other, gliding and slipping together, bending our bodies in formations that match one another. Our last days together loomed over us like an unspoken endgame. We would have to separate for a month before he visited me in March.

I closed my eyes and disappeared as my body engaged in the art of lovemaking. While I should be blossoming from pleasure, I often found myself spiraling, wondering if I have pushed myself too far. I tried to convince myself it is merely the repercussions of my past. My inability to feel pleasure. Putting all the responsibility and pressure on myself rather than my partner made it easier to cope with. I thought it was my burden to keep.

It didn't help that Gartner refused to lube up, even though I would frequently ask him to. I told him it would make it easier for me, but he simply said he prefers it without. The one time I successfully convinced him to use lubrication, he complained about the stickiness afterwards and refused to use it again. Again, I felt I had to push my own comfortability as a second priority.

After Gartner finished, I was left to lie underneath the weight of his body. I suddenly so desperately wished I could push him off me and return to myself. I tried to recall a time when this was not a reoccurring feeling in my sex life.

I have experienced pleasures on both ends of the spectrum: sex that made me comfortable and sex that made me severely uncomfortable. I just figured it was a give or take, almost like the luck of the draw. After each encounter I would be left to speculate my self-worth; thinking, "Is the type of love I deserve? Is this a mistake? Have I been left astray?"

My thoughts were interrupted then, as Gartner pushed himself up from me while kissing the back of my neck.

"I love you baby" he said as he left the bed to go clean himself off. I convinced myself that if he didn't love me, he would never say those words to me.

I tried to fall asleep, but the thought was bothering me more than I let on. I kept wondering if I so desperately wanted to be loved that I was willing to take my most vulnerable comfortability and sacrifice it, just to feel something for a fleeting moment.

The following morning my eyes were greeted with a gloomy sky. Rain fell at a steady pace from the heavy, dark clouds hovering above the city. I was forced to shutter the open windows to stop the water from seeping into the apartment. I sighed and checked the weather app on my phone out of curiosity. I wasn't too shocked to find out that it was raining in Orlando as well. I guessed it reflected my glum mood, spanning across both the east and west coast.

When Gartner arrived home from work later that day, he busied himself around the apartment, performing mundane chores. I recognized that he was an avoidant type and wondered why he would want to ruin the last few hours we had together before I had to fly on a red eye back to Orlando.

I decided to play coy as I asked him random questions about his day, which he answered apathetically. I decided to change my tactic and go for the most generic option: comment on the weather, specifically how it was rainy in both Orlando and Los Angeles, but once again silence was returned to me.

"What is up with you?" I finally asked, dropping my patience and directly addressing the problem.
"Nothing" he said curtly and returned to scrubbing the dishes he had busied himself with.

"Do not give me that," I started, already rolling my eyes. "We're supposed to be enjoying our last evening together and you've come home avoiding and evading me at all costs? You're hardly speaking to me and choosing to clean instead, wasting the last few hours I have with you for a month. I feel like this is ruining the last few weeks of the trip... So, what is up with you?" I felt lighter after letting all the frustration I felt out and waited for his reasoning.
Finally, he said, "that is really mean to say."
'That's it? That's all I get?' I thought to myself, getting annoyed again.

"Don't do this right now," I shook my head. "You came home obviously not yourself, not talking to me or interacting and for what reason? What did I do?" I didn't care that my voice was getting louder. I was over it.

"Nothing man. I just don't want you to leave," he whispered, then burst into a sob.
"So, you're choosing to ignore me?" I countered.
His head fell into his hands.

"I dunno how to do anything else, everyone I have ever loved has always left me or hurt me in some way. I am worried I will lose you too," he admitted sadly.

"Lose me? I have not given you an inclination suggesting there is any reason to worry about losing me. I'm sorry, Gartner, but I think you have let your overthinking ruin this day."

Gartner apologized then, realizing he had acted immaturely about the whole thing. Just then, I received a notification on my phone: my flight was delayed due to weather. And then as if it was a sign from the universe, my flight continued to be delayed throughout the next hour. Eventually I was allowed to rebook my flight the following day, free of charge. I felt overwhelmed but decided to view the flight change as a blessing, instead focusing on how it was providing me with another night in Gartner's bed.

The digital clock on the stove read 9:09 PM. Too late for us to go out, but too early for us to call it a night and go to sleep. I was thinking I did not want to end the night on a sour note.

"What should we do with the rest of the night, then?" I asked Gartner, trying to make my voice sound lighter than before.

"I have an idea..." he offered shyly.

Gartner moved from his bed to the center of the room and extended his hand out in my direction. I gave in easily, hoisting myself up from the couch and letting him pull me into his embrace. He curved one arm around my waist, holding my hand in the other.

"Alexa, play I Remember Everything" he said, with the strum of guitar from the opening chord of the song penetrating my eardrums instantaneously. My heart reverberates to the beat of the rhythm.

Gartner pulled me into him even closer, so we're nearly chest to chest. We danced around the apartment for what seemed like hours, smoothly drifting across the floor. Every so often he would spin me outward from him so I could twirl out, and once we extended as far as our limbs would allow, I'd use inertia to spin myself back into his arms. We continued to dance as the songs shuffled through a playlist of loving-slow ballads. After we had grown too tired, we stripped off our clothing and left them littered across the floor leading up to the bed as we climbed in. Before we fell asleep, we held onto one another, moving as one as if we were still dancing.

The next morning Gartner took me to brunch before dropping me off at the airport. It was a wholesome last few hours together, and I was grateful for the change in plans that allowed me to stay. Even if it was just for a little while longer. I fell asleep on the plane as the illuminated glow of the LA city lights faded behind me as I journey eastward, back home.

## To Live and Die in L.A.

Gartner and I had talked about getting married just about from the moment we met, and maybe that was my fault. The thing about me is that I have the capacity to love deeply, quickly, and powerfully.

My love can feel like a black hole, unbeknownst to even itself, collapsing in when the mass is too great. I've found that I can carry the weight of this collapsed mass if I need to. I move fast, I over-commit, and I say what I mean, and follow through. My only requirement for Gartner at the time was to meet my family before he proposed to me. I didn't think this was asking for too much, especially after he seemed perfectly capable of doing so.

At night while I was home in Florida, in between visits to California, I would go to the gym late in the evening and stay for an hour or more - sometimes showing up well past ten and staying till nearly one in the morning. On the short drive home, I would FaceTime Gartner as I was accustomed to, and we would sync up our TVs to watch the same shows.

One night I was staring at the dozen roses he sent me sitting on my kitchen counter when I had to ask: "Why were you single for so long?"

"I tried to date in LA, and it sucked," he said, clearly exasperated at the memory. "Everyone is a catfish! Their profile picture would be completely different from what they looked like in real life, and if I brought it up, they wouldn't even care! It happened too many times. And if it was the rare occasion that the person was not a catfish - they would just constantly be on their phone during the entire duration of the date. Not interested in creating dialogue, which is what I really liked about you when I first met you. You were interested in having a conversation with me," he sighed after giving the long-winded answer.

"What do you mean that they catfished you? You never suspected they were someone else or looked a different way?" I asked, curious.

"No, I always believed them, and am unsure how to explain catfish better," he snapped, annoyed at my questioning.

"You're just so nice and loving, is all. I have never dated anyone like you" I admitted "I just find it hard to believe that's why you were single for so long."

"So, no guy has ever treated you this well?" he asked before continuing, not willing to wait for my answer., "You must have been dating a bunch of losers."

"I dunno if I would say that" I responded, somewhat annoyed that he thought of my exes in a negative light.

"You know, my clients at the salon have all been saying that they think you love-bomb me, and that you're just using me to move to California," he admitted, his tone somewhat cold.

The statement was so random, so casually inserted into the conversation almost like it was rehearsed. The words rolled off Gartner's tongue and reverberated around in my head. I briefly wondered if he had spent so much time to himself that he failed to realize how incredibly rude and abrasive a statement like that could be perceived.

I felt as though I had been gaslit to question myself and wondered if it could be the truth. But no, I reminded myself. My first thought when I met Gartner was that I would not like him, and I was proven wrong. I loved Gartner. I did not have to think twice about that.

"I dunno why you would listen to your clients, I think they hardly know me. I think that's a hurtful thing for them to say," I argue back, not wanting to come off as the bad guy when just moments before, I was complimenting him. "I would never use anyone like they are suggesting, you should know that."

I tried to disguise the hurt I was feeling that he would even bring it up to me. I didn't think I performed very well, but then I realized he probably did not care either way. "I didn't say I agreed with them," he barked back.

I sighed, instead wondering if my getting flustered and defending myself was overdramatic and unnecessary.

Part of me contemplated why Gartner would ever say that to me, if he did not believe it himself, at least subconsciously. It had not previously crossed my mind that it could have been premeditated by him. Maybe Gartner was the one love bombing me. The problem though, was that when you truly love someone, you tend to believe them when they tell you they love you back.

After what felt like an unnecessary argument, I spent the next day's reading to pass the time. The heat was beginning to work its way into the daily Florida weather, with the humidity bringing thunderous afternoon storms.

Upon reflection, I knew I would miss these thunderstorms if I left Florida to live in California. Gartner had again asked me if I would move in with him, and he wanted me to do it soon. After the annoyance of our previous argument blew over like a Florida shower, I told him I would consider it. Maybe I could, I reasoned, but I figured in a few months from then.

I was ready to start over, that much I knew. In a way, I had been manifesting the move out West ever since I had gone to Coachella the year before.

I stuck to my original proposition, though. If Gartner wanted me to move, he would have to visit me in my home. I wanted him to get a clear understanding of the environment I was raised in. More than that - he needed to meet my family in person. On this I would not budge.

Before the month of March was over, Gartner agreed to fly down and meet my family for the first time. I had never felt so certain about someone in my life before, so I wanted to show him my home and all the things I did love about Florida. I wanted him to see where I came from, who raised me, and why I loved the way I did. I longed for him to understand how I got to where I was with him, with the intensity of my feelings and hopefulness for our future.

***

The weather during Gartner's visit was perfect. Not overwhelmingly hot, with crispy cool mornings. I chauffeured Gartner around Orlando, emphasizing old apartments and work locations that had built me up, places around my home that formed and molded me into the Florida boy that was standing before him.

I took Gartner to the resort I worked at one day. We spent an entire day around the massive complex referred to often as The World. From open to close we checked off the marquee attractions, stepping foot in all four parks in a singular day.

I wonder if Gartner realized how special this day truly meant to me, if he felt the same as I did. Or if he was indifferent towards the parks that in no way held the same sentimental value for him as it did for me. I wondered what it cost for him to show some sort of enjoyment for my interests. He never said much either way, so I chose to assume the best.

One morning Gartner and I drove out to Wekiva Springs, one of Florida's State Parks with crystal-clear water and a year-round temperature of 72 degrees. The perfect spot to enjoy a sunny day. I strapped the neon green kayak I was gifted for my birthday a few years back onto the roof rack of my car, prepared for a great day together.

Along the way we picked up Reni, a friend I had known for years, who I also originally met through Twitter. We considered one another our official travel buddy, cut from the same cloth and with similar personalities. We understood each other on a higher level than most, with our communication requiring little to no effort.

The spring water is known for being translucent, allowing patrons to peer through the water's surface down below. The colors reflect a vibrant turquoise as it connects to rivers and lakes, that muddy up to a dark blue, near black in color.

The sun was bright that day, the sky blue. Puffy, white clouds drifted in and out of our view and reflected on the glassy surface as our kayak glided through the water. Florida is already naturally stunning, but the access to water in varying capacities makes it uniquely beautiful to the state. From rivers, lakes, the springs, to the intercoastal and the ocean. Florida was truly a natural masterpiece.

I wanted to show Gartner those authentically beautiful parts of Florida, the parts I loved the most.

The day after the springs, I took Gartner to Cocoa beach, a quaint hippie beach town about forty minutes east of Orlando, just neighboring the Kennedy Space Center.

We met up with my cousins in the downtown area and had brunch at Fourth Street Gastrobar, an old gas station that eventually converted into an operational restaurant. My cousin, Laney, her husband, and their kids were all exactly like me. We've always thought and acted alike.
I knew Gartner would love meeting them.

"So, you think you'll move to California?" Laney asked me casually.

"I dunno," I said, "I do love it here, but a change might be nice. I have been thinking about moving, but I still haven't fully decided," I respond sheepishly.

"Well, I think you should move with me" Gartner chimed in, "I could maybe live here in Florida for a year, but then we could move back to California. But I really think you should just move with me. I would move you."

"You would move to Florida?" Laney asked Gartner, stuck on that part of his response.

"Yes, it is beautiful here and sometimes I find myself over California," he shrugged.

Laney gawked, as she has always loved California. She could not begin to imagine anyone currently living there who wished to move from the western paradise.

I started mulling over my options again. I would move to California, because I dreamed of it since I was little, and I had always wanted to know what life would be like living there.

On the other hand, I knew Los Angeles would not be my forever home. I hated being away from Florida and my family for extended periods of time, as much as I liked the idea of getting away from Florida. I had previously told myself the only way I would write and change my life was if I dropped everything and moved to a different place to start over. Was I being offered this opportunity now, from the man I was so happy to be with?

I often fantasized about moving to a small cabin in the woods, and sequestering myself inside the warmth of a cabin, or a small cottage on a secluded beach shore where I could engulf myself in salty damp walls. I imagined my life as a cozy hermit, spending my days writing from sunup to sundown. It felt like pure bliss, these dreams of mine.

When Gartner finally met my parents, I could tell how much my mother liked him from the moment he tried to sneak off at dinner to pay for our meal without anyone catching on. I exposed him to my mother, pointing him out to her as he snuck around the corner to find our waiter. I knew he had made a good impression, and my family would only encourage me to follow my heart when it came to him.

He was likable and forward, also honest and kind. He had the ability to be humble, which I initially thought was natural to his personality. Now I question if was ever genuine to his personality.

After he met my family, I knew I would move to California and start a life with Gartner in Los Angeles. Still, I felt uneasy within myself but had an unknown force pushing me forward. All signs were pointing towards the West Coast. With my family's blessing, there was nothing left standing in my way. I should have listened to my internal feelings. My mother always taught me to go with what I felt in my gut. Except this time, she was just as encouraging, making me second guess the conflicting thoughts I had about actually going.

A few days later Gartner flew back home. The day after he left, I was greeted with a beautiful bouquet of roses at my doorstep, with a card attached that read:

'I miss you already, Love Gartner.'

And my heart fluttered., I thought, 'this was it; I have picked the right guy finally.'

\*\*\*

Over time I grew more excited for the month ahead. I planned to spend the entire month of April in California, to fully test it out. I couldn't have been more thrilled to spend so much time with Gartner, to dance with him at Coachella, and to go to my first wedding in the state.

Before leaving for California, I bought a bag of powder from a friend downtown to bring with me to Coachella. Every so often I would dabble with altering substances. I never over did it - I had only ever gone too far once before, and that was a completely different substance altogether and the lesson was learned quickly.

The medical condition I was born with often-rejected various ingestibles from my body whenever I tried to regularly take them, which is why I originally started to smoke weed. It was the only substance that never made me feel sick. My body never rejected marijuana.

However, I found that I could dabble with other substances every so often, especially if I was meant to attend a music festival. But after some time, I started to realize the effects it had on my body, so I would use less. Even as a casual taker, the effects were noted. I used to feel envy surface within me as I watched my close friends partake in the drugs around, doing more than I could do myself.

When I was younger, I was perceived as the 'bad child' of the family. My family believed I had begun to abuse alcohol and drugs at a young age due to word of mouth (never mine). I simply bought alcohol for house parties and suddenly I was considered a drunk. I had only been intoxicated a few times in my youth, and my experience with marijuana was extremely limited. I only ever smoked a handful of times before I officially graduated high school.

After graduating I dabbled more frequently, and quickly realized what drugs were for me and which were not. Eventually I stopped altogether with recreational drugs, aside from marijuana. I felt comforted in the fact that the addiction gene did not carry within my parents, my sister, or me. But again, there was a time and place for everything, and I knew Coachella was one of them. It was nice to have something to look forward to.

Then on the fourth of April, my grandmother suffered a stroke. It was early afternoon. She called my dad through her confusion and said she had fallen and could not get herself up. Her house was closer to our own, and we arrived in ten long minutes that felt equivalent to a lifetime. There was steady rain as I jumped out of the vehicle, before my father could even put it in park. I peered through the front door's window, catching a small glimpse of my grandmother hunched over, her hand extended as she attempted to open the door with no success. It was a horrible sight to see, and every other thought I had disappeared, my sole focus now getting her help.

We finally located a loose window and were able to wriggle it free. My dad lifted me up and pushed me through the small opening. I landed on my feet, and I immediately went to my grandmother's side in a matter of seconds. I could instantly tell something was wrong, I shouted for my dad to call 911, with the house alarm for intruders blaring from the moment we broke in through the window. My father attempted to turn it off while I sat with my grandmother.

My grandmother's brown, wispy hair was half done. She had one leg of her floral pants pulled up, with the other leg left flapping loosely around unbeknownst to her. The left side of her face had slightly drooped, and I knew immediately that she had endured a stroke. I told this to my dad, who handed me the phone to speak with the emergency operator. I informed them she experienced a stroke and I gave them the one identifier I have always known, a left drooping face as evidence to support my claim.

The paramedics arrived and ran multiple tests. They did not need to confirm to me what I already knew, but they announced she had suffered a stroke anyway. Once the ambulance drove out of our line of vision, I informed my dad he needed to contact his brother and more challengingly enough, his sister. He agreed to call his brother but refused to call his sister.

My father's family is dysfunctional. Over the years they've often been plagued with drama thicker than their own blood. My grandmother and grandfather divorced years before I was born, and their livelihoods were shrouded in mystery. My grandmother never remarried. My grandpa went back to Puerto Rico where he was born and then married a woman less than half his age, agitating his children with the announcement. There were three children in total, two boys and a girl.

My Aunt Di was often perceived as a prude. In my younger years, I found myself seeking a deeper connection with her anyways. She would often pick me up so I could spend weekends with her, where we would go to the theme parks or visit the farmer's market in Winter Park.
One Sunday, my aunt and I spent the day lounging around her home. She had drunk too much wine and as she drove me home, she began to drive recklessly. I called out loudly for her to stop and compose herself. She quickly corrected herself and apologized, but the initial fear I felt lingered within my nervous system.

My father and his siblings were known to fight. I recalled a time when I watched my father and his brother tussle off the side of their boat before we were to cast off for a family trip to the Bahamas. They threw each other into the water after engaging in a dramatic scream-off in broad daylight. They made up just as soon as it had started, but that was common for my dad and uncle; a heated disagreement written off as a brotherly argument. With my Aunt Di, though, it was a different story. She often refused to forgive, and would only believe she was in the right, which never held over well with either my dad or uncle.

As much as my uncle and father would fight and make up, my aunt held grudges. The last time I spoke with my aunt before my grandmother's stroke was the summer back in June 2011, the year my sister graduated high school. My family hosted a joint birthday party for my father and graduation party for my sister at our home.

My Aunt Di arrived at the house with her dog. I instantly knew my father would be displeased. She had not asked him prior if she could bring the dog. Had she asked, he more than likely would have said yes, but it was the principle of her just showing up and assuming she could do whatever she wanted.

My father politely pulled her aside from the partygoers and informed her she should have asked before bringing her dog over. Before he could continue any further, she tore off in a fit and I witnessed their argument from afar. I followed Di as she stormed away from the back of the house where the party was being held up to the front yard where she had parked her vehicle. Just like that she was already leaving.

I approached her to just try and help her open the driveway gates that guarded my family's home, but she turned to me and said:

"I want you to listen to me clearly, I want nothing to do with my brother or his family ever again, which includes you. Do not ever contact me again and never speak to me again."

I began to cry, unable to understand how I could be lumped into a sibling argument, let alone one that was over bringing a dog to a party. It felt immature and unfair. When she noticed me crying, she degraded me further by saying:

"You should cry harder little gay boy," she snapped, with ice in her voice.

The hurt I felt as my aunt chastised me was out of shame. I wasn't out at this point, and somehow everyone else knew who I was deep down before I was ever able to speak it aloud for myself. The cruelness of the words struck deep and I gave into them, letting it consume me. How long had she known? How long had she mulled the thought over in her head? I was left to fear she talked about my own secret behind closed doors. Doors I wasn't quite ready to open yet.

My Aunt Isa from my mother's side chased my father's sister down the road as she attempted to flee after bashing my identity. My Aunt Isa never questioned the legitimacy of my claim; her intuition had set her up for this moment all along - she was prepared to slam her into a wall for what she said to me. As a woman who constantly praised peace over war, she was ready to end the war my father's sister had waged that day. Thankfully, we all kept my aunt's wishes and refrained from having any contact with her. At least, until this tragedy struck.

Mentally, I had already prepared myself for the day I would be forced to contact my father's sister again. I had forgiven her. I forgave everyone for what they did to me, even if it caused me shame. Aunt Di answered the phone after a single ring; I was surprised to find the number I saved as her contact worked. Yet all I heard on the other line was silence.

The static noise of an established connection over the line was the indicator she had answered the call. After a few "Hellos?" from me, I assumed she must be listening at the very least. I told her grandma had suffered a stroke, and what hospital she would be recovering at. No response still, and after thirty seconds, the call ended.

I visited my grandmother daily at the hospital. I would sit beside her as tubes and wires were attached to her body, supporting her livelihood. She was stretched across her bed and attached to the machines on either side of her. Her brown hair appeared even more dull than normal. Wrinkles had worn themselves into her face. I worried this could be the end of life for her.

The closer I got to thirty, the more I feared I would end up with no answers for the questions I sought. No tangible evidence for me to decipher. I wondered what all the secrecy is for in life, but then I realized I carried the burden of an abundance of secrets myself - thinking that some things should be kept to yourself, although maybe not indefinitely. There had been plenty of secrets exposed posthumously. There's nothing like a family emergency that puts time in perspective for a person.

As my sister and I aged, the relationships between my family and my grandmother would strain and wear. Accusations would be used as weapons and words would be the artillery. Years later when I was less self-involved with the shadows of my own life, I would wonder if it was all worth it for anyone in the family. The arguments, the hate. I accepted that I was also guilty of perpetuating arguments as well. But my sister and I were kids for most of them, and mistakes were meant to be made at a young age.

I still held onto fond memories of my grandmother, with pictures printed of us posing with silly faces on Frankenstein's Chair in the Studios park, or shopping on Park Avenue in Winter Park, or at the Florida Mall; she bought me a copy of Harry Potter and the Half-Blood Prince the morning of its release.

I recalled all the positive perceptions I had of her. Our family would take multiple vacations together, usually on a cruise ship. I enjoyed watching her smoke cigarettes, with a ring from her brightly colored lips staining the end of the filter. She maintained her generational up-keep, with her hair shiny and kept. She always wore nail polish to match her lips and gold, dangly earrings.

As we were entering the final stages of her life, I found myself yearning to be closer to her like I once was. I wondered what choices she made behind closed doors that got her where she was today. The doctors revealed she had a tattoo, an unknown and shocking revelation to me - she specifically commented negatively against my own tattoos on multiple occasions. I wondered what other secrets she kept, and if she would ever reveal them. I concluded that if I were so lucky to hear them, I swore they would die with me, too.

\*\*\*

I continued to visit with my grandmother up until I returned to Los Angeles on April 9th, a couple days before Coachella. I felt a slight tinge of guilt for leaving my grandmother before she was fully healed. Pink picked me up outside of LAX while Gartner worked. It had not been long since I saw him last. We were together in Florida just under two and half weeks prior, but we had grown even more inseparable through the distance.

Pink dropped me off at the apartment on Wilcox Place. Gartner had made me a key back in February so I could have access whenever I needed. I lugged my bags up the flight of stairs to the second floor and let myself into apartment three with the turn of my personal key.

Gartner's cat was sitting on the bed staring at me, flicking her tail in a polite greeting.

The apartment was an old, but comforting studio. Worn and polished wooden floors, steel appliances in the far end from the entrance. Leading from the main room to the bathroom was a small hallway containing storage space behind full-length, sliding mirror doors. A spacious studio apartment located in Los Angeles, complete with a personal parking space. It felt like a nice place to come home to, especially after the time I'd recently had in Florida.

To the right of the front door hung a small, 12x12 whiteboard on the wall, where Gartner wrote personal checklists and reminders. Written in neat blue handwriting was a message to me and Pink:

'Hey Babe, Welcome Home! I love you so much, I can't wait to hug/kiss you. You are my world! Thank you, Pink!'

"Awh, that's so sweet of him," Pink said after I read the message aloud.

Once Pink had left the apartment, I slid out my airport clothes, left only in my underwear. I slipped into Gartner's bed and fell asleep, only waking later to find Gartner standing over me, nudging me awake.

"Hey, you," he said sweetly as he landed a kiss on my forehead. A smile took hold of my face. I felt at peace for the first time in weeks.

He walked to the kitchen and started rummaging around in the fridge for ingredients to prepare dinner. After a few dreamy moments I hopped out of bed and threw on a pair of running shorts and an oversized camo t-shirt. When Gartner saw me dressed, his expression changed to a frown.

"What?" I ask him as I start to dress myself.

"You were not naked just now," he said.

"When I was just sleeping? Well yeah, you were not here, and I usually sleep in my underwear."

"You know I like it when you sleep naked though," he responded. I thought it was strange to bring this up again. I also did not want our first moments back together to start on the wrong foot.

I smiled, mainly to change the current energy I was receiving. "I'm sorry baby, I didn't think it mattered that much," I said, keeping my tone light.

"It doesn't matter," he said, turning away from me.

"But you frowned," I said, although I instantly thought I should have kept the thought to myself.

"Well, I just like it better when you are naked."

"Well, it was just me," I countered. "You know I'm willing to sleep naked for you, but it's not exactly the most comfortable thing for me all the time." I hoped explaining myself would erase the awkwardness between us.

He dropped the subject then. I mistook his quietness for indifference, but on the surface his feelings were blatantly displayed across his face. I loved Gartner, I felt it deep within me. The love that manifested between us rooted itself in the pit of my stomach like a budding rose and perturbed into all my organs. My lungs filled with rose petals, even while thorns poked at my flesh from the inside. It was gorgeous and deadly at the same time, and it made it difficult for me to breathe.

Gartner listened to me and encouraged my dreams. His actions reflected those of a caring lover. In the end, it was only at his expense - what he considered best for me was meant to be good enough for me to accept. I could never be contained or restricted, I knew that about myself. And I knew that would make our relationship difficult in the future. It was fine for the time being, but there would come a time we would have to face these contradictions head on.

I'll admit that I gave in when I could, letting myself shrink to keep us afloat. That's what I told myself as we fell asleep normally, with me naked in his bed. For the first time in our relationship, I felt the same immense guilt I felt after all my one-night stands and hookups that I used to curb my own depression with. I never chose to be hypersexual. No one chooses to use sex as a coping mechanism unless it was forced upon them. After all these years, you would think I would have returned to some sort of intimate normalcy.

I tried to find my voice to explain to Gartner how I felt, but the thoughts in my head were jumbled and I was unable to decipher their code. I was at a loss for words. My mind was like a hollow cavern so vast that the blackness of it swallowed all points of available light. I was flailing, hoping I could stay afloat and failing all the same. I could only tread dangerous waters for so long before I succumbed to my own exhaustion.

I remained in Gartner's bed feeling out of place and exposed the following morning. He left early in the morning for work. I pretended to sleep as he dressed himself for the day and once he left I sighed to myself, remaining in bed for the next few hours before I managed to push myself out of the covers and dressed myself. All the good feelings I felt the day before felt far away now.

Pink arrived shortly before noon, and we drove to Yeastie Boy Bagels truck in Los Feliz for breakfast. The morning was crisp and sunny, with the usual gray overcast dissipated, leaving the Los Angeles mornings now crystal blue, tinged with gold from the sunlight. The sun shone radiantly as it cascaded across the eastern mountain range.

We spent our morning together staggering in and out of various boutiques and clothing stores that can only be found along the historic Melrose Avenue as Pink shopped for last minute festival clothing. She perused the clothing racks throughout the stores for garments that would match her obvious aesthetic, pink.

The shopping was underwhelming with options. We decided to leave the shops on Melrose, and she dropped me back off at the apartment on Wilcox Place. Gartner waited for me with street tacos he got from a vendor by the Pavilions we frequented at the intersection of Melrose and Vine.

Feeling mentally exhausted again, I fell asleep with my head resting in Gartner's lap as he played video games into the night. I was unaware how much time had passed as he gently kissed me awake. My eyelids were heavy, and I blinked rapidly as I staggered to the bed and wiggled myself under the warmth of the bedsheets. I felt his warmth as he slid into bed next to me. I reached out for him, pulling him into me. I was ready to focus on the incredible weekend ahead of us.

The first alarm for Gartner woke us both up. Our bodies were still tangled together as if we were one. Gartner left for work and again Pink stopped by. We walked to the 24Hour Fitness off Sunset Boulevard and worked out in preparation for the weekend ahead. The gym was not as nice as my own back in Florida, but a view of the mountains and Hollywood sign made up for the outdated complex.

I packed my suitcase before Gartner arrived home from work. Once he arrived home, we loaded our suitcases into his Toyota Camry and joined the caravan of city weekend traffic due east to Palm Springs for the festival. We arrived at the condo located on the edge of a golf course. Palm Springs is littered with multiple sprawling green courses. Florida and California have retirement in common, and somehow the distance between Palm Springs and Orlando feels less than factual due to these similarities. My friends from the bay area had arrived earlier, Dina and De, a couple we refer to as their social handle known together as 'The Hungries.' They built their brand by food blogging, where it became their side hustle as the influencing industry came about with the advancement of social media and marketing.

Pink and Bondi showed up after everyone in the Airbnb had fallen asleep. In the morning, Gartner drove me to Dutch Bros. We grabbed coffees for everyone in our group and returned to the condo to get ready for the first day on the Polo Fields.

The festival flew by, and it was the best Coachella I attended yet. The music was progressive and pulsing. The sound waves beckoned the festivalgoers. Gartner and I danced in the crowd. As we walked from stage to stage, he would grab my hand and spin me outward, dust kicked up in my wake and then spun me inward again to kiss me on the cheek before we continued our walk to the next set.

The days were hot, with the desert sun beating down on us. The nights were cold and plagued with high winds that blew in from the mountains and rolled through the fields, sending a shiver down the spines of partygoers. I packed an extra set of clothes in a tote and brought them in with me each day. I changed as the sun set and the temperature plummeted.

The arch-line of balloons the festival was known for in viral photos sprawled across the festival grounds from the mainstage to the Sahara. As the day progressed the balloons moved closer to the main stage and once the night ended, they were all bunched together. The balloons served as an indication of time-telling for those lost in the illusive pattern of the festival.

Gartner asked me to keep the baggie I had brought between us. He implored me to keep it to myself, emphasizing that I should not share any of it with Bondi or Pink before they arrived the first night. I reluctantly went along with his request. Within my friend group, we reasonably shared with one another. I'd like to think we developed a kinship so powerful that we established unwritten rules we all abided by. So, what was originally a small and otherwise reasonable request from Gartner turned into an awkward position for me.

I felt uncomfortable yet again, and I could not discern why it mattered to Gartner if we shared with Bondi and Pink. It became obvious that Gartner and I had our own stash. Pretending like it did not exist in front of my friends created an awkward elephant in the room that needed to be addressed.

In a way, Gartner was everything I had ever wanted in a man. But I thought to myself that if he caused a rift in my friendships, the relationship was doomed. Then what would he be to me? I pushed the thought out of my mind, worried it would cause more bad than good if I continued to let the thoughts penetrate my consciousness. I made the decision to focus on enjoying the weekend with Gartner.

The two of us roamed the playa together while Pink and Bondi gallivanted around the festival grounds by themselves. Occasionally we ran into the girls during bathroom breaks at our established homebase.

The first night I smuggled in an entire bottle of champagne, and Gartner and I shared it amongst each other as we casually passed a joint between one another through the sips of bubbles. We danced through the night, unclear if it was the bubbles and weed or our intense devotion to each other that created this electric energy.

During the nighttime the desert sky was a deep black, with stars dotted across the vast open sky. The palm trees bristled fiercely in the wind as the music and commotion from the crowd stifled the noise the branches made as they thrashed amongst themselves.

At the end of each night, Gartner and I took a shower together, slipping and sliding against one another as we kissed underneath the cascading water. The dirt and dust washed off our bodies from the day. We would dry off and move under the bedsheets, rolling and wrestling around until we exhausted the energy within our bodies. We ended each night tucked into one another in a deep sleep.

One night as we cuddled together in the bed, we were too jazzed from the bumps we shared throughout the day. We had also microdosed mushrooms earlier, so sleep was not in sight for either of us that night.

Instead, I turned on the TV in our room and streamed Seinfeld, since Gartner does not enjoy my favorite, Sex and the City. Television shows playing in the background as I fell asleep always brought me comfort as a child, and it still did. I felt accomplished with the weekend so far. I felt that rotting around the festival grounds together strengthened our feelings for one another. I was at ease, and with the substance-courage I suddenly insisted on learning more about Gartner's past.

"Why did you move back from Chicago?" I asked him once before, but the answer he gave then was too simple, and I knew it was shrouded in a half-truth. I hoped now as the drugs coursed through our veins he would answer my question honestly.

"I left because I felt like I had nothing to leave behind me in Chicago. I felt like my friends were not reliable and cared too much about partying and not enough about anything else substantial," he said thoughtfully.
"What happened to your friends?"

"They stopped talking to me, and when I told them I was moving - none of them bothered to reach out to me. Is that not awful?" He asked, then said to me, "I spent my final weeks in Chicago alone."

"Yeah..." I said trailing off, not fully convinced. I wasn't sure if I would ever know Gartner the way I wished I could know him.

My prying resulted in zero results. I wished I could get a better read on Gartner, but part of me felt like he was not being honest about what had happened with his friends in Chicago. Gartner seemed to have a constant theme in all his relationships: they all ended. He always insisted it was the other individuals' involved fault. I wondered at what point that became a flaw in his personality? Would it make me a bad person if I could not continue to be with him because of that? The conflicting questions consumed me.

"Everyone in my life has been horrible and abusive to me," he said as he grasped my hand. I felt his body shake slightly as he continued: "Everyone in my life has always been awful to me and left me or treated me like I was nothing to them."

"But you never told me what exactly they did that was so awful. I know it hurts to talk about, but I would like to understand you better." I tried again.
"It is too painful to talk about, I don't know if I will ever be ready," he said solemnly.

"I understand that, but I fail to understand why you are unable to forgive them? Or even come to a resolve? Some sort of conversation with any of your friends or family who have hurt you to try to fix it?" I was confused at his ability to just move on, cutting ties completely.

"Because they do not deserve forgiveness for what they did to me. If you did something like that to me and I cut you off, it is forever," he said gravely.

At the moment my biggest fear was no longer having the ability to talk to Gartner again. If we broke up, would he never speak to me again? Even after all that we had been through? I realized at this moment Gartner and I had built a life together in Los Angeles. I think about my last relationship and how I never prepared myself for the relationship to end. I had no time to preserve it respectfully in my memory. I would not let that happen to me again.

I stared into Gartner's eyes, trying to capture the oceanic blue in my mind's eye forever. If there ever came a night where I fell asleep and he was no longer in my bed, I wanted to remember his eyes at the very least.

"Can you promise me something?" I asked while we were cuddled up in bed after our shower that second night of the festival.
"What is it?"

"If we ever break up, please do not cut me off and pretend I do not exist" I said, yearning for our love to be immortal.

"I can't promise you that," he said before he closed his eyes and fell asleep, nothing else for him to say. I fell asleep next to his physical body, while emotionally I felt light years away.

I recognized I must reconcile with the idea of Gartner removing himself from my life if we were to split, but it was hard for me to fathom. Of course I had ex-boyfriends that I no longer spoke to, but the idea of Gartner becoming a stranger made me uneasy.

I knew I must respect his wish to remain silent, but I also knew it would drive me mad.

On the last day of the festival we microdosed mushrooms and wandered through the sun-scorched, trampled grass.

I took a moment to ground myself. My third time at Coachella and my fifth time in Palm Springs - I never expected this to be my life. I was in love in the desert, thousands of miles away from my hometown. My skin was warm from the kiss of the sun shining down on us and my heart fluttered with every twirl Gartner danced me into.

We took a seat on a hill near the Sahara stage, with the main stage fireworks seeming more vivid under the influence of shrooms. I wondered if my eyesight improved under the influence of certain substances.

That weekend spent with Gartner was indescribable. A moment suspended and sealed within its own curated time blimp, preserving our love forever. We wandered around the Polo Fields as we giggled and kissed in corners as if we were school children exploring our feelings and emotions for the first time, relishing in a drawn-out kiss as if it were our last. Gartner was leading me into the great unknown, and it felt incredible. At night we fell asleep laughing with one another as we recounted the day and how nice it felt to be in love in the middle of a crowded music festival. It was too easy to let my doubts and fears slip away with an experience like this.

There is a theory that the more people there are in a room the more intimate the party is, and the less people there are, the more exposed you are. I understood the concept as Gartner and I lost ourselves within the massive sea of people.

We existed only with each other. Gartner and I were the only two people on the planet over the weekend.

The sun was high in the sky by the time we lazily drew ourselves from bed. Pink, Bondi, Gartner, and I stopped for breakfast at a Filipino diner before we drove to Joshua Tree for the remainder of our day. The mushrooms from the day before left us with residual shroom-giggles as the psychedelics continued to course through our body and work their way out of our system.

The giggles took over in the middle of our breakfast, all four of us sat around the table laughing, stuffing our mouths with eggs and sausage while we tried not to choke over the muffled giggles we could not contain.

My body vibrated, and I felt a pulse within me that connected me to my friends and Gartner. We avoided the prying eyes set on us from other patrons in the restaurant as we laughed uncontrollably. We were overcome with feelings of joy and gratitude, just happy to be there.

We took our time as we cruised through Joshua Tree. The windows were down so we could feel the sunlight warm our bodies while the fresh, springtime air nipped at us. Inside the national park we pulled off on the side of the road and ran around the scorched earth, kicking up dust in our wake that trailed into a puff cloud behind us.

We hiked past Jumping Chollas that littered the park and admired the tall, mighty Joshua Trees that bent and stretched in abstract ways, mimicking sea coral on dry land.

Bondi and Pink were ahead of Gartner and me. We watched as they giggled and bounced off each other's flamboyant behavior. Gartner grabbed ahold of my hand and twirls me into him, where we spin and spin, stepping into a dance until he lifts me up, spinning us both around in circles as the desert dust kicks up around us. In the moment it feels like a dream, a moment made for television that was curated exclusively for me. Gartner kissed me gently on the lips as he placed me back down on the ground. It felt like ecstasy.

We ran side by side, our hands spread out to imitate birds in flight. The dust from the scorched earth beneath our feet spewed out behind us and left a faint, brown cloud trailing in our wake. Gartner grabbed me again as we slowed down to a halt. He pivoted my body and spun me around in circles until we were both dizzy and left gasping for air.

We sat on the desert floor, opposite of each other. The blue sky that touched the earth was met with seemingly painted mountains, sharp and jagged across the skyline from years of wind erosion.

I never felt more grounded than in that moment. With the earth flat in all directions around me and the foothills of the mountains beginning to ascend, creating a base to ground myself.

The sky above me stretched for hundreds of thousands of miles across the earth. The clear space above us was so pure it could only be replicated in Gartner's eyes while they glistened in the sun looking back at me

The laughs of Bondi and Pink echoed from nearby, and I recognized their loyalty throughout our friendship, along with the value of having their personalities around, constantly keeping my spirit lifted.

I was successful in creating the life I had always dreamed. I never expected to fall in love with a California boy. I never expected to wander around Joshua Tree just because I could and it was convenient. I was exactly where I was meant to be. Everything had fallen into place.

I heard the wind whisper to me that everything was as it should be as it breezed through the Valley, flipping my wavy unkept brown hair from one side to the other. I caught a glimpse of Gartner's eyes in the sun and his electric blue irises beamed back at me. The sun warmed my skin, and the dust filled my lungs. I felt the dryness of the air in my hands. My skin pricked as goosebumps took over my arms, and I relished in the glow of the desert.

Gartner met me kneeling on the sandy floor. He leaned in and kissed me for a lengthy period of time, immeasurable by the Time Bandit. He pulled away and stared deep into my eyes before he smiled handsomely.

"Deeper than the Ocean," he said.

"Deeper than the Ocean," I repeated.

"Higher than the Sky."

"Higher than the Sky," I repeated.

"Bigger than the Universe" he said through his breath.

"Bigger than the Universe" I breathed back as I pushed closer to his lips again.

"And so much more," he said.

I sealed it with a kiss.

"My love, my love, my love, my love, my love, my love, my love, my love," I whispered against his lips.

The sun began to set ahead of us as we careened the highway back into Los Angeles. The desert, Coachella, and Joshua Tree were miles behind us, their healing nature having left us energized and rejuvenated as we coasted back into the city.

The week following Coachella was blissfully simple. Pink and I lounged around lazily in each other's apartments while Gartner was at work, and while Bondi slept for hours between her own shifts. We fell back into our typical weekly habits.

Soon it was time to leave for Rissa's wedding up north. Beforehand, Gartner and I hiked Runyon Canyon. The spring had brought out the blue skies, with the previous rains fortifying yellow flowers dotted across the coastal desert terrain. The hike was breathtaking, providing a clear view of LA and beyond. You could almost see through to Orange County. A smog-less day in a usually smoggy city was incredible. Los Angeles was meant to be bathed in sunlight and blue skies.

I loved the look and feel of Mediterranean desert biomes, the flora and fauna a shade of muted green. There were no vines or bushes overgrowing and overcrowding each other, fighting to be seen like they do back in Florida. The dirt crunched beneath my feet, so compacted even a shovel couldn't churn up the earth below its hard surface.

Before heading out to the wedding, Reni flew into LAX to meet up with our other friends for the second week of Coachella. Before she got in, I told her that Gartner and I would pick her up so we could grab lunch.

The night before our scheduled airport pickup, I told Gartner we needed to be up early in the morning so we would be on time to get Reni. I offered to drive myself so he could remain asleep, but he rejected the suggestion. So, as the morning sun rose and we were meant to leave, Gartner refused to wake up. Instead, he rolled over and promptly fell back asleep, facing the opposite direction.

I let ten minutes pass before I tried to wake him again. He stirred and opened his eyes. Sunshine blue as dazzling as an aquamarine sea peered up at me.

"Hey," I said, "We gotta head out soon, Reni has almost landed."

He sighed as he rolled out of bed and headed for the shower. Something felt off. But I did not want to press it. I followed him to the shower and joined him. Once I got out and dried off, I walked over to the small lockbox on the nightstand next to our bed and found a small bag of powder we had left over and untouched from Coachella.

"What are you doing?" he asked me.

"Just bringing this for the day with Reni," I replied, not thinking much of it.

"No, you are not," he said, this time with anger in his voice.

Maybe he had a valid reason, and maybe if Gartner would have just stated that he would prefer me not to bring it because of such a valid reason, it would have prevented the situation from exploding. But if there is one thing I have never liked, it's when someone tells me I cannot do something. I was the one that bought the powder and transported it from Florida to California, he had no say in that as far as I was concerned.

"Why not? I can do what I want," I said firmly.

"Well, Reni did not pay for it," he answered, just as stubbornly.

"Neither did you," I replied.

"I do not get why you have to argue with me, do not bring it with us" he grunted.

"I am not trying to argue, but I do not like it when people tell me what to do, even if they are my boyfriend. Besides, it is what my friends and I have always done. We share with one another," I explained, trying to get him to understand my reasoning.

We spent another ten minutes in a heated argument over whether my friends pay or should pay for the sharing of drugs. For me, I couldn't care less if my friends paid me or not. When you are part of my friend group, when we have spent so much time together, we are not stingy people. It's just the unspoken rule we all have with one another.

One thing that has bothered me about Gartner from the start was his opposition to people, specifically my friends. I did not think that sharing what you have amongst your closest friends and peers should be a controversial take.

"I do not get why you get like this; I feel like it is just because of Reni," I said in an accusing tone.

"I just do not like how y'all act together," was his response, which just infuriated me further.

I was stopped in my tracks. "Well, if you do not like how we are together that kinda worries me… we're basically the same person. So does that mean you will eventually not like me either?"

"If you act like her, maybe," he said coldly.

I decided not to press the issue and let it go. I swallowed the remaining arguments lodged in my throat, along with my pride. At this point we were running so late, I just didn't want to let Reni down by not being there to pick her up. I hoped Gartner would cool off on the drive to the airport.

When we finally picked up Reni, we headed into town to a sushi restaurant that Reni frequented when she visited Los Angeles. After the fight with Gartner that morning, he seemed to have resolved his frustrations; but I was still bothered by the fact that he expressed his dislike for Reni. She was one of my oldest and closest friends. I wished he hadn't gone with me that morning when I picked her up. I wanted space to myself, and time to hang out with her without the negative background thoughts that kept popping up in my head. After lunch, Reni was picked up by another friend going to Coachella, so I gave her a long, hug farewell. I was flying to San Jose for Rissa's wedding the following day and by the time I would be back in LA, Reni would already be on a flight back to Orlando. I hated that any time spent with her was tainted with a bad memory, but I tried to focus on the fact that we at least saw each other, even for a brief period.

***

Rissa's wedding was held in Gilroy, California: The Garlic Capital of the world. You would never guess that a town only an hour and a half away from San Francisco would give off a small-town boot and country aesthetic. But that was Gilroy. The town gave more of a Colorado vibe than a California one. It had rolling green hills that led to large ever green mountains teeming with alpine life.

For some reason, I felt uncomfortable in my own skin. I felt out of place, which was what I had been fearing since the bachelorette party. It seemed odd to me, actively being around one of my best friends for over ten years as I experienced such discomfort. I could tell Rissa was frustrated, or maybe she was just overwhelmed, but she was not her normal self.

At the rehearsal dinner I scurried her off. I made the move to steal her away from those who could not manage to understand the entirety of her inner monologue. It was my job to make sure she was okay, I had decided.

We stood off on a side street as she yelled to the stars about her frustrations. I listened intently as I hit the vape of THC I always kept on my person.

"Ugh, gimmie that," she said, stopping midsentence to snatch the vape out of my hand.

Rissa took a long hit and let it out, breathing harshly. I should note, it had been ten years since she last smoked. I giggled to myself. She was really going through it if she felt she should take a hit.

"I'm sorry," I said, trying to be a good friend for her at that moment.

"This is exactly why we did our vows and had a ceremony a few weeks ago, because I knew of course my actual wedding day would be frustrating as hell," she let out, exasperated.

"And so, fuck 'em!" I said, "that is your man already babe! Ain't no changing that."

We started laughing, because we knew the day was ridiculous. I hugged her, and we stood like that for a moment in an embrace before heading back to dinner.

I realized as we returned to the rehearsal dinner that my individual time with Rissa during the wedding weekend was limited, and a part of me felt hurt. I felt low on the totem pole of importance, even though I understood it was just the inner workings of my over-analytical and anxiety ridden brain telling me I was less than.

During the rehearsal dinner I sat between Nette and Roxi, Rissa's much younger sisters. Roxi had experienced intense epilepsy and seizures since birth. Rissa's parents had put me on seizure duty for the weekend. I held her medicine in my pocket in case of an emergency.

Halfway through dinner I turned to my left and noticed Roxi's head had drooped downwards. I immediately called for her mother and tapped Nette beside me so she could help as Roxi endured an elongated seizure, lasting several minutes. I held her hand while seated next to her, as she clutched and went in and out of the episode.

The buffet was served a few minutes before Roxi had her seizure. I found the selfishness of humankind to be unbearable as some of the attendants continued to get up and help themselves to heaping plates of food while Roxi was mid-seizure. If I was them, I would have remained seated until I knew she was back to good health.

After several minutes, Roxi relaxed back into normalcy. Family and friends stopped by the table to check in on her well-being. I made a mental note of those who did not and hypothetically curse them throughout the remainder of dinner in the private quarters of my mind.

The following morning, I was greeted by a typical gloomy California sky as I rubbed the sleep out of my eyes. As the girls prepared for the night ahead, I drove into town to run a last-minute errand for Rissa. I figured I would stop at a Dispensary while I was out and was shocked to discover I was in a dry town, with the nearest dispensary a twenty-five-minute drive away. I returned to the hotel and spent the remainder of time patiently waiting for the girls to finish getting ready so we could board the shuttle to the venue. By the time we loaded onto the bus to the Vineyard, the sun started to peak out from beyond gloomy clouds.

Unfortunately, Rissa's frustration with those around her only grew stronger throughout the day. Her feelings were justified, though. One bridesmaid prolonged the party from leaving the hotel because of her own makeup. Another bridesmaid gave the impression she was there as a commodity. She participated in the bare minimum and avoided helping Rissa altogether. As the day progressed, Rissa released her frustrations and I was pleased to witness her react to her own benefit. She moved on from the disappointment of her chosen party and focused on the importance of the day.

During the wedding's dinner reception, I was seated at a private table among the members of the bridal party who I found disingenuous. The conversation shifted uncomfortably to mundane small talk. I was overcome with shameful awkwardness when the date of the selfish bridesmaid asked me what I do for work. I fumbled over the words, eventually settling on declaring myself a bartender before I uncomfortably shuffled my feet and excused myself to the restroom.

Once I escaped the uneasiness of the bridal party's table, I found myself exploring the grounds of the vineyard. The venue was a small cottage farmhouse, surrounded by a large hillside vineyard with various citrus trees. The front yard had a barn and outdoor seating area to host the event. I plucked fruits from the trees throughout the night, hoping it would ease my nausea as I enjoyed a tangy treat.

I took in the view of the vast Northern California wilderness, the mountains nearly eclipsing the moon in their domination of the night skyline. I found Nette, Rissa's son, and her brother, Z, standing in the plowed earth of the vineyards about twenty feet from where I stood. I made my way over to them. It was a conscious effort to force myself into movement and conversation, as I felt my social battery had deteriorated and my discomfort had taken hold. The rest of the wedding night went by in a blur.

Upon arriving at Rissa's house in San Jose, I was unable to sleep for more than a few hours. The house they lived in, while large and spacious, had no central air conditioning. This was commonplace in Northern California as the temperatures would average in the low 50s and high 70s during the month of April. However, in stereotypical fashion as a born and raised Floridian, I never slept well without air conditioning.

I attempted to hide my awkwardness the remainder of the night and failed.

I sat feeling misplaced at my table, and hardly even touched the dance floor. I still struggled to determine why I felt down in the dumps. I felt the same wave of sadness take over my emotions that I had felt before Coachella. Was it the issues with my family? My grandma's health? The recent arguments with Gartner? I felt guilty and hoped I would not be remembered as a scorned guest at the wedding. Perhaps I was just being overcritical of myself again.

I decided to leave earlier than expected. I changed my flight to leave the following day in the afternoon. I felt guilty when I gave a sort of lie, saying that I did not feel well. I found myself desperately wishing to recede into the confines of Wilcox Place for the remainder of my time in California. I could no longer tolerate a large group of people. The hour-long flight south to Los Angeles was the last hurdle I had to overcome to subdue my anxiety and return to a comfortable setting. Once I made it to Gartner's apartment, I was convinced I would feel better.

I arrived back at the comfort of Gartner's apartment on Wilcox Place and fell asleep instantly. I remained there through the rest of the night and into the late morning the following day. When I finally came to, I felt refined, only to realize Gartner had already left for work. I vaguely recalled Garner's kiss to my forehead before he hurried out the door.

I pushed myself up and looked out the windows. The curtains were permanently held open to reveal the outside world, which provided a clear view inside for those who had a viewpoint of his window. In the beginning of our relationship, I asked Gartner if we could close the curtains, but he preferred to keep them open. At first, I considered it voyeuristic. Eventually, I deduced it to a dominant power structure he formulated for himself over time.

Clouds rolled into the city and remained hovering in place. Rain slowly drizzled and eventually turned into a steady pitter-patter against the window. Gartner arrived home later and found me slumped across the couch, fully engulfed in the world of the book I had brought with me for the trip.

Gartner started our conversation that day by complaining to me about his coworkers, slandering their skillset while he praised his own success and ego. He cited his colleagues' clothing choices as an example of something to critique. Gartner's colleagues wore expressive colors, while he chose to don a plain white shirt. He believed this allowed him to see the profile of the client reflected against a plain background, arguing that colors and graphics would just disrupt the silhouette. I allowed him to vent, grateful from the break of my own mind. I decided to focus on making food.

I prepared a chicken Caesar salad for dinner, while he continued to ramble on about his work frustrations. He let his guard down when he stated that he was not sure if he could sustain his hairstyling career much longer.

"I have been a hairstylist for over ten years and at this point I am in burnout mode," he said. I could relate, as I was burnt out from years of hospitality roles.
"What would you do instead?" I asked him.

"I don't know, this is the only job I have ever had. I put a lot of time into homing in on my craft," he said. He took a deep breath before he continued: "I wanted to be an actor, and my mom encouraged it, up until my dad did not. Can you imagine how that felt for me? Can you imagine having a family who never supported your dreams?"

I nodded understandingly, unsure how to navigate the conversation. I wondered if I was unable to provide the support to Gartner that he so desperately sought after. There were times I felt as though his charismatic charm blinded me to his in-authenticity. I ignored the thought and decided it would be best to try and support and uplift him.

"I am sorry, Gartner, I wish there was more I could say to comfort you. I can't fully understand how you feel because I never experienced that from my family... I held my dreams in my heart rather than verbalizing them, I was too afraid to speak to them out loud" I said.

"It doesn't feel good, and most days it sucks. My family was horrible to me, everyone in my life has been horrible to me," Gartner continued on this familiar conversational path.

"That is why I have always been alone. If I wasn't treated horribly, chances are they died of an overdose instead," he said solemnly.

"I hope you never say that about me," I said out loud before I could stop myself.

"Then don't do anything to me that would make me feel that way about you," he said simply, which irritated me. I tried not to let it show.

"I think you should be more forgiving," I said.

"You think I should forgive my parents for how horrible they were to me?" Gartner asked, incredulous.

"I think you should consider it; I think you should try to make some sort of amends; you often mention your parents - especially your mom. I think you miss them and your hometown more than you let on," I confessed, hoping it would reach the part of him that would finally let me in.

"My family was horrible to me, I can never forgive them," he said firmly. "The last time I saw my dad he helped me move into this apartment, and I thought he would be excited that I had moved back to Los Angeles and that we had the opportunity to bond. Everything was fine until he stepped foot in the apartment once and called it a shit hole. He argued with me on every slight inconvenience for him, so I eventually told him to leave and not come back."

"That was rude of him," I said carefully, considering my words before I continued: "Unfortunately our parents' generation do not understand the realities we are presented at our ages with the rising cost of living. I feel as though most people their age like to overreact. I am not excusing everything they have done, but that is your family, and you still love each other, that bond is eternal. My parents have fucked up a lot and I have forgiven them. I have fucked up just as much towards them and they have forgiven me. I think it would be good for you, Gartner, to try to find a way to forgive instead."

"You do not understand," he said harshly.

"Well, I am doing my best to try to," I responded, suddenly feeling like he was trying to make me into the bad guy.

"Listen to me and understand when I say I do not want anything to do with them, they were abusive, and that should be enough!" Gartner was raising his voice now.

I let the conversation drop and was again feeling dejected that I was unable to persuade his mindset. It must have been hard for him to make the choice to cut them off. I cut mine off for three months once and it was unbearable, I never felt so out of place. And sure, my family was not perfect, and they often did or said things that hurt my feelings or upset me. But they were always there at the end of the day - they always forgave me, and I always forgave them.

The next day the clouds had gone and the rain subsided. The forecaster for KTLA announced the city had its last rainy day, and the radar predicted clear and sunny skies for the remainder of the spring season well into summer. Later in the evening Gartner dropped me off at the airport for my flight home. A week later he was meant to visit me in Orlando for my nephew's first birthday.

## *Good for Me*

My nephew's first birthday took place on the 6<sup>th</sup> of May 2024. Gartner flew in for the occasion on a forty-eight-hour trip. I could tell my sister and mother were impressed when I told them he planned to fly in for the party because it was important to me. Gartner put forth the effort to be a part of my family. I knew they liked him just as much as I did after they met him back in March, but his continued devotion to my family and to me further cemented him into our livelihood.

After I picked Gartner up from the airport and we returned to my home, we took a nap before heading to Universal Studios Park. I had received complimentary tickets from a friend I used to work at the theme park with back in 2014.

I wanted Gartner to enjoy himself, but throughout the day I could not stop myself from wondering if he fully conceptualized the luxury of complimentary tickets to any of the parks in Orlando. If I never brought him, he would have never visited willingly.

At the end of the day, I asked what his favorite ride had been and in typical Gartner fashion, he did not answer. He had no tether to theme parks, something he had explicitly told me a handful of times. He only agreed to visit any theme parks because I wanted to. I wish he would have given me some semblance of an answer, but I never told him and maybe that was part of the problem.

"I never came to the parks as a kid; that's something you and your family have always done and loved. I'm just here because I love you - I would never go to one if it was not for you," he said to me again.

As he said the words I knew deep down, he had not aimed to hurt me, but I considered that Gartner had attributed his accompaniment to the parks with me as an act of service. He believed he channeled an exemplary boyfriend when he tagged along. What I wanted was for him to enjoy it himself, to see how much fun we could have together in this environment that was so familiar to me. Instead, it just seemed like he wanted to boost his own ego by doing what he thought he should.

Gartner and I stayed with my sister, mom, and my nephew, Wy in an overly large and modernly bland home in the touristy hub of Orlando. It was one of those places built to house large families playing tourist for extended periods of time. My sister had rented the property to host the party. The house was extravagant in terms of size - with eleven bedrooms and five bathrooms. It could have been seen as over the top for a one-year old's birthday, but we were all equally excited to celebrate Wyatt.

The partygoers from my mom's side of the family outnumbered the rest. If Gartner felt nervous about meeting the remainder of my family, he showed no sign of discomfort. My family instantly gravitated to him. They asked him questions about his personal life with sincere interest, like where he grew up and what he did for work. Halfway through a conversation about the town Gartner grew up in, my cousin turned to me and asked me when I would move out of Florida to Los Angeles. I was caught off guard, and that was her intention. My family had always been a calculated bunch. I chuckled uncomfortably and I met the quizzitive eyes of my family looking intently at me. I had a flashback then, to a memory from the week prior of myself hunched over my laptop, frantically submitting applications to jobs across the Los Angeles metro.

Luckily Gartner swooped in at the perfect moment and answered for me: "We have talked about moving. I originally wanted to leave Los Angeles, but I think I'll stay a bit longer. We agreed we could live there together for a while before eventually moving back to Florida. Because I know how important it is for Robert to be by his family," he said with dignified confidence. He did not stutter; he did not fumble his words. I was reminded how much he loved me as he delicately explained to my family that I would be moved away from Orlando.

My cousin Teri encouraged my move, and I felt at ease. I could feel the break in tension with my mother, who preferred me to remain as close to her as possible, where she could easily reach me if she needed to.

After the party ended my mom drove Gartner and me to the airport. Gartner flew home to Los Angeles, and I flew to New York City for another wedding. This wedding was a massive meetup of a collective group of friends that all met each other on Twitter, me included. The ceremony, reception, and after party were held in various venues split between Manhattan and Brooklyn.

I met the bride of the wedding, Trippy, on Twitter years ago, when we had both established ourselves into the dance music community that evolved on the social media site. Trippy met her husband Aus in the city, and together they would eventually move to Australia (where he was from) shortly after the wedding.

While staying in NYC I crashed on my friend Spunky's pull out couch in her one-bedroom apartment. It was in a pre-war building on the Upper East Side. I met Spunky in 2015, when we worked together at a resort in Orlando. We bonded over our shared love for the band Twenty-One Pilots and connected through our conductive enthusiastic energy.

She was born and raised in Scottsdale, Arizona. Her personality was blessed by the desert sun as a vibrant Leo. She had short blonde hair that bounced enthusiastically as she walked. Her radiant personality complimented her short height and stature. She may have been short, but she was mighty. That's where she got her nickname from me: Spunky, she was one hell of a spunky chick.

My flight landed late in the night. The captain of the plane looped around the city, flying high enough over the skyline for the skyscrapers to appear below, close enough to land upon if I were to open the exit door and jump.

Once I landed, I hailed a cab to Spunky's apartment. As soon as I was through her apartment door I was engulfed into an elongated and soulful hug, full of adoration and love. After we briefly reconnected, we walked to the Buffalo Wild Wings two blocks from us for takeout.

We lounged on the pull out in the living room and caught up on our most recent life updates. When Spunky lived in Florida we were inseparable, and our friendship strengthened easily. She met my family, and I met hers. We vacationed together, even referred to each other as our brother and sister. The last time Spunky and I were together was two years before in Palm Springs, of course for a bachelorette party. Since then, we both fell victim to the game of life and found ourselves far too busy to properly meet up.

I texted Gartner once I landed and again once I arrived at Spunky's apartment. Five hours later I had yet to receive a response. I checked his location and saw that he was back at Wilcox Place. I deduced he was tired and fell asleep upon entering the apartment. I eventually relaxed on the pull out, long after Spunky had fallen asleep. I felt euphoric as Sex and the City played on the television as I drifted to sleep.

In the morning, I checked my phone. With no text from Gartner, I knew something was wrong. I knew him well enough, and in a way, we were similar with our texting habits. His no response was the response he offered.

I dressed myself for the wedding in a brown ensemble complete with free-flowing pants that I began to feel subconscious about as the day progressed. I walked to the nearest subway station, braving a brisk and wet morning. The spring air had not fully left the city and the dewy remnants of

April showers pushed through The Big Apple, with rain forecasted for later that day.

I took the subway to Brooklyn. I visited New York City three times when I was in high school, but I had yet to visit one of the other boroughs. I got off at Prospect Park and wandered through the expansive space; a slice of heavenly nature that caused amnesia as your mind is tricked to forget you are in one of the largest cities in the world.

The wedding was widespread, with the ceremony held in the morning in a beautiful brick building on the outskirts of Prospect Park. The attendees were a lush group of people from the Twitter-verse along with a mixture of Trippy and Aus's family. The inside of the ceremonial room was a classic wooden interior, complete with simple chairs centered around a classically elegant central walkway that led to the altar. I was seated behind a mutual Twitter-friend I had followed for years - it was our first time actually meeting in real life. Around the room were people I had met when we were previously too intoxicated to string together grammatically correct sentences, and it had been years since those moments. We could effectively communicate while intoxicated now.

I was taken back to a time when we were able to dance freely with one another at a dodgy club in downtown Miami as 'Good for Me' by Above & Beyond queued Trippy's entrance down the aisle and to the altar. I thought if only our younger selves were able to see us now.

The reception was held outside Times Square near Penn Station, at a restaurant called Bourbon and Branch. Later, alters were held at a bar Trippy worked at called Nothing Really Matters. A year from then Aus and Trippy would be living in Australia, away from the divided United States. Thousands of miles that would separate foundational friendships.

Throughout the day I sent a string of texts to Gartner and still received zero responses.

I became overwhelmed by time, the illusive bandit that steals from us blindly. Ten years somehow felt like ten days, or even just five seconds ago.

Throughout the room I spotted past friends that I no longer spoke to. I kept an eye as some lingered across from me, as we pretended not to glance in each other's direction. I was aware of old crushes and flings as they floated around. I took shots and pictures with the same person I once danced with until ten in the morning at a club in downtown Miami.

Time had caught up to me, with the years laid out before me through friendships and now-strangers.
I feared thinking about my own perception too much. I worried I was intolerable to some. I could appear to be overdramatic or irritating or annoying to others around me.

I thought this of myself for so long that when Trippy invited me to the wedding a year ago, I audibly gasped and cried to myself in private. I did not expect to receive an invitation.

I realized I can be harder on myself than anyone else, with myself as my own worst critic. I knew I should be kinder to myself; I thought that I had made it this far already and that alone was impressive, given the circumstances.

I thought of Gartner again as I started to feel overwhelmed with my emotions. I stepped outside of the club into the stairway corridor - either leading to the subway below to my right or the New York streets above to my left.

The bar was uniquely placed and appeared smaller in scale from the outside. I thought it was a place that Gartner would love, so I decided to call him.

He answered after a few rings. I could tell by his low-energy response that he was not in a conversational mood. I shoved the sadness welling up inside me back down, because I did not want him to know that his reaction to hearing my voice had dimmed my spirits. It was the type of information I did not want anyone to ever know, let alone my boyfriend.

"Baby," I said, "the wedding has been so fun, I really miss you and- "I couldn't help it, I started to cry. "I just want to say," I choked down my tears, "I feel so thankful and loved to be here, I have always wanted this, and I am feeling so overwhelmed in a good way. I just wish you were here."

"I'm glad you are enjoying it," he said, monotone and short. "Go have fun baby, go back inside with your friends." The dryness in his voice was concrete.

"Okay, are you alright though?" I asked, concerned.

"Yeah, I'm fine, do not worry, we'll talk later." And just like that, he hung up the phone.

I knew something was off, but I chose to ignore it. I felt irked by his short response to my emotions. Gartner could have responded with a different cadence. I wondered if he felt jealous of my experience in New York with my friends.

During one of our many FaceTimes in the beginning of our relationship, Gartner told me he had a hard time maintaining friends, and in the same breath said that most of his friends from childhood had all but passed away to drug overdose.

He was born and raised in the Santa Cruz area. Gartner had confided in me about his life in the country mountain hills of Corralito's, California, until he later moved to Capitola.

Then Gartner left Santa Cruz and moved to Portland with his hometown boyfriend at the time. Eventually, Gartner left him and moved to Chicago where he began to establish himself as a personal hairstylist.

While living in Chicago, Gartner's childhood friends began to pass away from drug use. He once opened up to me about his experience at a funeral for a friend who had passed away. He flew from Chicago to Santa Cruz to attend, only to be told by another friend that he was unwanted at the gathering. The friends he had spent years with had ostracized him. It didn't make sense to me, how people could be so cruel to him during a time they clearly all needed each other.

When Gartner decided to move to Los Angeles from Chicago, the friends he made in the windy city suddenly ghosted him during his final few weeks there.

Abandoned, Gartner had felt abandoned and alone. I could look at him and see the hurt boy peek through every now and again, unaware how to express himself correctly when he feared he was losing another person in his life.

I tried my best to understand his thought process, because I loved him. I was determined to show him I loved him by knowing who he was in his soul. The sum of his existence decoded through my devoted adoration. I was able to guess some tid-bits of information I had gathered from him over the course of our relationship, but it was limited to expressions of basic subplots in his life that were shared in small snippets. It was never the entire story in full detail. I felt that I was unable to love him properly if he refused to open up to me fully.

I was still deep in thought when Reni exited out of the bar and found me in the corridor. She interrupted my train of thought, happily bringing my worrisome mind to the present function. She coaxed me back inside the party where the other patrons were dancing.

Reni climbed on top of a leather bench that spanned across the wall and shook her butt in the air. I knew she was able to tell I was off, not necessarily from the conversation with Gartner, but she was trying to take my mind off my self doubt clearly reflected on my face. I yelled cheerfully in support of her as she continued to dance above everyone else.

"So, what is up?" she asked after she climbed down from the bench.

"Nothing, Gartner is just being weird," I said coyly.

"You see!" she said exasperatedly, "Are you sure you can trust him?" she asked me.

"Yeah, he really is a good guy," I said, confidently. I wanted to believe it myself. I was still convinced I should believe in what we could be together. It didn't help knowing Reni's doubts about Gartner, given his own conflicting opinions about her.

"I get suspicious of him," she said then, trying not to upset me. "I do not want anything to happen to you, but if you are sure..." she said, shrugging.

"Yeah, I think he just has a lot of traumas and hasn't learned how to express himself correctly." I watched the disappointment in Reni's face take over. I laughed to myself internally- we were so similar, I would have reacted the same.

I wanted to remove myself from the situation and I felt a pit in my stomach to hide that Gartner was ignoring me. Who said this was the love I deserved? I stole a look at my friends around the room. People I had known for over ten years. I wondered if this would be the last time we were all gathered in the same place together. Reunions would be hard to accomplish once Trippy and Aus were in Australia.

The afters ended around three in the morning, after Trippy delivered a heartfelt speech transcribing our extended Twitter friendship history. The small bar was left filled with more friends than family, though a few of Aus's family remained. The entire lot of partygoers were intoxicated. The perfect night drew to a close. I took a final glance around the room of familiar faces and noted this could be the last time.

The Time Bandit struck again.

After the bar closed and we began to stumble out onto the streets to return to our respective accommodations, I decided to walk in the direction of the Upper East Side, where I eventually caught the Q train back to Spunky's apartment.

As I walked the city streets I took note of its stillness. One of the most heavily populated cities in the world, and yet there was no one bustling around this late at night. The night was crisp, with the air chilling my bony fingertips. The clouds from earlier had given way to indigo skies. There was nowhere else on earth that could have hosted such a momentous occasion other than New York City.

I took in the grandeur of being alone on the New York streets. I wondered yet again, how sustainable Gartner and I were. I wondered if he felt good about himself while he ignored me. I began to wonder if he purposefully tried to ruin my trip due to his own insecurities. The thought rattled my brain as I let myself into Spunky's apartment and collapsed onto the pull-out sofa, quickly falling into a restful sleep.

The following morning Spunky and I nabbed a breakfast sammie from a bodega close to her apartment. We took the subway towards Battery Park and lower Manhattan. We found Reni and her boyfriend, Fonz, waiting for us. We wandered the city, actively playing tourist as we visited iconic filming locations from the Sex and the City franchise, per my request.

In the evening Spunky and I met with friends I had not seen in a few years due to our busy schedules. Bebe, another Twitter friend who wasn't directly linked to the core group at the wedding, and Blu, a friend I met at my second high school.

After dinner at a Korean spot outside of Times Square, Bebe led us to Brooklyn where she lived. In my New York foods research, I found that Brooklyn housed a plethora of dairy-free options for me to indulge in.

We located a small vegan-friendly diner and ordered milkshakes with a side of loaded fries to share. Once the clock struck midnight, Spunky and Blu traveled back to their apartments together. Bebe and I walked back to her apartment just ten minutes from the diner.

When we got to her room, we took turns passing a baggie back and forth to one another. We tell each other casual updates from our lives after a few years apart.

Our friendship spanned ten years with quality memories to match. We spent one awkward New Years together in Bebe's family farm home in rural Kentucky. It happened after she had driven to a bordering state for a late-night booty call without consulting with her mother and subsequently crashed her vehicle into a ditch. We developed a concrete connection then, and it was truly everlasting.

"He has been annoying me lately, not gonna lie," I admitted out loud for the first time, knowing Bebe would understand I was talking about Gartner without saying his name.

"I fear he has spent a lot of time alone and that has not helped his communication or understanding skills. He has not had to work cooperatively with anyone other than his job, and I wonder if I jumped the gun. So far on this trip he has not helped me feel any better about being with him, as he continues to ignore me. I have hardly talked to him since I walked off the airplane when I got here. I've had an amazing trip-" I stifled a cry, "but I can't deny that it has been slightly tainted by how Gartner has treated me. I almost wonder if he did it on purpose because he is not here, but I do not want to believe that. I wanted to share these memories from this trip with him. But I feel as though I have not been able to do that" I said, exhausted. It felt like a release, finally expressing my thoughts to one person I could let my guard down with regarding Gartner. I did not want to hear perspectives from anyone else other than Bebe at the time.

"Why doesn't he have friends?" she asked, curious.

"He told me that they all died of overdose when he was younger, and he doesn't really talk to anyone in LA either. Except for his clients, who he claims are his friends, but I do not agree."

"I don't think that your clients can really be your true friends at the end of the day," she said.

Part of me agreed with Bebe, and I wondered if this was all worth the hassle. Before I left Los Angeles I applied for jobs around where Gartner lived. Something deep within me had told me that I was destined to live there and make a life with Gartner.

I hoped it would work, and for the first time in a long time I had believed in something other than the bare minimum. I deserved to fall in love in a different city and start anew. Gartner was my reason to experience the grandeur of the cosmos within me, infinitely unbound by my time with him. The city of LA and Gartner tugged at the invisible string attached to my heart. I had the will and Gartner was the way. I felt these contradicting thoughts flow through my consciousness for the rest of my trip.

I waited until I was back in Orlando to confront Gartner about his willful avoidance. He cowardly apologized in an effort to soothe my discomfort. I somehow could feel the control in my life slipping from my grasp. I rationalized his avoidance as jealousy, though I wasn't sure that made me feel any better. I willed my own ignorance to believe in the possibility my gut could be wrong. I ignored it, I owed it to myself to try. Maybe I could save myself and Gartner.

\*\*\*

After a few days home with my family in Orlando, I was seated on my couch, bored and unmoved. My phone vibrated and before I slid the button across the screen to answer the call, my sixth sense ignited and I was acutely aware that it would be a job offer in Los Angeles waiting for me on the other line.

The interview was quick. I was offered the job. When the interviewer asked me when I would be able to start orientation, my pulse quickened and informed the interviewer I could start at the end of the month.

Once the call ended, I jumped up and down in joyful elation. My wildest dreams were coming to fruition. I called Gartner immediately, excited to share my employment opportunity and begin our own version of a westward expansion. The sun was due to rise in the west for me, a new opportunity, California was the northern star at dawn.

"Hello gorgeous," he said with gusto as he answered.

"Hi baby, I wanted to let you know something exciting that just happened!"

"What is it?" he asked me apprehensively.

"I got a job offer in Los Angeles!"

"Oh my god babe! That's amazing!" He said elated, his cadence changed at a rapid rate with each word I spoke "Where are you? When do you start?"

"It's at The Market down the street from the apartment on Wilcox Place. I told them I could come after Memorial Day weekend, because I have a few shifts at the pop-up coffee spot and I do not want to leave them hanging. So, I figured I could drive myself that weekend to you."

"You cannot just do that," he said, his tone of voice changing sharply.

"Do what?" I asked, confused.

"You can't just suddenly decide when you want to move. I am the one who is moving you and that's not fair to me, I want to be there with you when you drive across the country."

"Oh... I'm sorry, I just thought it would be easy. I mean, I did not know I would get the job, and I figured this would be-"

"No, that is extremely shellfish of you," he cut me off before I was able to finish what I was saying. "Especially since I am the one spending money for you to move here..."

"I don't think it is that serious, I did not know you would be upset beca-"

Once again, Gartner cut me off: "How did you not think I would be upset? As if I would be okay with you driving alone across the country?"

"Well yeah, I mean it's not a fun drive, but I did not think you-"

"No, you didn't think," he cut in, the anger spewing from his voice.

The words began to stumble out with my need to explain things, to ease the situation. "I think you are overreacting to a simple remedy, and I am sorry to not consider your own feelings, but I was unaware that you felt so strongly. I was excited that I got offered the position, and maybe I should have told them I needed to talk it over first, but I also didn't want them to rescind the offer... I thought you would have been happy to finally have me there with you? When do you want me to move, then?"

"Well, since you got the job, why don't I just come next week?" he asked back.

"Next week? I don't think that's enough time." My pulse quickened, no longer from the excitement but from something else

"When will you have enough time, then?" he asked.

"Give me at least two weeks. I don't want to leave the coffee shop in a bad spot," I tried to reason with Gartner, which was feeling impossible.

"Fuck the coffee shop! They don't pay you well, and I can just pay you for the two days you were supposed to work anyway," he said, as if his money could always solve everything.

I found the arrogant statement off-putting, and I wondered how I had not noticed this side of Gartner before. This controlling and inherently selfish nature was not comforting to see. I wondered if he felt possessive of me. I asked myself if I had let my own overthinking interpret his reaction. I understood his frustration in a way, but part of me felt like he had ruined a good thing with his unsavory response. My intentions had been pure, why could he not see that?

I sat on my couch in silence as the disbelief from Gartner's reaction washed over me.
I realized my time left in Florida was diminishing, much quicker than I thought. The Time Bandit had struck yet again. I needed to pack my life into boxes and prepare to move. The guilt weighed on me as I had little over two weeks to tell my family I was going.

I was presented with a new challenge, aside from Gartner's attitude. I attempted to announce my move to Los Angeles to my family. Attempt one was informing my mother, who awkwardly danced around the subject. Unfortunately, it was not the first time I received a cold shoulder upon my announcement of relocation. Years prior when I broke the news to my family about my move to Denver, they reacted just as coldly.

I reconciled with strategic moves that came with my personal game of life. Every choice I made up to this point had led me here, so had the universe punished me for poor choice? Not everything is perfect, I knew that. Some things would take time to smooth out their sharp edges. I was prepared to face my family's opposition, even if I truly craved their support.

One week remained before relocation. My family had not yet acknowledged my plan. A hushed reality swept under the rug. I wished my mother would discuss the transition with me, share in my anticipation. It would have helped foster a sense of excitement about the new chapter in life. Out of all the people in my life, her support was particularly meaningful. Meanwhile, Gartner urged me to finalize the rental car reservation, which only increased my anxiety. Life continued to barrel forward at an alarming rate.

I met some friends at a local DJ showcase at a lesser-known club downtown. Reni stayed home for the evening, but Kash and KT were there. We drifted in and out of the crowd to the DJ booth, taking a shot at the decks.

I was unable to relax; my anxiety fired on all cylinders. My palms were sweaty, and the music only quickened my pulse and agitated my anxiety further. I left the venue to go outside. I should have felt suffocated from the thick spring air, but Florida's humidity was all-too familiar to me. In a way, it comforted me. My family's silent reaction juxtaposed to Gartner's boisterous one unnerved me. Two-halves of my heart were fighting an imbalance. When all I needed was verbal confirmation of support.

I spiraled through time, unable to control it at the speed I wish I could. The Time Bandit had control again. I wished Gartner respected my time and yet somehow, I knew he wished I was more respectful of his money. What was more valuable, time or money?

We argued all day before I made it to the show. I felt I was on the cusp of a mental breakdown. My family and I had avoided each other, and I felt Gartner ignored my mental decomposition. I could not focus on packing until my family verbally approved. We had always been there for each other. I knew they would support me overtime, but I needed to hear the confirmation from them personally. I was worried the move was too soon. I texted Gartner.

Gartner's advice to combat my parents was to pack my belongings up into boxes they can see, to deliver a strong message. I was frustrated with the lack of meaningful support. I felt forced to move faster through time, against my own comfortability. I expressed my discomfort and he dismissed me as if it was simply a part of growing up, a part of adulthood I had yet to experience for myself. This only aggravated me further.

Gartner and I continued to argue via text. I told him he did not understand the implications of my close-knit family bond. The reality was not as simple as it would be if I had no family ties. No tether to a life that time and blood built.

Gartner told me I should not blame him for misunderstanding the predicament, or for the stubborn nature of my family. I told him I was facing a difficult scenario, and I felt he lacked empathy for my situation.

I called him hoping we could move beyond the tense moment. We were both nervous for the anticipated move, and it was clearly going to be an adjustment for us both. I understood the concept of a pressure cooker.

I texted him to answer me and received no response via text. I tried to call him and received no answer. I called again, and after he ignored attempt two, I tried a few more times, only to be left with the sound of his voicemail. After the fifth call, Gartner finally texted me:

> You really hurt my feelings, texting me all that while I am out with my friends,
> making me feel guilty for things I didn't do. I am so frustrated with how you
> invalidated my own feelings, I don't want to talk on the phone.

I texted him back:

> I am sorry Gartner; I wasn't trying to do that, and I am overwhelmed. I thought we were okay? I am sorry for my freak out earlier.

Gartner:

> You are causing me to feel guilty about my family and invalidating my feelings. Leave me the fuck alone, you are being the biggest asshole.

Another attempt to call him was met with rejection. I called two more times consecutively, and after the third attempt he answered. I sighed out a sense of relief. I momentarily thought it was the end of us, before we even had a real chance to start. Gartner sobbed as he explained how deeply I hurt him. He expressed that he had been excited for our future, at least before tonight.

How did we allow ourselves to reach this boiling point? Part of me was ashamed as I begged for his forgiveness. I feared the embarrassment of a star-crossed love affair.

The night was wet, and the Florida tropic summer had begun to show its boggy head in the central region. Dew attached itself to blades of grass around the parking lot and the tarmac had a slicked, glossy appearance as moisture seeped into the concrete. I paced back and forth outside as I continued to argue with Gartner. I hoped my friends would stay inside, ignorant to my discomfort.

I apologized several more times. I realized the increasingly difficult nature it was to interact with him when he was this emotional. My apologies were met with rejection, and he refused to believe my sincerity. It felt like we had to talk in circles, me begging for him to hear me out while just kept saying how much of an asshole I was being. It didn't feel fair. I couldn't understand how the day had taken such a drastic shift - we should have been celebrating my new job, the start of our new lives together.

After I was able to keep him on the phone long enough, I managed to quell his tears. He had finally calmed down enough that I felt confident in my ability to patchwork enough damage to continue my apology later. I decided at that point to let him rest. We were let down by one another, but I wondered if he failed to realize he let me down as well. Everything seemed to be falling on me - when again, I was the one about to pack up and move across the country to be with him.

Time passed for us to say a peaceful goodnight to each other. I slipped back inside and found my friends, who were crowded around the DJ booth to watch one of the girls spin that we knew from the downtown community.

If any of my friends wondered where I had been for an hour while I argued with Gartner, they failed to ask. I sighed a sense of relief to myself for not having to expose the real reason behind my prolonged disappearance. I realized the mood had died and considered that maybe I had outgrown the life I had known. After thirty minutes, I left without saying goodbye. On the drive home I thought perhaps that was what Gartner had wanted all along.

I called Gartner again once I got home. I was shocked, he answered. A muffled sniffle was his response. I told him how sorry I was for upsetting him but tried to explain how he also upset me. I apologized sincerely for what I said and professed my love to him by committing to overcome any obstacle we faced.

I confessed that I was suffering from high amounts of anxiety pertaining to the move. Untapped fears of being left on the street and alone after an argument began to creep from the doubtful corners of my mind. Gartner vowed to never let anything like that happen, but I had undeniable skepticism. I put all my faith into him, which could be seen as a foolish choice for a potentially disastrous love.

Once he calmed down further, he brought out his productive side. Putting the plans into motion. He booked the rental car, and I felt a shift in myself. Suddenly his mood had lifted so quickly. My critical thinking skills had succumbed to the woes of my adoration. I had little to no time to consider the outcome, I just knew I had to try. I owed it to myself. By the following week, I would be a California resident. Gartner was helping to make that happen.

A few days prior to the move, just as we had worked through the argument from before, Gartner confessed that he was impatiently waiting to propose to me. I had been researching wedding venues for some time already without telling him. I knew he wanted to marry me just as much as I did him. It was like once we had things that were so exciting to look forward to, the stress and worries from before began to melt away.

I had met someone who was as excited to plan a wedding as I was, making my heart erupt into a frenzy of butterflies. I had not felt so hopelessly in love since high school. I thought I would marry my first boyfriend then too, and maybe that was a sign for me then. The deity of hidden meanings had taken an affliction to my suffering.

As Gartner and I continued to discuss our future together, he suddenly pivoted mid-sentence and insinuated that he had worries about my lack of accountability, claiming that he feared I would slack off in laziness.

If it had not been for our fight the night before, I would have found a way to argue his lack of confidence in me. Just because I had not been working in Orlando - due to a tumultuous job market - that did not equate to a lack in work ethic. It was hurtful that he would immediately jump to this conclusion.

Gartner told me he'd wait to see how dedicated of a worker I was when the time came, and of course this irritated me further, but I chose not to push it. Part of me was used to people underestimating me, to the point where sometimes I felt as though I underestimated myself.

Gartner sent a long text message as he boarded his flight to Orlando for the moving day:

> I want to apologize and write you a letter saying everything because you really deserve some love and
> understanding these past few days and I have not
> been a good boyfriend to you at all emotionally especially when you need it right now and
> I am so sorry for that baby.
>
> First off, I want to apologize for my behavior.

I have been a lot to say the least; extremely bratty, needy,
 insecure and having selective hearing to the max.
For real, I am not liking who I have been lately and I
have been really thinking about this all and wondering
where I dropped myself/confidence only
to realize that I am completely self-sabotaging myself
by pushing you away hard subconsciously.

As you know, my whole life I have been really hurt by
 the ones who were supposed to love me to the point
that I am absolutely terrified, of love or being loved.
I am terrified of giving myself to someone and I'm terrified
of rejection from someone I love.

I have always been like this since I can remember.
isolating myself, running away from my problems and
devouring myself in my depression thoughts and anxieties.
 It is all I knew and understood to do cause I never had
peace or the support I needed to get through. I really
 don't want to be like that anymore and you have been
helping me so much.

You genuinely are the best thing to ever happen to me.
You are healing my inner child and trauma so much
everyday. You give me so much love and understanding.
 You are everything I could have ever asked for.
Thank you so much for everything you do.
I really couldn't explain my appreciation for you
 and how thankful I am to have you in my life.

I promise to be your rock from here on out.
I genuinely want this moving experience to be really
bonding and for us to fall even more in love with each other.
I promise to have your back and give you an ear that won't
be so selective to my best of my abilities. I really want you.
I really really love you. I will fight for you. I will by your side
to the end and I cannot wait to marry you.

Forever my baby.

## *The Thoroughfare*

The morning Gartner landed for the big move was a gloomy day in May. I read his text message over and my stomach churned. My gut knew of the dangers before I could consciously recognize them. Humans are intelligent creatures, but we are often blind to our own destinies. On self-reflection, I thought I deserved the type of love Gartner offered me. So, I destabilized my intuition. I texted Gartner back and thanked him for his apology. I vowed to stand by his side indefinitely, till death do us part, devoted even before there was a ring. I wondered if I should have thrown in the towel, if I should have stayed in Florida. But I persisted, I had to know for myself. Curiosity killed the cat, after all.

We loaded the car in a steady drizzle, as the sky cried with signs of renewal. My dad helped us pack our boxes into the vehicle and I was able to see the man beneath the fearless mask he often wore. I felt a pang of discomfort. Once we left my parents' house, I had Gartner stop to see my mother at her work. She hugged me goodbye and instantly started crying. I knew she would miss me. I would miss her, too. She hugged me tight, offering me a warm embrace. If I had no one else to love me in this life, I knew my mother always would.

As we pulled away and we began our drive west, I watched my mother in the sideview mirror of the rental car. She continued to wipe her eyes. As I witnessed her crying, I cried to myself and felt that same sense of discomfort again. I allowed myself to feel guilty, for indulging in my selfish desire to seek out a new life built on love. We turned a corner and she slipped from view.

*** 

After the night we fought, my body internalized the anxiety that seeped itself into the confines of my skin and bones, like a sticky substance stuck to the inner fibers of my being. I couldn't stop sobbing as we made the drive out of Florida. I had a deep love for my home, and I was anxious for what was to come with the move ahead. He tried to calm me down by rubbing my back with his free hand while the other steered us towards our future. My last weeks in Florida had slipped through my fingertips so quickly, the Time Bandit had shown itself again.

At one point while we had argued, I blurted out that I thought Gartner spent too much time alone, which had diminished his will to compromise. If I had not suggested it to him, would he have ever thought about it? Or did he already know? Had I struck an insecurity of his? I never meant to hurt him but maybe that's all I did. No one told me this about growing up, how many wars you would have with yourself over your own right and wrongs. I hoped it would not return to haunt me.

Gartner and I were flawed from the moment we first met. I was broke, jobless, and utterly depressed. And that was how Gartner had continued to perceive me. After our first date I had been exhausted, I was unable to sleep for more than a few hours at a time, beginning months before I even met him. Then I began to sleep miraculously, finding a peaceful slumber when I was with him. I thought he was the remedy, the answer to my problems.

Throughout our relationship Gartner would remind me of the proclamation I made to him. My vulnerability was used as a weapon against me. I cautioned letting my guard down around him afterwards. We had promised to love one another, and I hoped we could see it through. I was determined for the both of us.

During our long drive, we stopped in Pascagoula, Mississippi to visit my long-term friend, Hutch, who had recently moved to the coastal town. Hutch and I met on Twitter through mutual friends, and our adoration for dance music. She and I were there for each other in our foundational youth, we scoured Miami and New Orleans together. We made childish mistakes together, where freshly out of our teenage youth we explored the new world.

We reached her home just before ten at night and remained till well past midnight. We stretched our legs and let her dog, Ghost run amuck around the large yard. Hutch and I caught up with one another after it had been a few years. The Time Bandit can be observed in all facets of life.

Our visit was short and I was unable to coordinate the thoughts in my head with the voice from my mouth. Hutch led us to our rental and before I opened the door she hugged me tightly in a warm embrace. I squeezed her back. She is tall and boisterous; her eyes are big and fawn-like, and her short, blonde hair bobs and weaves as she talks with gusto. I felt her shoulders shake as she started to cry, and I cried with her.

"You are gonna be okay, don't worry," she said to me. "I am proud of you." I let out a sob and nodded my head. I was at a loss for words. She turned to Gartner and made direct eye contact: "Do not hurt him," she said in a protective voice, before turning on her heel and returning to her home.

"What are you feeling right now?" Gartner asked me as we drove down the dark Mississippi streets.
"Overwhelmed" I breathed.
"Why? What was all that about?"

"She just told me she was proud of me; I have not heard that much before," I said. "She knows what I have been through, and I think we both thought this would never happen for me."

"Why would you think something like this could never happen?"

"I don't know, it's a silly thing to think, I know" I said.

I grabbed a tissue from inside the lockbox and blew my nose. "She knows everything about me, what happened to me before I had even met her, things from my past that I just do not talk about."

"Do you think you are unlovable?" Gartner asked me then.

"No," I say confidently, "I think people have not perceived me in the light I should be seen in... I feel almost as if I am constantly in a shadow."

"Why do you say that?" he asked me.

"Because it's mostly true... Look, when I was a kid, I used to lie to try and cover up my sexuality... and it never went over well. Sometimes I think if I had never done that and had just been more honest with myself and others, then maybe I would not be this fucked up," I said with conviction.

We were quiet the rest of the ride that night.

The following morning, we awoke to a foggy sky at the Best Western in the central business district of New Orleans. I had been to New Orleans many times with Hutch, and it felt unnatural to not be with her in the Big Easy for once. Gartner had never been to the deep south before we met.

I guided him on a brief walking tour of the French Quarter. We ended in Jackson Square as we admired the Cathedral-Basilica of Saint Louis King of France. The resilient cathedral stood proudly against the robust Mississippi river.

Before we left, Gartner approached the Cathedral wall and placed the palm of his hand against the exterior of the building. I watched his chest rise as he steadied himself and controlled his breathing. I assumed this was his own form of worship.

Gartner insisted on driving most of the route to California. After we stopped for food outside of San Antonio, I took over the wheel as I caravaned us through the western outskirts of San Antonio and further into central Texas.

As Gartner rested in the passenger seat, I was left to ponder the several times in my life I experienced unbelievable encounters. The encounters felt like they could only be explained by forces of natural ether, powered by the earth and cosmos. Matter warped by our own lived-in observations. Freshly eighteen, my vice was marijuana. I had never endured a hangover from the plant and that was enough for me to continue smoking over drinking alcohol.

It was a bitterly cold January circa 2016, and I found myself at a house party hosted by a coworker from the Studios park. Earlier in the day, my friend picked up from a local dealer who carried a backpack with various strains of weed with him. He displayed the varieties in an organized snack box. Before dispensaries we had scrawny white dudes with unkept curly hair, a backpack full of weed, and a car as our dealer.

A hit of the cheese-variant strain we purchased had me rocked. I found myself locked in a spacious closet away from the overstimulating house party. After midnight I streamed a new album that had been released. I slipped my headphones in and laid my head back, breathing deeply in the dark and cold closet. I find comfort in this simplicity.

I drifted into a dreamscape where I experienced what some refer to as a spiritual awakening, or at least some sort of message. I was handed tools and explanations that defined and explained my human existence. I was told my destiny was not intertwined with love; instead, I was destined to be my own true love.

When this meta information was downloaded, I transcribed the experience to my close friend at the time, who responded with skeptical judgement. I decided to lock the memory away, for fear of being judged more than once.

I had hoped the universe was wrong that night, or that maybe I had just smoked too strong a strain. I kept my gaze focused on the road ahead, now back to the present moment of the drive. The Texas highway was dark, and the sky was teamed with starlight.

Observing the cosmos from the stretch of Texas highway was breathtaking. The number of stars covering the sky convinced me that life was not impossible. There was life and love to be found in every corner of the universe.

During a stopover in Arizona, Gartner and I were fortunate to be offered accommodation from Spunky's mother, in her townhome in Scottsdale while she was between renters. The cross-country road-trip had left me restless, and the anxiety induced from the anticipation leading up to the move worsened my exhaustion. I began to feel guilty for rejecting Gartner's advances each night, claiming it was because I was too tired from the lack of sleep and tenuous drive.

We took our time waking up in the morning, allowing ourselves the ability to sleep in. We embarked on the final leg of the journey that afternoon, and I was aware that by the end of the night, I would be an official 'Angeleno.' Before we began our drive, we took my dog Ghost to hike a nearby trail.

Right before we left the townhouse, after having groomed ourselves from the hike, I was finally in a place to give into Gartner's continued advances. We made passionate love to each other. It felt good, like my energy had doubled after a peaceful rest in such a comfortable setting.

Only once we made it to the west of the Phoenix metro area did the sun start to set over the Western mountain tops. Vibrant red and orange hues of the desert reflected naturally against the golden hour.

We played a variation of carpool karaoke which led me to belt the lyrics to Ethel Cain's entire discography, both released and unreleased. Gartner recorded me as I sang along. I tried to pretend I didn't notice; I disliked being recorded but I loved Gartner, and I knew this was something he wanted for himself to personally have. He gave positive comments on my singing but deep down I didn't believe in my abilities. I knew I was meant to be a writer. I did admire the potential Gartner saw in me that I often felt blind to.

When we were an hour out from the apartment on Wilcox Place, Gartner asked: "So if my cat and your cats don't get along, would you be okay giving your cats away?"

The way the words rolled off his tongue, so casually, upset my stomach. I felt physically ill. He smirked and let out a laugh. I tried to figure out if he was serious or not.

"Are you kidding?" I asked in disbelief, "I would never ask you to do that with your cat if it would be the other way around and you were to move to Florida" I said.

I could tell then that he was not joking, and it infuriated me. My heart sank. I would never get rid of my cats, and I would not hesitate to leave Gartner if this was what he was asking of me. I would make the impossible walk back to Orlando if I had to, with all of my animals in tow. That was a line I drew. How dare him even try to cross it, I thought to myself.

The sun was setting in the distance, just over the Pacific Ocean. We crested over the final mountain top as we began our descent into the greater Los Angeles area. There were warning signs for steep grading inclines along the side of the road as we curved through the mountainside further into the metro.

"I cannot believe you'd ever ask me that" I said finally, "I would break up with you."

His face darkened, "I can't believe you would leave me over that" he said, serious and stern. "Saying you would break up with me is cruel... I would never do that to you." It felt like we were on different planets of understanding each other, of the severity of what he was asking me.

"I can't believe you'd ask me to give up my cats." I emphasized, "So easily, so casually - instead of even thinking to suggest anything else? I think that is so selfish of you to say." "I don't agree," he said stubbornly, shaking his head like I was the one in the wrong. "I can't believe you would leave over that." If it was possible for my mouth to drop further, it would have. I couldn't believe we had gotten this far, had driven across the entire country, for him to drop this bullshit on me right before I was meant to be living with him. It felt like a sick trap.

"I can't believe this," I let out, exasperated. "You know my personality and how I am with my animals! It's beyond me that you would ever think otherwise, quite honestly." I peered behind my shoulder, taking in a protective glance at both the cats in the backseat. Of course I would do anything to keep them. Even if it meant axing this entire plan with Gartner. Of that, I was sure. It took everything in me not to pull on the emergency break, grab all my shit, and find the next route back to Florida.

I had adopted my cats the summer of 2020, during peak COVID-19 time. When I went to adopt the cats, my original intention was to get two male cats. Then I spotted a plump, small gray and white kitten hiding in the back of her cage at the shelter. I asked the shelter attendant to let me interact with her in the private room and while inside, the cat hid herself underneath an obstruction from the wall that provided a covering for her head. The attendant suggested bringing in the plump cat's sister because she comforted her.

The attendant brought in the slender and curious-natured sibling, which eased her sister's tension instantly. The shelter was running a two-for-one special on cats. Suddenly both the plump and slender cats came home with me that evening. I named them Zu and La. I adored them from the moment I brought them home. I would never part from them.

Gartner could clearly sense the rage radiating off my body.
"They will probably get along," Gartner said then, pivoting.
"You are the one who said it," I remarked. I was fuming.

I felt a tug on the string connected to my heart, coming from the swamps of Florida. I wondered if my mother was at the end of the string, sensing something I hadn't yet seen.

I should have felt some emotion other than numbness as we whizzed past the lights on the 101, but it felt like we were speeding toward a future I could not control. The Time Bandit was in control again. I felt like I was merely an idle passenger, moving along without the ability to say or do anything. A bystander in what was meant to be the new life I was orchestrating. A part of my subconscious knew that our end was on the horizon. I expected it to last longer; I wanted it to last forever. Hadn't I? In hindsight it felt like an inconvenient probability.

Before I left Florida, my mom told me to have an exit plan in case Gartner, and I met an untimely demise. At first, I felt somewhat insulted at this, feeling as if the most important person in my life was already counting on the end. That she didn't believe in our love, didn't believe in me. Technically I did have one, so there was a fail-safe at least. I always had the ability to phone-a-friend and couch surf until I figured something else out. It was an idea of a plan, with people who would not leave me on the street. That seemed good enough for me.

This may have not been what my mom had intended by her definition of a plan, but it was enough for me to at least to guarantee my safety for her. Again, it hurt that this was even a topic of conversation before I left Florida, or that I was truly considering it again before I even made it back into the apartment that would soon be my own.

It was past nightfall when we arrived at our shared home on Wilcox Place. We took Ghost up first, both of us assured he would not attack Gartner's cat, Jude. Ghost quickly took his place on the couch. We then brought up each cat one by one and locked them in the boxed hallway between the main room and the bathroom. Jude and my cats could get used to each other's scent through the door. I decided they could remain in peace by themselves for the night while they grew accustomed to each other.

Ghost and Jude were instantly fine with one another. Of course, Ghost was naturally too curious and forward. He invaded Jude's personal space, causing her to swat him with her paw before she bounced off under the bed. Still, nothing major. I knew they would be pals in no time.

It brought comfort to me knowing that at the very least, Ghost and Jude would get along. I passed it off as a sign that

Jude and my cats would be fine as well, sparing my relationship in the meantime. I wondered if a bitter end was spelled out in the starless Los Angeles sky - maybe the lifeless sky was a sign. There were suddenly no more stars in the heavens to capture the intensity of our love, or what was left of it.

*** 

The summer was hot and dry, and the sun baked my skin each day if I stood beneath the rays for too long. The city was a desert beneath the sunshine, fortified by a concrete and glass jungle.

We unpacked my clothes and decorations on our first weekend officially living together. The weekend fell into West Hollywood Pride. In all my years as a member of the queer community, I had only been to pride once before, in Denver. I found them to be generic and corporate-centric. Before the first night of pride, we drove down to Los Angeles City Hall early Friday morning to complete the case hearing for Gartner's name change. The process was quick. The giant courthouse was fortified with wooden panels and clean white accents. His name change was granted, and immediately after we drove to the Hollywood DMV to complete his identification card change.

My first few days in the city and I had already visited the courthouse and DMV. Childhood actor Drake Bell stood before Gartner in line while we waited for his turn to submit his documents. I chuckled to myself quietly, thinking this was the LA life I had envisioned.

I ended up being exhausted during the duration of the pride festival. Gartner arrived early and remained until the venue closed. Truthfully, I would have done the opposite if I wasn't with him. I preferred to rest heavily during the day and show up towards the sunset.

On the last night of the festival, we left early, both too tired from the move. We had exhausted ourselves from all the unpacking, plus waking up early in the morning to complete his name change. I could tell Gartner was annoyed because he expected me to have more energy, but it had been depleted and I needed to sleep. I felt bad I had upset him and once we returned home, I made it up to him with a sensational kiss.

Gartner and I spent our days off at Palisades Beach. We would drive west on Wilshire Boulevard and park along Marguerita Avenue. The houses along the avenue were big and luscious, their yards dotted with fruit trees and colorful flowers, all surrounded by pristine grass. The area we parked in began at the incline to the mountain's peak. The shoreline was a steep cliffside that dropped to the beach below.

We walked across Ocean Avenue and through Palisades Park. The beaches in California might not be my favorite compared to Florida, but parts of the shoreline were undeniably gorgeous. The sand on the beach was almost a muted yellow color, as if kissed by the golden, western sunshine.

We played frisbee and swam in the water, which was much colder than the Atlantic. When I was in the eighth grade my family visited California for the first time. I ran towards the ocean at full speed without understanding the temperature difference and shocked my body once my feet hit the ice-like water. I never repeated that same mistake again. For lunch, Gartner and I packed homemade sandwiches, pasta salad, and honey mangoes. I sipped a Vanilla Coke to help swallow it down. Those little things were a nice routine, something to keep me grounded and feel like I was making the right choice being there.

During those first few days in June, I couldn't deny that I felt off kilter. I woke in the mornings feeling more nauseous and tired than usual. The day ahead would loom over me. One afternoon after I got home from work, I felt depleted. I indulged in a nap until I suddenly woke up harshly, gasping for air. Gartner was on the couch playing video games. I startled him in my wake.

"Are you okay?" He asked after I found my bearings.

I breathed out heavily, expelling my lungs of the oxygen it housed. I rubbed my eyes before I responded.

"What day is it again?" I asked.

"June 11th," Gartner said to me.

I sighed guiltily. I realized I had been blissfully unaware of the impending date. Is that not what people wish for in the end, anyway? To forget the things that haunt you. I assumed it was pure luck. My brain found the ability to move on, but not everyone had been as lucky. The memory came back suddenly then, hitting me like a truck. It felt like forever ago but also felt like it was just yesterday.

June 11th, 2016

My shift at the animal park was mentally exhausting. I argued with my then-boyfriend for the last two hours of my shift. I was crying. In the end my manager let me wander around the park, seeing how distressed I was. I slipped off once the evening rush had begun to die down to collect myself.

My shift ended late, and I clocked out close to 11:30 pm. I walked fifteen-minutes to my car, parked relatively close in the front of the employee lot. I often arrived early to find a decent parking space before every shift, playing a game I coined as: 'Parking Wars.'

I took the long route home; I had no need to rush. There was not much waiting for me at my home other than my bed. I had packed a bowl before I left the employee parking lot and took my time striking the lighter and igniting the weed. I placed the bowl to my lips and inhaled.

My windows were down, allowing the hot humid summer air to fill my lungs just like the smoke I inhaled. I stuck my hand out the side of the window slightly, letting the moisture in the air collect on my hand. The moon shone in the distance over me, keeping its polarizing gaze locked on my location as if it were my own personal spotlight.

I traveled north on Palm Parkway before I came up to the Altis apartments where my friend Xina lived. I was in charge of walking her dog while she was out of town. I fed her cat and her boyfriend's dog and sat on the couch. I cried then, letting the tears flow from my eyes and drip onto my white undershirt. I felt overwhelmed with life. I thought I should stop for a drink somewhere on my way home. I checked the specials at the local gay bars in Orlando: Parliament House, Savoy, Southern Nights, and Pulse, but decided it best I go home.

I checked the time after I sat in silence sulking in my own emotions: fifteen minutes past twelve.

June 12th, 2016
12:21 am

I said goodbye to Xina's pets and informed them I would be back in the morning before work, as if they could understand me. I hoped they could.

I heaved myself into my truck with tired limbs. I packed another bowl before I left the complex and drove north towards the Sand Lake merge-ramp onto Interstate 4. I was in the second turning lane on the right side, waiting for the light to turn green. I glanced in the direction of the Whole Foods to my right before turning my gaze to the left.

A silver sedan was waiting for the light to turn green next to me. Suddenly my eyes locked on the woman in the passenger seat. Her face was covered with her hands and at first, I thought she might have been praying; but her hands remained covering her face for far too long and suddenly I realized the man in the driver's seat beside her was verbally assaulting her. I watched as his vein popped out of his temple and neck, visible specks of spit flying in different directions. His violent demeanor was threatening.

Something did not feel right. I thought maybe I should try to help her somehow, but then I thought I should move my gaze before the man caught me staring at them, but it was already too late. His eyes met mine, and I felt them burn into me. His eyes would engrave themselves into my memory, imprinting there for a lifetime. I changed my focus as the light turned green.

The man then jolted his vehicle in front of my truck, causing me to slam on my brakes. t I just barely missed a direct hit. I continued to drive through the light as the insane driver steered his vehicle back to his original lane, simultaneously cutting off another vehicle as he did so. He steered onto the entrance ramp and swerved past another car, causing the other vehicle to swerve over the painted white line to avoid colliding with the erratic man.

The driver slammed on his brakes, and I caught up to him quickly. I stared directly at him. Through the night and tinted windows, I could make out the white of his teeth as he continued to berate the woman next to him. I thought to myself that this was not normal, and it was not safe. He sped the vehicle up again and cut across three lanes of traffic before nearly clipping another vehicle in his wake.

Up ahead as I merged onto the interstate, I caught a glimpse of the car ahead of me on the left and watched as his hazard lights turned on. They flashed violently with his movement. His brake lights continued to flash, and the car directly behind him swerved around his right as they narrowly avoided a crash. I wondered why he was dramatically braking but then understood that he wanted to wait for me to approach him. He spotted my easily identified truck and veered his vehicle over to my lane, nearly missing another crash into two separate cars in the process. Then he attempted to crash into my vehicle.

I tried to race past him, veering all the way to the left and punching my gas petal to the floor. My adrenaline had spiked; I forgot how to breathe. I saw him floor his gas pedal and swerve his vehicle back toward my truck. I slammed on my brakes again, causing the cars behind us to swerve around to avoid hitting either of us. The other drivers blew their horns at the aggressive driver.

The emergency flashers were still blinking rapidly as he weaved through traffic. He sped up again as I drew back, hoping that would be the end. I pulled out my phone and dialed 9-1-1 into the keypad before I pressed the call button. If not just to protect myself, but all the other people on the highway who were clearly in danger around this man.

I was on the phone with the operator, describing the aggressive driver who nearly caused several accidents. I explained the woman I saw in the passenger seat who had been hiding behind their hands, clearly in fear.

I told the operator about the emergency flashers on the vehicle and how I witnessed the car screech across three lanes on the interstate, nearly colliding with four different vehicles. I begged the operator to send police after the person just as I drove underneath the bridge with illuminated letters spelling out: O R L A N D O, the official welcoming sign for visitors entering the city limits.

The car veered off John Young Parkway. I traveled below the speed limit, so the driver was not tempted to antagonize me again. I watched as the man turned left at the light off the exit far too fast, out of my eyesight. The operator and I finished our report, and I hoped an officer would catch them.

I texted my mom even though I knew she was asleep and told her about the aggressive driver. When I got home, I fell asleep as soon as my head touched my pillow. What a wild night, I thought.

7:05 am.

My eyes were dry and had crusted over. I got inefficient sleep the night before. I realized I needed to quit one of my two jobs, since working in two separate parks was more than challenging, it was near impossible. I was exhausted. I grabbed my phone and snoozed the alarm. I pushed my upper body upright in bed before I began to scroll on Twitter.

I saw the tweet from My News 13 first. A shooting. It had taken place overnight at a downtown Orlando nightclub. I kept scrolling, as shootings were unfortunately not uncommon in Florida. At first, I brushed the tweet off as a small, isolated incident. That was when I saw another tweet from Mayor Buddy Deyer, where he stated that a mass casualty shooting had taken place at Pulse nightclub. My heart shattered. I felt my pulse quicken and a white heat take over my body.

I powered on my TV and immediately WESH 2 News displayed the incident across the screen. The headline: Breaking News: Mass Shooting, possible terrorist attack. I let out a scream as my eyes proceeded to overflow with tears. I sobbed for the first gay club I ever experienced. I stared in desperation and disbelief at the screen. Footage of a bartender who had given me water with lemon wedges when I was still too young to drink was being shown carried away by other patrons who made it out of the club. The bartender's leg was tied with a makeshift bandage from someone's shirt, with blood leaking out from the cloth. The visual was absorbed into my memory.

I woke my parents from their sleep, crying as I told them to turn on the news. They were quiet as they watched the newscasters give a grim update. They shared a look between each other. I was acutely aware of the life-altering events unfolding before our eyes.

Despite everything I dressed myself for work. I was late, I was unable to move from my bed as I watched the morning news. Unable to process the events unfolding in my childhood home, at the club I had first explored the comfort of my sexuality without limitation. The sun was bright, and the day was hot. What an oddly beautiful day, I thought. It was strange that there could be such good weather on such a terrible day, but I supposed mother nature existed in her own authority. We were merely subjected to its own power unwillingly.

I cried as I steered my car onto the 408 Expressway, my eyes a blurred mess. I questioned my ability to drive or perform my job comfortably that day. I pulled over on the side of the highway, boarded by a grassy field and flung myself out of the truck as I slammed the shifter into park. I fell to the grass and began to throw up. I continued to heave for several minutes, unable to sedate my emotions.

My phone rang then, breaking me from the nauseated spell. It was one of my childhood friends that found themselves with me in our youth; together we had found our place in queerdom.

"What is going on?" They asked me through a shaken voice.

"I do not know, I just threw up on the side of the highway," I said shakily, wiping the corners of my mouth.

"Kay-J is dead," they said to me then. For the second time that day, time froze.

I vomited again, unable to process this new information. How could one of my childhood friends be dead?

"What happened? Were they there? At- at Pulse?" The words stung as they left my throat.

"No, but I don't know if that makes it better…" they said, trying to keep from crying themselves.

"Car accident," they said finally, after a few moments of silence. I couldn't remember the rest of the phone call, if we said anything more or just sat in this confused, depressed state together.

I tried to find the silver lining and realized there was none. There was no way for me to make light of any of the events that had unfolded. I swallowed the tears and bile back down into my esophagus, long enough to get back in my car. I somehow made the thirty-five-minute drive that remained to work. I needed something to focus on, something to keep me from the horrors that were now reality.

In the backlot of the ocean park, the energy was low. Various team members sat huddled together peering at their phones. No audible conversations were had, everyone just communicated through emotional expressions. A collective feeling of solemnness and loss.

I walked past a small group huddled off to the side as one of the members burst into tears, the other patrons grabbing hold of them. They fell to their knees and wept, unable to control their emotions.

My coworkers and I sat huddled in the shape of a circle; life had been sucked from our livelihoods. Our manager approached us and immediately began to cry before they could utter a single word to us. I glanced around the group and took a moment to realize how thankful I was to be able to feel the sun on my face, there in that moment with them.

My phone vibrated continuously throughout the day. I answered in front of guests, not caring if they cared. Luckily, they understood the severity. After each phone call, the guest in front of me would offer a kind smile, as the news was global information by then. They knew what had happened. Everyone did.

On my way home I took the exit to Michigan street off I-4 and drove east towards Orange Avenue. The SWAT team had installed barriers two blocks in either direction from the center of Pulse. I walked the perimeter and saw others like me. They shuffled around as they attempted to understand the atrocities that plagued reality.

June 13th, 2024

After I relived the nightmare of that day so many years prior, my anxiety subdued. I slept better than the previous nights before. On nights when Gartner and I were off work early we would drive to George Wolfberg Park and take Ghost on a hike. We'd take our time meandering through the small canyon to the edge of the cliffside that overlooked the Pacific below.

On other days we would walk Ghost down Santa Monica Blvd to Hollywood Forever Cemetery, where we would stop by Judy Garland's burial site. We always wrote a heartfelt message in the notebook that stood on a podium in front of her final resting place, provided by the cemetery.

Our summer nights would end with takeout from Kung Pao Bistro or street tacos from a vendor by the Pavilions for dinner. We enjoyed gluttony while \ streaming re-runs of Drag Race, afterwards falling asleep together after sharing a joint. Some days after the beach we drove to El Condor to visit Bondi while she was behind the bar. Pink would be there already to meet us. We would indulge in mediocre Americanized Mexican food and down mezcal margaritas that Bondi specialized in. Pink was branded with a signature pink drink in hand, strawberry margarita with a sugar rim.

On days when I worked past the evening into nightfall, Gartner walked Ghost down to see me at The Market. If I worked late at night, I would find him waiting for me outside in his Toyota Camry. It was a comfortable reminder that he loved and cared for me.

Nighttime in Los Angeles was my favorite. Lights illuminated the city and set it aglow. The mountain tops sparkled as streetlamps and house lights created pathways down the slopes that would shine as a decorative beacon in the night. I interpreted the trail of lights as a mosaic of rivers and streams.

Between the LA alleyways you could catch fleeting glimpses of the Hollywood sign as you passed the gaps in-between buildings. As the sun set, the temperature cooled. The breeze from the mountains pushed in, and palm trees rustled in their gusts. The sound eased my anxiety.

I was amazed by mountains, something Florida lacked. I admired how manmade developments and structures rarely reached the towering summit peaks. They were left for glory, lifted high above everything else.

Some days if I was off work before the afternoon, Pink would meet me at Wilcox Place, and we would walk north to the 24Hour Fitness on Sunset. After the gym we would spend the afternoon at her apartment pool or at the Pan Pacific Park across from The Grove. We would flag a vendor down and buy a coke to sip on. We tanned, leisurely lounging in the soft grass. I read a book. Palm trees swayed lazily against the crystal-clear blue sky.

I purchased Gartner and I tickets to the Ethel Cain concert at the Greek Theater in late June. The venue was nestled in the mountains of Griffith Park, placed in the valley of two large hills. Concert-crashers crowded the highest peak opposite of the stage on the hillside, their positions amongst the trees given away by the lights from their phones.

I wondered where they hiked from, thinking it would be the kind of local knowledge I wish I could know. The trade secret would be hard to come by, guarded by Angelenos who would only pass down the tribal knowledge to their friends or family. Bats flew high above us as dusk turned the sky from blue to gray, then purple to black. For once I felt closer to Florida than I had since my move to California.

Back in Florida I would watch the same class of bats fly freely over my parents' home and across the thick woods that surrounded the street I grew up on. I breathed a sense of relief, thinking I was exactly where I was meant to be. After years of waiting, my life compass had pointed me West, towards a life of expansion.

After the concert we sparked a joint as we walked to the parked car, close to Bondi's apartment in Los Feliz. On our drive home we drove through Tommy's Burgers on Hollywood Boulevard for takeout. Particularly on that night, I sensed the beauty of Los Angeles that was carried in the wind. Lore surrounded the magic of LA, and that night I felt the tiniest flicker of it pulsating through my veins. The city had a defined vibe, you knew you were in Los Angeles no matter what neighborhood you were in. The architecture and stylization of the neighborhoods was pronounced.

After we finished our burgers, we danced to Ethel Cain as it streamed from Gartner's Alexa setup. The old wood floors creaked beneath our feet as we shuffled to match each other's steps. The night was chilly from the Spring winds that blew in from the Pacific, but Gartner's arms provided warmth as we continued to dance in a sweet embrace.

If our work schedules aligned and we had a Saturday off, we did our laundry up the road from Wilcox on Sunset boulevard. Gartner had developed a ritual for his laundry. I always enjoyed observing the people at the laundromat. The smell of freshly cleaned clothes and sheets brought comfort to my weekends. I could see the appeal for Gartner, as well. It was peaceful and provided a sense of community, all those lives coexisting with one another. The early summer months in Los Angeles had cooler temperatures than what I experienced in Florida. I often wore a hoodie paired with running shorts. I was always cold in the morning, but by midday it warmed enough to wear shorts.

While our laundry washed, we walked across the street to the Home Depot and Target. Sometimes we would grab Panda Express for lunch afterwards so we could return to our apartment and lounge lazily.

I often thought about how fascinating it must have been to grow up in Los Angeles with Targets you had to access through a multi-leveled concourse that provided a view of the Griffith observatory. Then being able to look to the left and see the Hollywood Sign in the distance, staggered against the Hollywood Hills. Viewpoints in Los Angeles were definitely a plus. Viewpoints in Florida only provided sights of flat, widespread greenery - it was clear the winner was Los Angeles.

Gartner loved the beach, and we shared that trait in common. My dad raised my sister and me on boats in Florida. Now that I lived so close to the beach in California, we would spend hours of our day playing frisbee in the shallow wake of the Pacific Ocean. After I grew bored of frisbee, I would collect kelp that had washed along the shoreline, popping their bulbous ends. As the sun creeped from East to West, we would witness it set just as we pulled away in the direction of our apartment on Wilcox Place.

Our summer remained consistent with activities. Beach, Takeout, El Condor, Dancing, Joint, Takeout, Beach, Hike, Shim Sham, Pavilions, Laundry, Beach. It was a cycle I grew accustomed to. The repetition became a familiar pattern.

One weekend Gartner drove south to San Diego for a wedding he had been invited to, pre-relationship. I was left alone in the apartment on Wilcox place and was thankful to get some alone time. I loved Gartner, but I found comfort in solidarity at times.

I spent my morning in and out of sleep, and in the afternoon, I walked to the complex a few blocks over that housed The Market and let myself up to the pool. I slipped in behind tenants, unrecognized among the already-crowded pool deck.

Nearly all the chairs were occupied. I spotted a small conversation pit with a bench available in the left corner. I seated myself and tanned while reading a book. Between paragraphs I observed the people socializing on the deck. It was a peaceful day, people watching and losing myself in a book. Closer to sunset, I returned home to the apartment. After a quick walk with Ghost around the block, I knocked out in deep rest.

On the second night Gartner was away, he called me. I recognized the sound of his intoxication quickly. He mumbled words to me over the phone that I hardly understood. He expressed his intense desire for his family's validation. He confessed he was triggered when a family member of the groomsmen made a heartfelt declaration of love to him during the ceremony.

In a potentially twisted way, I wondered if Gartner caused his emotional fit. I wondered what his family could have done to traumatize him so deeply that it triggered him during a harmonious celebration. I compared it to my own experiences with family and found it inadequate.

Gartner had only ever confided in me with half-detailed explanations of the abuse he experienced. I was ashamed to question the validity of his experiences. And who the hell was I? I fought with myself internally over the thought. I was never warranted an explanation. I had shared some of my deepest fears and dreams with Gartner, and at times I felt like I had not received the same in return. I wondered if rawness equated intimacy. I wondered if there was a reason he wouldn't fully let me in.

I regularly found similarities between him and I. We wanted to be perceived at our allowance. We wanted to retreat from the outside world, but at the same time had an affinity for connection.

***

Another one of my favorite Los Angeles traits were the towering palm trees that dominated the skyline. As you cruised the metro you could often spot a palm towering in any direction.

I was preoccupied admiring a lone palm perched on a hilltop during one of our drives home from the beach, and as I went to pass the joint we were smoking to Gartner, the wind caught an ember. In its gust it landed on the passenger seat, burning a small hole in the fabric.

Gartner instantly blamed me for the burn. I felt the energy from the sunshine-fueled day being stripped away as quickly as I was able to extinguish the burn in the chair with my bare hand.

Gartner continued to scold me for the burn mark. Our day was ruined by the silent treatment he gave me the remainder of our journey home. The awkward tension soon amounted to discomfort. I pretended to nap when we arrived home. Later the same week, someone sideswiped his car in a hit and run at a parking garage, damaging his passenger door.

Gartner continued to criticize me for the burn mark even a few weeks after the incident. He went as far as insinuating I often caused destruction. I chose to ignore the harsh words, not wanting to make things worse.

I developed a routine to walk Ghost in the morning and evening. Sometimes Gartner walked him. When I first moved in, Gartner was excited to walk Ghost. However, his feelings quickly changed. On the walk I would smell the scent of Jasmine flowers wafting through the air. My nostrils filled with the sweet aroma, and I breathed it in deeply, allowing the pungent smell to ease my nerves.

It was then I noticed the large quantity of Jasmine bushels clustered along the borders of the sidewalks and fencelines around our neighborhood. The city was covered in Jasmine plants. The flower's bloom brought me great comfort. Annually in the months of May and June, Jasmines filled the Los Angeles air with its sweet scent.

If I could take something back to Orlando with me from Los Angeles it would be the Jasmine bloom around the city. I would plant them in all my favorite places in Florida.

Assimilation into the California workforce proved difficult for me. I found making connections with my peers challenging, and a conflict with the manager of The Market created a toxic work environment.

After several despairing weeks, the manager was let go due to complaints filed with corporate regarding her discriminatory behavior. I felt slighted by my first experience in the Los Angeles workforce, but after time I began to tolerate the quirks that gave the Hollywood locations its unique charm.

The store attracted various transients that perused through the aisles, stealing various items. Other patrons would yell at shoppers who were simply minding their business, until they were chased out by management or security.

I nicknamed one hectic regular Harley Quinn, because of her tattered hair that was displaced between two pigtails and decorated with bows on either side of her head. Her makeup ran down her face, from her eyes over cheeks as if she had just applied fresh makeup and immediately wet her face after. She would steal a prepared sushi box and eat it with her bare hands as she exited the store, screaming obscenities at anyone who tried to stop her.

When the store did not erupt into chaotic specter, the aisles were quiet. The energy was stoic and the nights felt elongated. I found daily tasks to pass my time as I grew bored with cosplaying as a grocery clerk. One evening, I told Gartner I felt stagnant at The Market and wanted to get back into the service industry. He discouraged exploring the service industry and emphasized the practicality of The Market being in close proximity to the apartment.

## *The Arid Summer*

Over Independence Day, my parents flew Gartner and I to Orlando, to masque a favor for house sitting as a vacation. They were traveling to Puerto Rico to visit my father's family. The weeks leading up to our departure, I struggled to convince Gartner to join me on the trip. He tried to argue money as a reason to stay home, even with the offer of a free pet sitter and all-expenses paid trip.

For weeks Gartner scoured for an excusable reason to avoid the Florida trip. I counteracted each argument, eventually convincing him to join me. Although I should have saved my energy. I should have let him stay in Los Angeles.

The trip to Florida was simple. We spent our time relaxing around my parents' house in the cool air conditioning. We visited Cocoa Beach to escape the heat and continue our summer beach habit. On the Fourth we hosted a cook-out, and grilled burger patties and hot dogs for my friends. Reni, her boyfriend Le, and Kash showed up throughout the day and remained well into the late morning hours after midnight.

Princess had been in town over the summer, visiting her parents while the writer's strike was at its peak in Los Angeles. Eventually Pink left with a friend we graduated with, Dana, to another Fourth of July party. Just after as time drew closer to midnight and the silence between the bangs of firework explosions lengthened, Gartner and I drove to the end of the street to a pop-up firework stand. We took advantage of the high-discount sale as the holiday night ended. Once home, we spent the next hour aggravating our neighbors with explosive bangs from our discounted purchase.

On our last day in Florida before returning to California, we spent at the beach with my sister and nephew. The Florida sun baked my skin and refreshed me. The Florida humidity comforted me in a nostalgic way and naturally moisturized my skin. On the other hand, the dry California air caused my skin to dry out and turn ashy.

We spent our time swimming in the warm Atlantic water. I waded into the ocean before I swam a few feet out. I admired the Florida shoreline. There were no mountains in sight, no domineering skyline like at Palisades Beach. Just water, sky, and a sandy shore that followed the curvature of the Earth.

Adjusting to life in California had not been what I expected, and it was comforting to have found myself feeling at peace in a familiar setting. It felt nice to wade the Florida waters after spending the first half of summer wading in the California waves.

On the plane ride home, I realized my birthday would arrive soon. We had more than a month left to the day, but the Time Bandit was elusive. The weeks slipped by quicker than I could have imagined. For my birthday, I wanted to find a connection to Florida to indulge in for that day, to help me adjust and to curb the feelings of homesickness. I settled on celebrating at the resort in Anaheim.

The summer weather settled into the coastal desert city. If wind blew in from the coast, the moisture was leeched from the breeze before it reached inner Hollywood.

"Let's go see Twisters!" I said excitedly to Gartner. "It can be the kickoff to my birthday."

"Birthday?" Gartner questions. "Your birthday is not for another month."

"Yeah, I get a birthday month, and I'm activating it now," I joked.

"No, you get one day for your birthday and that's it, "he responded, shocking me.

I laughed it off as a joke, but there was a serious underlying tone to his voice. His cadence suggested annoyance with me for suggesting something as foolish as a birthday month.

I ironically mocked the idea of a birthday month but found myself partaking in them from time to time. Sometimes I wanted to celebrate my age for longer than other years. The way I saw it, there was no limit to celebrations. I wondered if his family saw birthdays from a narrow viewpoint, and this was his reasoning for taking my suggestion so poorly.

Gartner eventually agreed to watch the movie, when it wasn't considered part of my birthday. We decided to go to the theater at the Grove. We had been to the Grove once before, back in April after Coachella. The marketplace was the home to the original farmer's market which had eclectic food and craft vendors. The Grove reminded me of Downtown Disney. Perfectly manicured and pristine. I had expectations for the inside of the theater's design, but only to be let down. Los Angeles was known for movies, with the inside of theaters along Hollywood Boulevard always decadent and extravagant. On the other hand, the theater at the Grove was generic. I expected the theater to offer some sort of competition to the regal theaters only a few miles away.

After the movie as we were leaving the parking garage, the automated payment machine had a glitch and shut down on us in the middle of the transaction. Gartner pressed the call button for security, and as we waited for them, cars began to line behind us from disrupting the flow of traffic. It spanned up the ramp to the second level and curved beyond my eyesight, causing a roadblock.

Far too many minutes passed and the drivers behind us grew impatient. Various horns started to honk at us as the drivers became more irritated with the lack of movement.

In the car directly behind us I caught the passenger expressively talking about our car. Their gestures were easily identifiable, matching the words as I read their lips. I wondered how they failed to realize the gate had malfunctioned. I grew irritated as the driver behind us blared their horn. I turned around to yell back at them out the window that the machine was broken, but Gartner pulled me back in.

"Do not yell at them," he said to me, clearly aggravated. There was a harshness in his voice I had not heard from him before.

"You do not need to grab me," I said. I didn't understand how he could be mad at me in this situation.

The car behind us honked again, and I turned again to yell before Gartner stopped me. He raised his voice at me - and I felt my blood boil. We started to bicker with one another, back and forth. The car behind us started to beep their horn repetitively again. I began to turn in my seat to yell back at them once more from the window. And that was when he threw his fist at me. I realized as I turned around to see him drawing back in fear, that he realized what he had done. I sputtered and stared at him. It happened quickly; I blinked rapidly, unsure of what to say or do. His face changed from one emotion to another too quickly for me to infer what he was thinking. His hands were shaking.

I thought through the emotions that circled through my mind, the other cars and broken machine now long forgotten. There was only one course of action that could be taken at the time.

"Just take me home," I said, refusing to look at him.

We sat in silence as the security lazily walked in front of us and scanned their badge on the gate, allowing it to finally pop open. We left without paying, and I suppose that was the only good thing that came from the day.

I was thousands of miles away from home, and I felt immensely alone. I told myself I should leave, but I was faced with the fear that I had nowhere to go. And for the first time since I moved, I really wondered if I made a mistake. My back felt sore and my muscles were slightly agitated.

The silence was violent as Gartner drove us home. I watched the buildings blur past as he drove down La Brea. The sunny, smog-less day had quickly turned suffocating. I felt it was hard to breathe.

For a moment I was jealous of the people living their normal lives as they walked down the sidewalk. I began to question my feelings for Gartner, which caused a pit in my stomach. Did I love him anymore? Should I love him anymore? I quickly realized that that was an irrelevant thought. Of course I loved him, the issue was not whether I loved him, but if I trusted him. This was somehow harder to distinguish. I chose to believe I could trust him. If I couldn't trust him, I knew what we had would end. But after the incident in the garage, I was unsure if that trust would return.

How many chances was I willing to give? When did I draw the line? I needed more money, I thought as I began to spiral. Once we were back inside the apartment, I scooped Ghost into my arms and carried him to the couch to cuddle.

Gartner apologized and I only half listened. I felt like I had let myself down. Yet again, I let a man physically hurt me. I didn't think I would be able to be intimate or vulnerable with Gartner again. It had already started to feel like a chore. As long as I could remember, I felt this way with every partner. How much our past shaped our future overwhelmed me. It seemed like there were some things we could not control.

November 2009

I lost my virginity at thirteen years old. The boy I lost it to was fifteen. He was conventionally handsome. He was tall, with a pearl-white smile and flat, brown hair that had a natural shine to it. In the mornings when he styled his hair it would fall in different placements that seemed tasseled and misplaced across his forehead. His voice was clear and carried an unstable force with its vibration. He had blue-gray eyes that glinted in the sun. Only once you got closer to him you realized his freckles were irregular and his skin was puffy, a tell-tale sign of adolescence doing its job.

He lived down the road from my parents' house. He and another boy I knew since our sandbox days would ride their bikes the half mile to my house. We would play around with various items from my dad's garage like a moped, dirt bike, or skateboards. Other times we would hike through my backyard and out into the undeveloped woods that lined my parents' property.

One day, the boy arrived alone. He was persistent about coming over to my house. I remember finding it odd, as I received multiple texts from him in a row. I was at a school event as I texted him back on my red flip phone. Before my parents even picked me up, he told me he was on his way to my house. Once my parents had pulled up to the house, he waited outside for several minutes. We went to the back house together that my father had built as an addition to the property.

Everything happened quickly, then. He started by asking about the first sexual encounter I had over summer, with an older boy who I gave oral sex to.
"Head is head," he said, shrugging.
"Sure," I said, wanting to sound cooler than I felt. My pulse had quickened, and I felt unsure how to proceed. He was handsome. Did I have a crush on him?

"Wanna give me head?" He said casually, like he had been rehearsing the line for a play. As if he had been planning to ask me for weeks since he found out about the first guy I had hooked up with.

My pulse doubled. He was devilishly handsome. We had always been friends, and he had always just appeared to me as the straight, jock boy. He was friendly, and we had grown up together. His sister and my sister were in the same

124

grade, they were friends. We were friends. My head spun around the decision he was waiting for me to give.

"You would have to be hard first," I said. I instantly regretted the statement. I sounded like I was trying to play it cool, which I was, but I did not want him to know.

"I have been hard since I first walked in the door," he said as he stared at me from across the room. He stood in the door frame of the bedroom with his hands stretched up to the top, his fingers gripping the wooden frame. His shirt stretched, revealing a nonexistent happy trail that led to the logo on his Adidas soccer pants. I focused on the symbol.
"So?" he asked expectantly.

I hesitated to say no. Before I knew what was happening, he had moved to sit opposite of me on the couch. I was unaware when I decided to sit down myself.

"I am freshly shaved," he said to me. "It feels great when you've just shaved and it's all smooth."

He pulled his Adidas soccer pants to the cusp of his penis, revealing smooth pink skin. I wondered if he was unable to grow hair easily, considering he had no happy trail either, even if he claimed to shave before. I wondered if I wanted to see him naked, since I had never thought of him that way before. He was extremely handsome, but was out of my league - so how was this happening?

"Come on, blow me," he said again as he pulled his pants down further. He exposed his erect penis to me. It was not large, actually much smaller than my own which I had not expected. He appeared to be under four inches.

I subconsciously knew that day would end poorly for me, but another part of me didn't want to lose him as a friend. I was nervous that if I did not go through with what he wanted, that he would not speak to me again. Another part of me was worried he would want to continue to have sex after the first time. It felt like I was stuck between a wall and a hard place. No decision felt like the right one.

He was staring at me while touching himself and I thought that I needed to act quickly. I stood up and shuffled around the room. "I am nervous," I admitted, avoiding his piercing stare.

"Hey, it is me," he tried to sound reassuring. "It'll be fine. Besides, I'm sure you are good at it."

I realized he would probably not stop, even if I rejected him. He would likely come back another day and then it would happen. Maybe some things were written into the stars, even if it didn't feel like something that would end on a positive note. If that was one of them, I wondered about the lesson I was meant to learn.

I walked back to him, got on my knees, and began performing oral sex. My mouth was dry, and it felt like sandpaper. I was nervous about performing poorly because I would be embarrassed, but then I thought I did not want to perform the act at all.

I stopped myself: "I can't do this," I said.

"You can't stop," he said in an assertive tone.

"I can't do this," I said, shaking my head. I had no idea what lay ahead for me that day when I first woke up. I wondered if it was always like this, starting a day, you thought was going to be normal, just to have it end up being one you would never forget.

"Do it for me," he said then. "Let me fuck you."

My heart plummeted. Stars began to cloud my vision. Why the fuck would he ever ask me that? I wondered. I tried to think of an excuse to get out of it. I never had sex with anyone before. I was not sure I understood how it worked for gay people. Does this mean he was gay? Too many thoughts swirled around my head as I tried to steady myself.

"You have to have a condom," I said firmly. It was the best way to assure it wouldn't happen, and in no way did I think he would have one. I was convinced of this, and I didn't have one either. I thought this was the perfect excuse to get out of this unexpected mess.

"I have one," he said simply, pulling a metallic packaging from his pants pocket.

My heart shattered as I felt my insides grow weak and queasy. The stars increased in my vision; everything was going blurry. I wanted time to stop. I wanted to fast forward through time, to skip past this unwanted reality. Wasn't I meant to feel excited about my first time? I wondered. Wasn't I meant to have a say in who I chose to give myself to? I wished I had never answered his text. I wished I was anywhere but there.

"Where did that come from?" I asked, thinking this was far too convenient to be a coincidence.

"This boy in gym class gave it to me the other day in the locker room. I forgot I had it in my pants till now," he shrugged again, acting far too casual for the circumstances.

Years later, I would come to understand that the entire day was premeditated. I lost my virginity that day, to a boy who knew nothing about sex and nothing about me. The pain radiated through my body with each individual push. I felt no pleasure, no comfort, no safety. He ripped away my first time like it was an unwanted Band-Aid. And I would forever resent him for that. Afterwards I stayed on the couch as he washed himself off. He slipped out the door just as casually as he had come in.

"Do better next time I come for you," he said to me on his way out, as if in warning.

I laid there for a few minutes, or maybe it was hours. Time was no longer a concept I understood. I was stuck, frozen. When I finally entered my house later, I felt like I had lived through my entire life. I felt different, but somehow nothing was different other than my insides, and no one was aware except for me and the other person involved. I sat on the couch with my family as images flicked by on the TV screen. The light faded from the day and set with the sun, ending what was left of me with it.

When I got the courage to make my way to the bathroom and inspect myself, it had been over an hour since I had moved. It ached to walk. I stripped my clothes off and examined myself in the mirror. No bruises at least, but I also hadn't tried to fight him. I would not have been able to. I was strong and compact, but I was small. Much smaller than him.

Once a person was over a certain height over me, I had a low chance of winning in a fight against them.

I figured I needed to wash up and began by taking a wad of toilet paper to wipe my underside. It stung as the paper glided against my skin. I pulled the paper up to my vision to inspect, and it was covered in a glob of blood. I shuttered and threw the wad into the toilet. I wiped again with another wad of paper and again came blood. This time it was significantly less, and by the third wipe I was clear. If only I could do the same with my memory, I thought. I sat on the toilet and rested my head in my hands. I sighed deeply.

July 2024

I hate surprises. I told Gartner to tell me in advance when he planned to propose to me - not the exact date or place, but at least an idea. I could guess if I wanted to know when he would. He was not very secretive. His mind was quiet, but his actions were loud. I knew he would propose to me in New York. I wondered why he had spent weeks arguing with me over booking the flight to the city but in the end, I had convinced him yet again to go on vacation with me.

I was set to visit New York, with or without him. If he chose to come with me, we would have a free place to stay, anyway. Blu, a friend of mine from high school, moved away to Texas a few months after we met in our junior year, but we still kept in touch. Spunky's thirtieth birthday was the weekend of our arrival. She invited me to her birthday party in the city, along with Blu and Bebe after they had been introduced at Trippy and Aus's wedding.

The ring cost him close to three-thousand dollars. I had a faint panic attack. I would have never thought to spend so much on a gold band, even if I could. My reaction was not what he had suspected, and I knew my face had given away too much, so I decided I should accept my fate.

"You did not have to spend that much on me, y'know?" I said, wondering if I sounded ungrateful. Part of me wished he would have talked to me about the cost first. I was not a flashy person, but Gartner had an essence of bougie to him.

"You are worth it," he said to me. Then he looked me in the eye and said, "I want the same ring."

I was forced to maintain his gaze. We locked in on one another's pupils, his eyes turning a shade of stormy blue. I saw myself struggling to breathe as I thrashed against the waves in his eyes. They crashed over and over with nowhere left to go but to topple on top of me. I treaded the water until my limbs failed me.

"Okay," I said through a tight smile as I drowned. I wondered how he could expect me to afford a three-thousand-dollar ring when I was not making a tipped wage in Los Angeles.

"Do you think you could afford it?" He asked me with a quizzical tone that implied he already suspected my answer to be no.

My stomach churned with uneasiness, and I thought this was when I started to see a different side of him that I could not quite understand. Was love worth all of this? I decided to move on, and figure it out later. Then I realized I had a growing list of things to figure out.

Even the cats had adjustments. While no major cat fights had perspired since we let them interact with each other, Jude antagonized both of my kitties often. I witnessed her charge after Zu, wrestling one another before they ran off in separate directions after Zu would fight back. Jude was the culprit multiple times. Gartner never believed me when I told him, he always insisted it was Zu. Jude and Gartner were similar to each other.

*** 

Before we left for New York, the remainder of our summer we spent at the beach. Gartner and I bought popsicles from vendors that pushed their oversized IGLOO coolers across the sand as they sold crisp sodas, ice creams, and other treats to patrons on the beach. We walked alongside the palm trees in Palisades Park near the cliffside as we overlooked the beach below. Down the coast was Long Beach, and up the coast lay Malibu and Big Sur beyond it.

When we returned home from the beach we would take Ghost on a long walk around the neighborhood, sometimes walking east down Santa Monica to the Hollywood Forever Cemetery before they closed.

As we wandered the massive cemetery, we walked past water fountains and the stones marking those who had already lived their lives and moved on. The local peacocks that live on the grounds frolicked around, hopping along the tops of the gravestones.

There was a center path that cut through the middle of a large portion of the graves and led to a roundabout fountain followed by a row of wind chimes. Each time we visited the cemetery we would walk the same route and gently brush the chimes as they clanged together. They continued to sing their vibrational song as we kept on our walk.

On the evening, we returned from a walk and booked our flight to New York, Gartner complained about the price right as we completed the purchase. I reminded him that he had gone back and forth on buying the flights for weeks. We could have easily bought them earlier. I lightly reminded him that at the end of the day, we were traveling from Los Angeles to New York City during peak summer travel. It was bound to be expensive, and the prolonged wait to purchase our tickets did not help the cost. He grumbled a stubborn response, seeming to forget it had taken time to even convince him to travel with me.

## *Love in the Big Apple*

We landed in Newark Airport around dinner time and took the Metrolink into Penn Station. We stayed with Blu in her apartment on the Upper East Side, close to where Spunky lived. Her apartment lacked central air-conditioning, and the city was overwhelmingly hot and humid. I never expected the city to be so intensely hot. Even as a Florida boy, I was shocked. We walked to a bodega for a deli sandwich after placing our things in Blu's apartment, then took a late-night stroll to Central Park.

Gartner craned his neck to see the non-existent stars in the jet-black sky above. His child-like, idealistic view of the world continued to make me fall in love with him. He had a quirk of physically touching an object of importance, so he could feel its energy. I found it adorable, and it made my stomach tingle in adoration. That was how I knew he was born in California, which made me love him even more.

The last time I felt any child-like wonder was lost to me. Which might have been embarrassing and slightly pathetic to reveal. Why was it so hard to recall when I had once felt like a kid? Part of me felt like I was robbed of adolescence, forced to adapt to a life that was inherently adult by its apparent taboo nature. I wondered if Gartner had ever felt the same.
He had expressed his discomfort growing up to me. One night while we were alone, he confessed that he once considered he had been forced to identify as gay due to the bullying he endured at a young age. I wondered if that was a shared experience with other queer people. But then I wondered a lot of things, like if he felt forced to love me.

We spent our vacation days roaming the city. We ate hot dogs throughout the day and visited bodegas for various deli-meat sandwiches when we were hungry. Blu led us on a fundamental tour of the city, providing Gartner with an authentic first visit. We stopped at the Metropolitan Museum of Art and the Highline. I watched bees flutter around the flowers and overgrown grass as the daily joggers and bicyclists passed by. The city was hot and the days were long.

We met my friends, Bebe and Kova, at The Peking Duck on Mott Street for dinner. We ravaged seven courses that ended with roast duck. Afterwards we wandered drunkenly around NYC as the moon shone down upon us, guiding us on our journey home the night before Spunky's birthday party.

We celebrated Spunky's birthday on the first of August, exactly twenty days before my own birthday. We danced to early 2000s music while we toasted champagne to one another. The party was a success, and I felt as though the city was mine, as if I had been a local the entire time. It was nice to feel as though I had extended my roots to New York City, another city I could call a second home.

Gartner purchased us tickets to The Edge at the Hudson Yards after one of his clients had suggested we visit the observation deck. The day we went, Gartner purchased Blu a last-minute ticket to tag along with us. The weather, however, was equal to a Florida rainstorm, thundering down in thick blankets of water. We decided it was best to change our tickets to the following day. Later I wondered if it was some kind of sign sent to me, blissfully unaware of the subtle foreshadowing.

The next day we were on the top of the world in New York City. I was overlooking the Hudson River when I went to turn around to say something to Gartner. That's when I found him on one knee, holding out a box containing a golden band before me.

I knew it would happen - but I was blissfully unaware of when it would happen. We had discussed it taking place in New York, with the romantic air of it all. It interfered with his original plan to propose to me in Santa Cruz, but clearly, he was okay with it. The moment Gartner got on one knee; it was like my body had registered how high in altitude we were at the moment. My legs felt like jelly, my pulse quickened, and my words caught in my throat.

Gartner spoke to me but as his mouth moved, the words were inaudible to me. The realization that I had been wishing for this moment caused me to give an audible, "Yes." I thought to myself that I deserved love, I deserved this, I deserved Gartner. I said yes because I was in love. I believed that Gartner would fulfill my needs in life, as a partner and a lover.

I was numb, holding my breath while he slid the ring onto my finger. He lifted me up and flung me high into the air as we shared a kiss to signify our forever. Blu was close by, and I guess that was why he had her join us that day. She photographed us together as we overlooked the skyline and the Hudson River. Part of me felt like Gartner might have been upset with my diluted reaction, but I had felt a shock run through my body. I was nervous. I hoped he wouldn't be able to tell, but later as we watched the video Blu recorded, it looked pretty obvious.

After our engagement, Gartner asked me if I would post about it on social media. It made me wonder if he had taken the time to understand me. It was not something I would do. I wanted people to know how excited I was to be engaged with a wonderful man, but I hated the idea of putting that part of my personal life on display, especially online. We were still pretty early on in our relationship, and part of me feared that I would carry the weight of shame and embarrassment if we ended. I found it strange that Gartner would want me to post our engagement so exclusively and quickly online. Gartner had no social media presence himself, after all.

I ended up not posting our engagement announcement on Facebook or Instagram, and I wondered if that hurt him. I posted about it on Twitter, which I explained to him held more significance to me than any of the other socials. He refused honesty. Part of me was worried I would one day have to admit to humility, but was that not a normal fear for everyone?

I wondered if Gartner only measured my love by how much I expressed it to others around me. Part of me felt like Gartner wanted me to publicly declare and express my love to him from the highest mountain top.

I felt infinitely in love with Gartner, so much so I could hardly find the words to describe the feelings. As loud as I was, in the moments of sincerity where my vulnerability was at its peak, my expression was diminished.

I wanted to be the devoted lover that Gartner desired. I wondered if I would be enough for him? I wondered if I needed to remove every part of my life that interfered with my devotion and time for him, in order for him to feel comfortable? From the moment Gartner had proposed to me, I feared I would never be able to give him the love he desired. I hoped he was able to recognize that my ability to love him existed beyond expression.

He had told me once he would love me no matter who I was. He asked me if I had ever considered transitioning, and if I had he would continue to support me and love me. I wondered if I had the strength to do the same.

We flew home to Los Angeles the day after he proposed. I was ready to sleep in my bed with Gartner and our animals. In a couple weeks it would be my birthday.

## *When it Matters Most*

I've cried on my birthday several times in my life. Each time I mentally drew a tally mark to keep track of the additional times I'd been brought to tears on my birthday. I was thousands of miles away from Florida and my family, what I considered to be the largest part of my comfort. Then I realized I was unbelievably uncomfortable in what should have been a safe space for myself in Los Angeles. Which made it all inherently worse.

I was seated on the curb outside of Wilcox Place. I found a walnut on the ground, with a perfectly in-tact casing surrounding the walnut inside. In a way, I wished I could ball up into a hard, exterior shell. That way I could be confided away from the fight Gartner and I were in. If I was the walnut, I wouldn't be crying on my birthday.

Earlier in the day we began our usual walk with Ghost to the Hollywood Forever Cemetery. I had been discussing hypothetical sex work, when he turned to me and without letting me finish my initial thought said:

"We are done with this conversation, change the subject now."

I asked him not to dismiss me. I would never tell him to stop talking and to change the subject as forcefully as he did. He began to swear. I was irritable and angry, but I did not agree with him. Somehow, we started arguing on the sidewalk of Santa Monica Boulevard during rush hour traffic.

I watched as cars rolled past us slowly, on their commutes to and from work. Parents grabbed their children from school and headed home as they watched Gartner and I argue on the side of the road. I felt embarrassed, and attempted to calm Gartner down, wanting more than anything to be home at the moment.

He swore that I was the irate one. I only felt that way in the moment because when trying to have a conversation with my fiancé, I had instead received a cease and desist. I felt less than. I wondered what I could have possibly been angry about before this. It was my birthday; I had money in my bank account. Earlier in the day I had put my brain to work and spent time writing. It was a great start to what was meant to be my day. I assumed Gartner was fueled with jealousy over the hypothetical topic of conversation.

While we argued, Gartner grabbed Ghost's leash and attempted to walk ahead of me with him. I was aggravated by his actions. If we broke up, Ghost would come back to Florida with me, he was my dog after all.

"Give me my dog," I said frustrated.

"Our dog," Gartner responded without giving me the leash.

"Look, I dunno what is going on with you right now, but that is my dog when this is all over. I adopted him, I took him to the vet appointments, I am sorry, Gartner, but he is mine." I stood with my hands on my hips, waiting for this very obvious information to become clear to him.

He stomped over to me and pushed the leash into my hand, then turned on his heel around the corner, veering right in the opposite direction of our apartment. I continued my walk home and let myself into Apartment three, which felt a lot less like my own recently.

When Gartner arrived back home, I could tell he was in a state of manic panic. His voice was shaky, and I could tell he understood where he had messed up. He was crying while he apologized for everything he had said, and I just wanted him to stop. I wanted silence and to be left alone.

If I had the means to run away in the moment, I would have. That was not an option for me. I understood that I did this to myself. After a while he calmed down enough to stop crying. I pulled out a puzzle I brought with me from Florida and streamed a movie on the TV screen. I decided to end the night together, whether he or I liked it or not. I thought that was what relationships were meant to be. Built on compromise and coming together to move on, even if it was your birthday and you were not in the wrong.

***

The next few days drifted by blandly. Gartner and I were as normal as we could be. I decided not to tell mom about the fight we had on my birthday. I told my sister that things were much better, and I assumed that she believed me. I wondered if that should make me feel better or not. I should have been honest, but again, I was scared. I wondered if I should tell either of them about the day at the Grove when Gartner hit me.

Earlier in the year before I moved, my sister bought me tickets to see Twenty-One Pilots as a birthday gift. Gartner was upset about paying for his own ticket, but like every argument we had over money, he eventually moved on.

The day before Gartner and I attended the Twenty-One Pilots concert I streamed the livestream experience from their Scaled and Icy performance on YouTube. While the livestream played in the background, Gartner and I began to roll around together under the bedsheets. Halfway through, Gartner asked me to turn off the livestream because it killed his hard-on: "They depress me," he said.

Somehow, I felt he wanted me to dislike everything that had raised me.

"This was my birthday, fuck," I thought.

From the moment we got the tickets, Gartner did not want to go to the show. As their album rolled out and singles were released, Gartner dismissed each one, expressing how unimpressed he was with each song. In a way, I understood it was not about the album, even if the album was not as good as I had hoped for. Gartner did not want to spend the money on experiences he was not interested in, even if it was for me and a special occasion like for my birthday.

While I could understand him being upset, his reaction was unnecessary. I hated how he made me feel for wanting to experience something that would provide me with fleeting happiness. He was frustrated about the idea of joining me for the show, which already hurt since they were one of my favorite bands. But I should have realized his emotional frequency would translate to the day of the concert.

I took the day off from work and even though I suggested for Gartner to do the same, he did not. When he arrived home, his energy was off - he was acting as if he was a shell of himself. He complained about his day, claiming that he hated his job. He said he could not keep working for his 'abusive boss.'

I attempted to cheer him up and failed. Anything I said was met with a counteractive response, there was clearly no winning the battle with him. When it was time to go we Ubered to the Intuit Dome where the Clancy Tour took place. As the driver caravaned us through the city, I grabbed Gartner's hand. He held it for a few seconds before letting go and fiddled with his phone instead. The ride was long and spent in silence. I knew Gartner was in a foul mood. It was obvious he felt sour about my birthday festivities and did not want to attend the concert.

I felt myself growing irritated, but my anxiety took over instead. How could he tell me he loved me and then act so standoffish? Why did he constantly feel the need to take away from every positive experience I was meant to have? I felt myself wanting to cry, and I stared out the window as we rolled through the small street hills to Inglewood. I looked back to Gartner, who was staring out the other window. Two people who claimed they loved each other and yet could not look less in love. Could not even make eye contact with each other. My heart skipped and my anxiety peaked. Suddenly an intense rush of insatiable need to feel his touch washed over me.

I pushed my leg over to him in an attempt to rest my calf against his. He shuffled his leg away from mine and closer to his passenger side window. I shifted in my seat uncomfortably. I was unable to comprehend his mood; he was so closed off from me.

I thought that must have been the hurt boy inside him responding to me, the boy who constantly felt abandoned. He closed himself off like an impenetrable wall. He felt better alone, with no one left to let him down. I've been there before, alone in a crowded room and while I find comfort in being alone, I would happily take the risk of feeling hurt to feel alive and loved in the moments that mattered. I wasn't sure if it was the same for him.

I once thought I had been betrayed by everyone; my parents included. Now I practiced forgiveness as often as I could. I forgave most of the people in my life, as people deserved second chances. It was all our first time living in reality. In the end we will meet our supposed maker, and that entity would decide our own consequences through their judgement, so the same goes for anyone who wronged me and vice versa.

I wondered what it was like to be like Gartner. I wondered about his experiences that had led him to draw the line, and I wondered how he determined the line? How many chances he gave until he was unable to forgive any further? He seemed exasperated by the effort he had already put forth.

I prayed I could forgive myself and all the others who had wronged me before it turned on me. That type of energy could hibernate within you, building with each individual hurt endured after the initial punch. I looked toward Gartner again, his blonde hair and gorgeous blue eyes sparkling despite the gray clouding his mind. Somehow, I thought I was the reason for his blues, but I did not know what I did to cause it.

The Uber driver dropped us off at the Costco up the street from the venue. We used my membership to buy hotdogs and walked the rest of the way to the entrance, which was technologically advanced. Cameras scanned ticketholder's faces to gain entry. Facial recognition seemed to be at the forefront of all transactions within the venue. The place was bigger on the inside than it appeared on the outside. Gartner refused to hold my hand as we walked through the tunnels to our seat in the lower bowl.

Gartner sat down in his seat and put on a pair of sunglasses.

"It's too bright in here, the lights are hurting my eyes," he said to me. It was not something for me to argue over. After several recent instances of Gartner going out of his way to hurt me, I decided to give in and accept the night for what it was.

I tried to shrug off my hurt and enjoy the concert. Gartner remained seated the duration of the show, only standing for two songs. I stood by myself as I belted the lyrics and wished with every note that I was by myself instead of with him.

At the end of the show, I asked Gartner to take a picture with me, his arms were crossed and in the first shot he gave a sarcastic smile. I asked him to give a proper smile and he obliged, but reluctantly. His sunglasses remained on his face.

Pink picked us up from the show afterwards. Gartner took his place in the back of the car and remained silent as she steered us towards the apartment on Wilcox Place.

Before Pink could even begin to put her car in park, Gartner was out of the car waving goodbye. I watched as he punched the door code into our apartment keypad, disappearing into Apartment three.

"He has been really fucking annoying all night," I said quickly. "Yeah, I noticed as soon as you got in the car. He seemed off," she said.

"Thanks for the ride home, I'll call you when I take Ghost on a walk because I doubt that he will walk him," I said before climbing out.

I closed Pink's passenger door behind me and crossed in front of her car before she drove off. I punched the same code into the keypad and the door unlocked for me. I let myself in and climbed the flight of stairs to the number three apartment on the second landing of the stairs.

Once inside, I saw Gartner was in bed already. He had stripped his clothes off, threw them into the hamper, and climbed into bed faster than I could say goodbye to Pink and make it up the stairs myself.

I sighed while I grabbed the dog leash off the key holder next to the door and walked over to where Ghost was on the couch. I clipped the leash onto his collar and led him outside for a walk. I called Pink once I was outside to explain how the concert went. How he had acted like an energy vampire, sucking the life out of the whole experience. How he wore sunglasses the entire evening, refused to hold my hand, and remained seated throughout the performance. As I repeated the events out loud, I aggravated myself further. I was finally able to process just how shitty the entire evening played out.

Pink listened to me as I vetted my complaints. She knew it was complicated. Her advice was simple, do what was best for me and she would stand by me. Easier said than done, and I wondered if she was worried for me. Or maybe I was projecting my own worry that I had begun to develop.

I sighed repeatedly to calm myself down once Ghost and I returned from our walk. As the minutes slipped past in the dark silence, I grew more frustrated with the events of the night.

"I hated how you acted today," I broke the silence, it would have to be me to do so, I realized.

Gartner remained silent.

"You've really hurt me throughout my birthday," I continued, needing him to know how I felt. "I was so excited for tonight and you just sat there; you did not care about the significance of it to me. Even if it was just for me, you ruined it and that upset me."

"I worked all day, and I was just tired," he said finally.

I scoffed in disbelief.

"Your overall body language and mannerisms told me otherwise, and maybe being tired was a small factor of it, but you just did not care to be there." I continued to push, needing him to realize he was in the wrong here.

"You said to yourself, you did not enjoy the new album," he said to me, as if that were to make everything better somehow.

He appeared to be grasping for straws to excuse his behavior.

"At first no, I didn't," I said, "but they are my favorite band and after tonight I really enjoyed the album more after hearing it live."

"I was just tired," he sighed heavily and rolled over to avoid eye contact.

"Okay, I am not going to argue with you but the way you are acting right now says otherwise and honestly, I just want you to know that I am really upset, you ruined tonight for me for no reason, and I wish I had gone by myself," I said.

Part of me regretted the harshness of reality as I felt I would rather be alone.

"That is really mean to say man," he said to me. "I know you are upset, but I wish you could hear how mean and hurtful you are."

I considered his words, the weight of them rolling around in my gut like rotten food. My fear had come true as I acted like my easily agitated father and I wondered if I had been harsh in the moment. Then I remembered I was supposed to have had a wonderous, memorable night with my supposed fiancé, and instead it became a tainted memory. Another argument I let deflate out of my system, just wanting to move onto the next day. Wanting to get on with the next thought that wasn't feeling so frustrated towards the person I was meant to do life with.

When I finally joined him in bed, I felt Gartner scooch his way over to me. For someone who desperately wanted to be alone, he was terrible at recognizing when others wanted to be alone themselves. I wished he could understand and accept that sometimes I wanted to be alone, not only from him, but everyone.

The next morning, I woke with a thought planted in my head, insisting that I purchase a ticket and attend night two of the Twenty-One Pilots show. This time by myself. Aside from the Gartner drama, the crowd as a whole night one was lackluster. I wanted a do-over.

Gartner left early for work that morning. I worked a shift at The Market and after I showered and dressed myself into a comfortable outfit for the day, Gartner had still yet to come home. Pink picked me up and I texted Gartner to let him know I had gone with Pink. I decided not to tell him I would be going to see Twenty-One Pilots again that night. Part of me believed he wouldn't be happy for me. Part of me didn't care.

Pink and I hung out at her place, watching Sex and the City and lazily passing a joint back and forth between ourselves. Gartner texted me and asked if he could call me. Not necessarily a response to my text about being by myself for the night, but at least he had communicated. I texted him back yes and a few seconds later my phone vibrated.
"Hey," I said.

"So, you don't want to be around me tonight?" he asked, and I could already tell that he was frustrated and reactive.

"Yeah, just a me-date, I feel overwhelmed and just want to spend time by myself," I responded, feeling proud of myself for asserting my needs.

"I wanted to hang out with you and try to make up for last night," he said.

I considered asking him if he wanted to try to re-do the night prior and buy a ticket to come to the concert with me but ultimately decided against it. If he was meant to come with me, it would happen. Part of me thought that if Gartner was a man who loved me and understood what the band meant to me, he would offer it himself, suggesting purchasing the tickets to night two for us himself.

There were moments where you had to be your own knight in shining armor, and I believed that night was one of them for myself. In a world that was difficult to digest, music was one of the few constant goods I had in my life. Gartner did not understand what it meant to be devoted to an artist and connect with their art, he had said it once himself before.

What I hoped happened, never happened. Gartner hung up the phone on me, in a passive aggressive manner. Pink dropped me off at home after the phone call ended. I had to walk Ghost and Gartner was working late. I decided I would purchase the ticket on the way to the show.

Gartner repeatedly called my phone while I was on the walk with Ghost.
I did not answer, my chest hurt. I was not sure what I would say - I needed more time to think to myself. After rejecting his third call, he texted me:
I would like to see you before you leave for your night to yourself if I can, that's why I was calling.

I was nearly done with my walk; I looped around the neighborhood and turned right down the street we lived on. I spotted Gartner's car in the designated parking spot. I decided to call him back. I do not want to spring up on him at the moment with all of our tension, but he didn't answer. I considered it fair, since I had not been proactive in answering his calls that day either.

We were both acting annoyingly sensitive, and neither of us would end up happy at that rate.

I punched our code into the door keypad and began the ascension up the stairs to the second floor. Gartner rounded the corner from the first landing as I was about to climb up, but he averted his gaze from mine which instantly aggravated me. He tried to maneuver past me as Ghost begged for his attention. I stood there confused, and he nearly made it to the courtyard before I got him to stop. I could feel the tears welling up in my eyes. He was halfway out the front door to the complex and I could tell he was full of anxiety ridden rage.

"What are you doing?" I asked him.

"You do not want to answer my calls!" he yelled back.

"I just needed a moment! You act like this every time we talk, you just get mad at me! I'm just trying to breathe for a fucking moment and figure out what to do!" I snapped back.

This was unhealthy. I wanted it to end, I had yet to enjoy a singular minute of my birthday and at that point, I was ready to book a one-way flight back to Florida the next day. I could tell his anxiety had gotten the best of him, he had a visible shake to him, and his eyes were glazed over. I wondered who hurt him so badly that he reacted so explosively when he feared he was losing control over a person or situation.

As much as I wanted to be happy, I wanted Gartner to be happier. I worried he wallowed so deeply in his own sadness that he had lost his ability to differentiate between melancholy and elation.

I wondered if there was a scientific study that could document the transferring of emotional sadness from one individual to another. As an empathetic person, I worried my inner conscience had begun to mirror the sadness detected beneath Gartner's exterior. At the beginning of our relationship in January, his hope for a better life where he could love and be loved had come true - so how had we gotten to where we were in that moment?

"You were my birthday wish," he told me one night back in April, while he held me in bed., "I wished for a boyfriend, and then you were mine," he admitted sheepishly.

I wondered where that man had gone then, the one who wished for me. I realized I let things go quickly and easily for him. It was the opposite. I wondered if I held a grudge against him, if I held out against his anger, how he would react.

In a perfect world, Gartner would have presented me with a grand gesture. I fantasized coming home after night two of the show to a house covered in red roses and hyacinths, Sex and the City streaming on the TV, and a sweet treat from MagPies Soft Serve or Erin McKenna's Bakery waiting for me. A sign to show he really knew me and cared about my happiness outside of just his own.

I stood on the curb of Wilcox Place. Ghost pulled against his leash as he tried to get to Gartner in his car. Gartner slammed the car door shut in my face as I approached him, started the ignition and jerked the gear shift back into reverse. He looked at me and we locked eyes. I stared into his stormy blue gaze as their shine dulled back at me. Instead of adoration reflected in his stare, he looked at me with repulse.

I was crying, with tears falling down my face and landing on the pavement below me. I entered an out of body phenomenon and watched as the scene unfolded around me. I was the seagull in the sky flying by above us, I was the alley cat grazing through the small patch of grass across the street as two humans argued.

I watched as the man I was to marry pressed the gas and pulled away from me. I turned to face him in the street as he flipped the gear into drive and drove south towards Santa Monica Boulevard. I stood shocked that someone could tear away from the person they loved so quickly. The ring on my finger felt heavy and lead-like as it poisoned my hand.

I felt the embarrassment wash over me as I stood alone with Ghost on the curb. Hadn't he said he wanted to see me before I left for the night? And then he was the one to immediately ignore me and storm off? Soon after the initial shock, the shame set in. After a few frozen moments I found the strength within me to move my legs. I furiously punched the door code into the keypad and took myself up to the apartment. I took note of the few people standing around, pretending to mind their business as they watched our lovers' quarrel unfold.

I let myself into Apartment three and scanned the room, letting out a huff of air and taking a seat on the couch. Ghost climbed on top of my legs and sprawled out across them. His body formed an elbow-noodle shape from one end to the other.

I could never imagine leaving someone in the same way Gartner had left me. I imagined how it was perceived from those on the outside. The image was engraved into my head like an overwhelming movie relay on a constant loop. I thought to myself if that was the love I had been destined for, then the universe could take it back.

I worried that if I called my mom and told her everything that had occurred in the past week with Gartner, she would not believe me. Logically I knew that would not happen. I realized that maybe I felt that way because I wished it was not true myself. I had been blinded by the idea of Gartner, that he was the man who loved me to infinity.

I was left to ask myself the same question yet again: How much was enough? Realistically, I had nowhere to go. I was thousands of miles away from my family, closer to the age thirty than my early twenties, and hardly any money in savings. I felt stuck. Stuck in this apartment, stuck in California, and stuck in this relationship. Wasn't this all I had wanted at one point? I couldn't believe how drastically the year had changed.

My chest ached at the idea of our relationship. Was it a waste of time? I immediately felt a pang of regret, thinking about how I could have been so selfish to want an immediate end after it got tough? I was reminded this was not our first argument, and I had been more forgiving than Gartner.

I decided not to tell Pink what happened earlier with Gartner when she picked me up. I did not want to add fuel to the fire, and if I was to marry Gartner, I had to adjust to the bad. Good could not exist without some necessary evil. I was convinced of this.

I texted Gartner:

> I need you to stop acting like this, I don't understand what is going on in your current headspace right now and for that I am sorry. I

am sorry for anything I said that made you upset. I never want to make you upset, and I have only been reacting to how you have treated me over this past week when I am supposed to be celebrating my birthday. I hope you can forgive and forget because that is all I want to do at this point. I made a vow to you, and I plan to keep it.

I pressed send as I contemplated my forgiveness. It physically pained me to consider the concept of being mean to a person I loved, even if it was because they were hurting me deeply. I found myself gasping for air, expressing my discontent. I was unable to withstand it. I caved into an explosion of emotions over the hurt that has been harboring within me and in the end, I felt terrible for myself.

I converted my state of mind as I hopped in the front seat of Pinks beat up Honda Fit. She referred to the vehicle as her art car. The interior was covered in glitter and art supplies from her various festival exhibitions. She often joked that when she bought a new car, she would use her current car as a mobile art installation.

She uniquely attributed her driving skills to me and the day I taught her to drive in the rain ten years prior in Miami. I liked that my life was mirrored by my past. In both present day and 2015, I was in Pink's car riding in the passenger seat in one of America's biggest cities - then Miami and at that moment Los Angeles.

Pink dropped me off across the street from the same venue as the night before, just as the sun was setting. I dashed inside. I had ten minutes before the show began and it was just enough time for me to make it to my seat. I bought the ticket last minute and the seat was in the lower club level. I was led deep beneath the venue. I was unnerved as I traveled through what could be considered a basement, something we do not have in Florida.

I was led through a row of doors that appeared to resemble corporate meeting rooms, each one labeled "CLUB

ROOM" followed by a corresponding number. It took me up a small flight of stairs where I emerged on the left side of the stage, three rows up from the floor. I paid less for that ticket than nearly any other Twenty-One Pilots ticket I had bought before. I felt a sense of calm wash over me as I instantly realized I had made the right choice in attending the concert alone. I thought I was being rewarded for the rotten night before.

I memorized every lyric to the songs. I recited the words so easily along with the band performing it live on stage. So much so that during a brief interlude, a man two rows in front of me turned back to me and yelled back in compliment: "Dude, you are going bar for bar! Do you want to come down here and sit by me? There is no one here," he held out his arms suggestively at the empty seats beside him.

Instead of thinking I answered: "Sure!" and scuffled down to the first row. We were right next to the railing, the only thing keeping us separated from the pit and stage just a few feet below.

The guy carried on a conversation once I took my spot and I wondered if I should tell him I had a fiancé but decided against it, it would not matter either way. I was grateful for the better seat and someone being kind to me.

After the show was over, I slipped into the crowd like a fish in a river. I let the current move me as if I were water moving through rocks in a riverbed, squeezing between gaps of the other attendees. I made it to the outside courtyard of the venue in several minutes. Pink was waiting for me on the other side of Century Boulevard.

Once I was safely in her vehicle, Pink drove west towards Hollywood and Wilcox Place. I noticed my nerves had doubled and started to fidget. I doubted Pink would mention it—she knew I would speak up if I wanted to. I ended up saying nothing. As midnight approached, I walked upstairs to the apartment after getting dropped off. Gartner was awake, and the tension was palpable. I could not understand his anger; I wanted to enjoy my birthday without interference.

"So how was night two?" he asked me. The bitterness in his voice instantly soured my mood.

I responded as if I was oblivious to his energy: "It was good, the vibes were definitely off yesterday."
"I wish you would have told me I would have-" he started, but this time I was the one to cut him off.

"What exactly, Gartner? I don't mean to be rude, but what would you have done? Asked to go again and make up for last night? I wanted to be alone, Pink could have gone if she wanted to, and you know that," I said.

He remained in bed, silent. He flicked on one of the salt rock lamps I had brought with me from Florida. I used to leave them on for twenty-four hours a day until I moved in with Gartner.

"You ruined yesterday and for no reason. You ruined every celebration to do with my birthday. I have no clue why you would think I would invite you after these last few days? And then you left me. You locked your door and pulled away in your car while our neighbors watched... All because I didn't respond to your text quick enough? I mean what could you do? I even told you I didn't want to fight... that I wanted to make up and you still just left me there, as I cried."

His face was full of tears; they dripped down to the bedsheets he had covered himself up with. I thought of my night at the show alone, and the guy who invited me to sit with him. For a moment I debated telling Gartner about it. I feared that would cause me to appear malicious and decided against it. I was unable to focus on the drama he caused when I was trying to enjoy the last of my birthday festivities.

"I am sorry," he said. "Do you still want me to come with you to the Halloween festival at the resort tomorrow?"

"I dunno, honestly," I said, staying quiet for a beat before I continued. "I want to spend every day with you, Gartner, but I can't do that if this is how you are always going to be."

"I understand," he said. "I am sorry I ruined your birthday." The desperation in his voice convinced me of his sympathy.

My energy had been depleted, I couldn't respond. I wasn't sure if it was okay. It was embarrassing to spend the majority of my birthday crying. I realized I felt immensely alone. Was my mother right? I hoped she wasn't. I didn't want to give up on what we had built. If I gave up, I feared being alone forever. I argued with myself in the confines of my mind as I drifted asleep.

The next morning Gartner left the apartment before I could turn over in bed. I checked the time as I rubbed the sleep out of my eyes and realized it was only eight in the morning. I rolled over and fell back asleep. When I woke up again, I decided to call Gartner.

"Hey," I said.

"Hi."

"Why did you leave so early this morning?"

"I didn't think you'd want to wake up next to me and I thought you would want your space," he said, a sadness in his voice.

"I don't want any of that, I wanted space yesterday and that's why I went to the concert by myself, I already told you that." I was trying to understand why he was still attempting to perpetuate an argument.

"I am sorry, what do you want to do about tonight, then?"

"I will have Pink and Bondi pick me up," I said, my mind already made up. "I'll ride with them and we will meet you there."

"Yeah, okay, if you even meet up with me. I think you will ditch me," he said then, the icy tone returned in his voice.

"I dunno why you would say that" I said, annoyed.

"I am sorry, I will see you later," he said before ending the call.

As the sun began to warm the late August morning, I pushed myself out of bed to take a shower. I let the hot water run down my body as I mulled over the previous weeks in my head. Why was it so hard to love? Why was it so complicated? I wanted to blame his family for the hurt they caused him. I wanted to message his mother on Facebook and ask her what happened between them. I was scared I would hear a different story from her than what he had told me. I wouldn't be able to discern the truths from the lies.

If Gartner discovered I had gone around his back to contact his mother, he'd be furious. I was unsure just how his fury would play out. He would not be happy. To be fair, I would not be happy if Gartner did that to me if I was in his shoes.

After the shower I threw on the outfit I had planned for the night. I planned the outfit nearly five minutes after we purchased the tickets for the resort's Halloween festival after we returned home from New York. I examined myself in the full-length mirror. I wore a decorative resort t-shirt I had bought a few years back in Orlando, never previously worn, a pair of brown pants with white stitching, and a purple bandana to match the purple accents on my shirt. I completed the look with my green sling bag. I felt pathetic as I dressed myself alone in the apartment. I sighed, feeling defeated. Maybe I should have stayed in Florida. I took a deep breath and reminded myself that I should at least try.

I wiped my face after realizing I had been crying. I stared blankly at the reflection that peered back at me. I gave myself one final look before walking downstairs to meet Bondi and Pinker as they waited patiently for me in the car.

Bondi cruised the 101, heading south towards downtown Los Angeles. We passed the monstrous city skyline. I keep myself occupied to ignore checking Gartner's location. I was not prepared to see if he was committed to the night ahead.

"So, what happened dude? What was his beef?" Bondi asked me as she eyed me from her rearview mirror. I chuckled at her effort to cheer me up.

"I dunno dude," I said, still unsure for myself. "For the past two weeks he has been terrible to deal with."

"I am confused, why is he giving you such a hard time?"

"He tried to say some unsavory shit about y'all. I think he is under the impression that y'all are a bad influence on me. I was over it, and that's what started the fight when we tried to walk Ghost before my birthday. Then it just spiraled after that."

"I was unaware we had beef, but alright," Bondi said, Pink nodding her head in agreement.

"At the concert, he was being stand-offish after I picked y'all up," Pink said.

"Yeah, and that was the other half of it, even at Knotts he was being annoying, remember?" I said back.

"Yeah, and that made no sense, it was your birthday. Why did he have an attitude about everything that day?"

"Can I be honest? Sometimes I think he does not want me to be friends with you both," I admit, not wanting to hear the words myself.

"Yeah, I noticed that, like why was he so mad at you for hanging out with me that day after the concert?" Pink asked.

"I don't know what that was all about either," I said, shaking my head in the back seat. "I think sometimes he wants me all to himself, but I have never been like that. I've always been able to have my boyfriends befriend my friends, but with him it's difficult. I think he has just been alone and without a healthy, long-standing relationship for so long that he doesn't understand what it means to have a stable one - which leads him to freaking out over the slightest inconvenience." There I was, making excuses for his behavior again.

"Yo, that would actually make a lot of sense," Bondi said, "Like when he was acting mad weird about the baggie during Coachella." I was surprised this was finally being brought up.

"Yeah, that was fucking weird too, and you know he doesn't like Reni?" I said, now feeling the need to address everything with them.

"Why doesn't he like her?" Pink asked.

"He says we are too alike."

"That's even more weird," Bondi said, "You think he is coming to meet us? It would be kinda fucked if he doesn't."
"I dunno," I said as I let out an exasperated breath.

Part of me hoped Gartner surprised me at the entrance to the park, presenting a grand gesture. Even if it were to petrify me a bit. I twisted the ring on my finger - I had almost forgotten it was there. I hadn't taken it off, and I was not sure if that made Gartner feel better or not. If he truly loved me, I thought he would show me that day.

I was distracted when my phone started vibrating. I answered once I saw it was him:
"Hey, what is up?" I asked.

"Hey," he said. His voice shook and had a higher pitch than normal. I could tell he was anxious. "I think I am going the wrong way; do I need to be on the 60?" he asked.

"No baby, you wanna stay on the 5 all the way down, it leads to its own exit after Euclid," I said back, hoping to calm his mind. Somehow hearing his voice had already broken my annoyed spell with him. I instantly wanted him to be okay.

"Ugh, I think the GPS told me wrong, I knew that was right... I am sorry for bothering you. Okay, I will see you there." He said before hanging up the phone.

I caught Bondi's eyes on me in her rearview. She lifted her eyebrow as she probed the phone call. I returned a smile. "It is fine," I said, "He just got lost." She directed her gaze back to the road.

I tried to stifle the sigh that escaped my mouth and stared at the mountains to my left as we passed by The Citadel. All the continued drama, and for what? I hated to hear Gartner's voice shake like that. I could tell how severely anxious he felt. His delivery and cadence was backed by fake courage he mustered, to not give away that he had been crying before calling me. The perfectionist within him gave it away. I could see through his plastic shell.

I hated the idea of him crying, but then I reminded myself of the afternoon that led us to this point. How he was able to drive away from me after slamming the door in my face and then locking me out. I remember the feeling of standing there in disbelief as my face welled with tears. How much forgiveness could he continue to ask for? How much was I willing to give?

I could never abandon Gartner, but I didn't have to endure a shoddy birthday just because…. Well, why? Why was he so mad? I couldn't discern where the anger perpetuated from. The only conclusion I kept coming to was that he was jealous of the attention being on me. But how selfish and fucked up would that make him? Love should not be hard; it should not be difficult. Your chest should not ache under a constant state of nerves. I was starting to question if I understood the concept of love.

I decided to forgive him for myself. I mustered the strength I needed to move on. I forgave his actions but found it did not matter to him. I had a feeling then, that our relationship would fundamentally change. The Time Bandit had started a countdown to the end, without my knowledge or consent.

I felt uncomfortable as I thought about the shame I would feel if I were to give up on us. I moved my life to Los Angeles for him, for love. Carrie Bradshaw would be proud, and that alone gave me an ironic strength. I packed my pets and my mug collection into boxes and threw my clothes into trash bags and moved for a love that was promised to me, because I believed him. That should have been enough.

I believed the love Gartner gave to me had been sent to me by the universe. The collection of mystical atoms and energy had decided I needed him in the moment, and I wondered if I had been suffering a karmic judgement. I hoped the night would end better than the days before. I hoped somehow Gartner had found it in him to forgive me. I also wondered again what it was I was meant to be forgiven for.

Bondi parked her car in the resort's parking structure, and we made our way down the multitude of escalators, and for a second I was reminded of the game 'chutes and ladders.' I thought that might be where they got the idea for the game.

We reached the bottom floor where the tram to the resort awaited.

We found Gartner waiting for us at the bottom of the escalators before the security line. I could tell from his demeanor that he was anxious. I decided in the moment how I felt. His guard was down, and I could see him for who he was. And I loved him. I knew then just as I did before, how much I adored him. He was meant for me. I would have to be the one with stable courage in the moment. I was unsure if I was satisfied with my decision. If I expressed discomfort or a negative feeling towards Gartner, I had the feeling he would leave and I would never see him again, and I was not sure if I could handle that.

Somehow between our first meet up and where we were at that moment, I developed the will to live through him. This was a pattern that was dangerous for me. I wondered if my mother had seen the potential outcome before I could. I felt as if I was back in high school, begging for someone to love me because I couldn't do it for myself.

I eventually learned to love myself, but only after I did the mental work and learned how to appreciate the parts of me that had been so hard to accept. I loved myself because I understood the lived experience was not finite. My skin and body would decompose, and my spirit would proceed to absorb another life somewhere in the dirt or sea.

I thought about self-love and reflection and decided I would refuse to embrace Gartner in a hug. Instead, I decided to pull myself out of the mental gutter and make the most out of the evening. I used my natural tone of voice with an upbeat attitude to simulate a sense of calm. Several times I've had to act indifferent through complex discomfort, so I figured I could act my way through the night.

"You ready silly goose?" I said, plastering a smile on my face.

"Yeah, I was looking at the map and there are a few things I wanted to do..." he trailed off, apprehensively.

"I am sure we will get through a lot," I responded, shrugging.

The resort was decorated and adorned with Halloween decor. The color palette was orange, purple, and black, utilizing additional spooky decorations. It felt strange to celebrate Halloween in August, but I was happy to celebrate the mid-point of my birthday itinerary in a familiar and comforting location.

Throughout the night, I knew I was successful in convincing Gartner I was no longer upset. I found a way to move around it and accepted that I had two options: one which involved moving on mentally from the situation itself or moving on from Gartner. I chose to move on from the situation. I would choose him every time because I believed in him. Every fight and every hurt feeling, I would instead focus on seeing who he was on the inside.

I observed Gartner as he interacted with his environment and felt admiration for his generosity towards strangers. I couldn't deny he had a caring nature. He had the ability to strike up a conversation with anyone around him. I loved the way his face beamed when he located me in a crowd. I was impressed with his fluidity, and his ability to disappear into a crowd as easily as I could.

After ending the night with the Halloween parade, I decided to ride home with Gartner. Despite the venting session in the car with Bondi and Pink, I was ready to move forward and end the night with him, on a good note. The night gave way to the dry, fall air that started to move into the city. I took Ghost for a walk around the neighborhood when we got home, and I felt hopeful. The future we had ahead of us had just begun to ignite. I figured this was what it meant to be an adult in a relationship, seeing through the bad and complicated, and looking to the future instead. I wanted Gartner to be a part of my future.

\*\*\*

A week later, I received a job offer for a coffee house at the resort I had decided to apply to on a whim. After mulling it over with Gartner, I accepted the position - I hoped it would bring a sense of normalcy to my new life in California. I hoped this new job would act as a rock and ground me as a resort job once had in Orlando. I thought the familiarity would help with my assimilation. Unfortunately, I quickly learned it was the opposite of what I had hoped for, but I was thankful for the opportunity, nonetheless.

The nerdiest personality trait I have is my obsessive nature with theme parks. In all fairness, my love had been conceived at a young age. The pillars of the park community existed in the very backyard of my own home in Orlando, since the city was known as the Theme Park Capital of the world.

Skipping school on weekdays, late-night weekends on coasters, and first dates with friends, family, or ex-lovers all took place throughout the various parks in the Orlando area. As I got older and realized that there was a limited job market, I accepted my first position at the Studios Park in 2014.

I realized my working life could exist within the parks until I was buried in my grave. Tourism had no end, and Orlando was not slowing down anytime soon on its expansion of theme parks - or the need to have people work at them. I told this to Gartner once in a moment of vulnerability, but he gave me a quizzical look in return and laughed - proceeding to poke fun at me.

It was understandable to find a theme park job silly, but part of me often felt that he thought he was superior to me as a hairdresser. He defined his job as a career and compared my career path as less than.

I had not given much thought to a career beyond my serving gigs, although I had always wanted to be a writer. While I never thought it was a plausible route, Gartner encouraged me to write. However, I had not been able to write more than a few paragraphs before I found myself stalling. At that point, I figured it was best to focus on the job I actually had.

The drive to the resort from our apartment on Wilcox Place became commonplace, and I looked forward to the days I was scheduled to work. My favorite part of the drive was racing through the hillsides from the 101 to the I-5 interchange. I loved seeing the view of the Sixth Street Bridge leading to the downtown skyline.

Some nights, Gartner would have food prepared for dinner. He learned how to make my favorite chicken Caesar salad, and stuck to the recipe as an easy, go-to meal. Other times I would stop and grab take out from Raising Canes on Euclid or street tacos by the Pavilions. We would watch a movie or catch up on the latest drag queen television series while we ate together. I enjoyed our domestic bliss in moments like these.

We continued our nightly traditions, until one night I decided I should try to dig further into Gartner's past. We had reached a point in the relationship where I needed to know more about who he was at his core. I knew it would only cause me to love him more. I wondered how he had become so tight lipped, how he spent so many years keeping his feelings and secrets to himself. I wanted to know them and take them in as my own. I wanted to redirect the tension he felt away from him. I wanted to be his sense of comfort, and solace.

One night, Gartner told me more about his first love. The night he got his first boyfriend - after the scheme they planned to break up with their girlfriends and date each other - Gartner had gone home to tell his parents. He wanted to be honest with them but was met with unforgiving ignorance from their end.

He told me he spent his younger, formative years avoiding his home. He would take the last bus from the city center of Santa Cruz back to his home in Corralitos. He confided in me about the bullying he endured at the mercy of his brother, and how their relationship diminished over time. He often reiterated that he would never accept an apology from his brother. I tried to place myself in his shoes to imagine a similar scenario with my own sister but came up short. I could not fathom life without my sister. I would always forgive her just as I forgave everyone, and maybe that was my greatest flaw.

I wondered what details he elected not to share with me, or if he had forgotten some fragments due to repercussions within his mental capacity. I listened to Gartner as he spoke with intent. Every piece of emotional detail he chose to share with me I held in my heart and wondered how I could atone for it. I always wanted to love him wholly and fully, and I wondered if I could ever keep up with the type of unconditional love he needed.

Thousands of miles separated the different livelihoods Gartner and I were raised in. It feels abstract to understand the dynamics a person endured throughout their life. I grew up with the egregious misconception that California was a haven for queers of all kinds, only to realize the same amount of bigotry existed in California as it did back in Florida. I had the displeasure of experiencing this firsthand, when a customer called me a faggot one early morning shift at The Market.

After living in Los Angeles for a few months, I realized that once you moved past the apparent structural and cultural differences, Orlando and Los Angeles shared a lot of similarities. Try as each city might to be uniquely identifiable, we were still one country. Some people grew up with mountains, others with swamps, and others grew up in deserts or in lush green forests. No matter if a state existed three time zones apart from another, you could find the American flag flying high in each place.

September 2024

Before probing Gartner in an effort to understand him more, I asked him what he wanted to do for his birthday. We discussed road tripping North to his hometown of Santa Cruz. We considered our options for the duration of the trip and activities. San Jose was close to Santa Cruz, so Gartner suggested we visited Rissa while we were there. After I lightened the mood with his birthday plans, I began to ask about his friends he no longer spoke to. In response he asked for my phone and began to search their profiles on Instagram.

He found their profiles easily and began to scroll through their feed. It wasn't long before he found a picture of him and his friend together, both in drag, half-beat, ready for a night out in Boystown, Chicago.

Gartner showed off more pictures of himself before I knew him, swiping through other profiles of friends he no longer spoke to. They all resided in Chicago. That was one of the few instances I confirmed his life from the stories he told me. When you date someone with no social media presence, how can you deduce what is true or not? Simply off the individual's promised word? I was not sure people would believe that anymore. It was strange in this modern era, feeling like you couldn't take someone at face value unless they had a curated profile to back it up. But I felt a sense of ease wash over me as I realized that not everything he told me had been a lie. Then a pang of guilt came over me for having doubted him in the first place.

As Gartner scrolled through memories of his past, I could sense he had a longing of desperation within him that came across in an excited smile. He showed me glimpses of the life he once lived. The version of himself that existed in Chicago. He was proud of his accomplishments while living in the midwestern metropolis, and it showed through his enthusiasm as he told me stories about the nights spent fumbling through clubs in Boystown.

He missed his friends, that was clear. As the holidays approached and he spent more time with my family, I wondered if he had been triggered into thinking about his past and found himself longing to rekindle his relationship with his own family. He never admitted it to me, though.

Since the first night, he had asked me to scroll the profiles of his family and friends on Facebook and Instagram on multiple occasions. I checked in on his mother often after he showed me her profile, wondering if she would ever post about her son.

"Why have you not spoken to them?" I asked boldly one night.

"Well, my mom emails me, but I don't respond. My friends in Chicago do not know where I am. After I left, I changed my number," he said simply.

"I was having a hard time understanding," I admitted.

"You have mentioned previously that you received an email from your mom, but not that they were consistent? And why did you change your number after leaving Chicago anyway?"

"Yeah, she emails me every other month or so," Gartner explained, which surprised me. "She sends me two hundred dollars for car insurance, even though I dropped the plan I was on and never told her. I pocket the money she sends me. When I left Chicago, I felt betrayed and abused by my friends there. I think they all struggled with addictions and couldn't treat me right in the end. I tried to set up a moment for us to say goodbye, but they never returned my messages, so I got a new number on my first day in Los Angeles."

I couldn't hide my shock at this new information. The money from his mom, the immediate ability in changing his number to cut off any possible communication with his friends in Chicago. I wasn't sure how it would sit with me.

"If your mother constantly emails you with money deposits, then she doesn't sound as bad as you have made her out to be," I said before I had time to think about how it could make him react. "And as for your friends, I am sorry that happened. I wish I could understand more clearly what went down between you all, but I understand you have no desire to talk about it if you have not already. I've just been curious about your life and your past, that's all." I can tell he was irritated at this point, but I continued to ask him questions anyways. It felt like we could be getting somewhere.

"I don't want to upset you," I said calmly, "But sometimes I can tell that you really miss your mom and that you love her... I know the situation with your dad and brother is more difficult, but I feel like I am lost on why you can't talk to your mom. I am sure she is worried about you... and..." I trailed off, studying his face, trying to catch a read on his emotion before I continued. "I think you miss your friends, and I think sometimes you shut people out too quickly. I hurt for you thinking about that, because you are such a good person and you deserve friendship and happiness."

"The only way I would ever talk to my brother or father is if they apologized to me for everything they ever said to me..." Gartner responded, his mood already visibly souring. "And even then, it would take a lot more than an apology for my brother. He was vile towards me."

"And as for my friendships - I am used to it now. All my friends in Santa Cruz were terrible, and most have overdosed and died by now," he continued. "I mean you saw the people I was friends with in Chicago, they all look terrible... Everyone just sucks" he finished. I sat on this, trying to figure out what to say next.

"I won't tell you what to do, but I think you are hurting yourself in the long run," I offered, trying to be the supportive fiancé I would want for myself. "You obviously want to talk to your mom, and I think you should find it within yourself to be more forgiving. You are a good person, Gartner, and I do not know everything that has happened to you in your life, mainly because you have not expressed it even when I have explicitly asked. But I think you'll feel better if you talk to them. I think maybe you should try to reach out to some of the friends you had. It could be good for you, and even if you can't fix the relationships, at least you can say you've tried and have received a type of closure from it."

"No, I've gone to a therapist, and they said it was my family and friends' fault," his annoyed tone was back, Gartner clearly not wanting to see things from anyone's perspective but his own. "I was not in the wrong, and now I have moved on. They would have to apologize to me."

I figured I needed to accept that he would never provide me with the answers I sought after. The conversation had hit the usual wall he used to guard himself. My biggest fear was if we were to break up. I once again worried that I would be left alone and Gartner would disappear, without a trace. It seemed like such an easy thing for him to do.

I feared I had turned the mood sour. I reclaimed my seat on the couch and turned my attention back to the book I was reading. Gartner sprawled across the bed and pulled Jude into him, kissing her softly as he stroked her fur. I understood that what I said affected his mental consciousness.

I watched a man who had never been able to heal his inner child long for the gratification as he wept into oblivion. He cried passionately as tears streamed from his eyes. There was no drought in the city of Los Angeles that night.

I wished I could be the healing force for Gartner, but I started to wonder if I would ever be able to scratch the surface of his emotional boundaries. Humans desperately try to bottle their emotions up, and pray they never crack and reveal what hurts them most.

I was unsuccessful in my probing venture. Gartner would keep his memories locked away, the secrets from those years stored within his mind. I could tell he did not understand my domineering devotion to him. This was my partner, my fiancé. I felt like we should be sharing everything with each other, including our sorrows. I wanted to help heal his wounds and be a sense of comfort for the things that kept him unhappy. Yet, it wasn't enough, I felt like I was plastic, molded into something I couldn't define outside of the confines of the box it was concealed in.

"You look sad," I said finally as I studied him from the couch. I was distracted by my thoughts, which kept interrupting my reading.

"What you said to me was extremely hurtful," he said, suddenly making it all my fault.

"I am sorry, I had no malicious intent," I said, a little bewildered. "I guess for me it's difficult to imagine myself in the same position as you and reacting the same way you do. I don't think I have it in me to ever stop talking to my family or cutting off ties with friends. They are all such important parts of my life."

Gartner relinquished himself to silence. I couldn't tell if it was because he had decided to move on, or if it was because he felt irritated with me. I have found my understanding of humans to be generally accurate. I could get a read on a person easily, and I read body language instinctively. I could utilize contextualized knowledge gained through a casual conversation and interaction with a person to understand them through cultural anthropology. However, it had gotten increasingly difficult to determine what Gartner was thinking.

How could Gartner deny himself parts of life just because he could not handle the negative emotions conceived the moment an inconvenience transpired? I hoped he would never do the same to me. I couldn't bear the thought of him loathing me to the point of never speaking to me again. I would not be able to go through life with zero communication, zero idea of the day he took his last breath.

We had created something, forged something incredible from nothing. I felt my anxiety heighten, first in the pit of my stomach. Something felt spoiled inside of me, as if I had consumed rotten food. It spread quickly to my heart and lungs, passing through my veins into a numbness. I became a shell of myself, consumed by my own doubt.

"If we ever broke up, would you speak to me after?" I asked cowardly.

He looked at me with an expression on his face that confirmed I knew what his answer would be before he could tell me himself. I feel a tug on my heartstrings. I had unfortunately gotten myself in too deep. I wanted to retreat and protect myself before I got hurt, but I knew it was too late as he said: "I want to say I will, because I love you and I know you would want to stay friends, but I can't do that for you and I am sorry for that."

I felt as though I lost a battle I had unknowingly fought. I could not imagine building something like what Gartner and I had, and ending it so quickly at my own expense, ceasing contact instantly. The fragility of our relationship suddenly loomed over me.

\*\*\*

Gartner never told me not to work at the resort, but he never encouraged it either. I had always been curious if he had wanted to say no but chose not to out of fear of an argument between us. When I told him where I had been offered a job, he did not react the way I had hoped. I wanted him to be excited for me but received the opposite response.

My work location was the original hotel, which complimented my past in Florida. I once worked for the sister hotel to the original, a contemporary take on what hotels could look like. My property orientation trainer guided us around the grounds of the resort. It was not as large as the Orlando resort, so I discovered my bearings easily - acutely aware of where I was at all times on property. After we toured the two parks and shopping district, we collected our wardrobe-issued work shoes. Once we completed the wardrobe customizations we walked to the employee bus stop for a lift back to the hotel to complete training.

It was an open-air bus that carried us between various drop off points across the resort. My trainer was a short woman in her early forties, who wore hair extension clip-ons that caused more of a distraction than a nonchalant enhancement. Her energy matched those I did not necessarily click with, and I could tell we had vastly different opinions on things already.

But the sun was shining, and I was beginning to feel excited about my journey ahead with the resort when my trainer turned to me out of the blue and said: "I am extremely racist." I tried to suppress the expression that overcame my face. I laughed it off uncomfortably as I gaslit myself into wondering if I had understood her correctly. I thought to myself how this was not the California they boasted about on television.

I decided to keep my mouth shut for the duration of the tour, as I would rather not make a dramatic scene before even starting my first shift. I settled on addressing the issue with managers later, privately. I sighed. I wondered if I needed to move on from the resort and its influence on my life. The thought hurt my heart, with memories that existed in the walls from here to Florida dutifully fortified within my psyche. I was not sure I could leave them behind, even if it no longer suited who I was.

I liked the drive to and from the resort. Depending on the time of day it could take over an hour to get to either destination. I was accustomed to long commutes and enjoyed the comfort of being alone, and the freedom it provided. Once I arrived home, I told Gartner about the racist comment from the trainer and without missing a beat he told me to quit. I realized I would hear those words from him frequently and wondered if I would eventually quit because he wanted me to, even if it was before I was ready.

I accustomed Gartner to my own traditions. We spent our nights at the haunt hosted by the studio park. It became another ritual of ours to have dinner and rest until eight at night, then walking north on Wilcox Avenue to Hollywood Boulevard where we caught a lift on the metro to Studio City. I never paid for the metro; I would slip through the gates behind Gartner as he scanned his own metro pass. Police hardly patrolled the stations, and no one seemed to pay attention to me anytime I scooted in behind Gartner before the turnstile closed.

I felt a tug on my heart string once I recognized I have been completing a bucket list goal I dreamed of as a child. In my wildest dreams, I would have never believed I would be a Los Angeles resident attending a haunt at the parent park of the studios park I grew up attending in Orlando.

The weather shifted and it finally felt like fall in Los Angeles. The delayed autumn weather reminded me of Florida: comfortable and warm during the day, cold and breezy at night.

One brisk, fall night we walked up Hollywood Boulevard to the TCL Chinese Theater. In a way I felt connected to the neighborhood, as if in a past life this was my native home. The parks back home in Orlando resembled so much of the studio's history that there was a realistic replica of the Chinese Theater in my neighborhood's backyard. The lobby of the theater was large and decorated with plush velvet red hues and gold accents that adorned the luxurious interior. Various movie props and artifacts were strung about in glass cases in the central lobby.

The inside of the theater was grand, with a high ceiling fashioned with decorative woodwork in a circle formation that spiraled outwards. The theater curtains were a deep rose-red, with gold trim, gold palm trees, and bamboo designs woven throughout the expensive fabric.

After seeing a movie, we walked to the metro and visited the haunt again. I could tell Gartner would rather be sleeping. Sometimes I felt as though Gartner forced himself to participate. I would have been fine going to the haunt by myself.

As much as I loved spending time with Gartner, there were times when I just wanted to be alone and left to feel things intimately. I could sit on a walkway amongst decorative trees, camouflaged with the night and have the option to reflect on the past year. I thought of my friends who were more than likely at Hollywood's counterpart park back in Orlando. I imagined them enjoying themselves as they ran from house to house. I wondered if Gartner would have felt differently about the haunt if we were surrounded by more people. I wondered if there was any way he would enjoy it more.

I found that the months began to drag on, even with all the fun being had. Adapting to the west coast had not gone over as well as I originally thought it would. I found myself struggling to connect with my peers and the job market, while more easily accessible, had been proven to be just as poorly run as back in Orlando. Was there anywhere left in the states for us to turn to for a better life? It seemed that even the bigger cities were just as defunct.

## No Glory in the West

In early October, Gartner and I met Bondi and Pink out for Bondi's birthday dinner. I was not acting myself, jolted by the realities of my ideal relationship crumbling with each passing sunset, and each sunrise presenting a new challenge to keep us afloat.

My assimilation into Los Angeles had become cumbersome to navigate. I was apprehensive of my honesty. My social battery had depleted and just like at Rissa's wedding, I knew I was observed by others as an outcast in the crowd of people. I was unable to keep up with the life I wanted to enjoy with the jobs I had, and solely due to Gartner's request, tipped service jobs were out of the question. I started to realize that the life Gartner had promised me was transitioning into an entirely different facet. Yet I failed to express my discomfort.

After dinner we relocated the party to Shim Sham, a local bar off Beverly Boulevard that Bondi had worked at since its inaugural inception a year prior.

Bondi quickly became wasted and we pulled an Irish goodbye after a few shared drinks. Gartner wanted to leave before we even arrived, and I half wondered if I should have attended the party by myself. However it was cramped with the amount of people in the small bar, so I figured it was probably best we left anyway. Even if I was by myself, I probably would have felt the same. It was getting to the point where I enjoyed little, even the time meant to be spent celebrating my closest friends.

Bondi wouldn't notice if we said goodbye to her. She was popular for good reason. Every step she took throughout the bar, a patron stopped her and wished her a happy birthday. As I made my way towards the exit, Bondi happened to walk past and noticed our covert escape without a farewell. She stopped and hugged both Gartner and I and kissed me sloppily on the cheek. \She declared her love for me, then sashayed off immediately in the direction of the bathrooms.

*\*\**

I should have understood money would be an issue for Gartner from the start. Before he moved me across the country, we discussed my finances. After a year of unemployment, I had just finally started to get my finances back on track.

Gartner and I originally agreed for me to pay half of the rent after my birthday. However, in July I gave him $250 after getting ahead of my bills sooner than expected. This was after I had worked a few weeks at The Market.

Before the move Gartner expressed concern with my work ethic. After a year of unemployment his skepticism was warranted, but I wanted him to believe in me.
"I'll believe it when I see it," he said.

My family was not rich, but my parents always showered my sister and I with riches. They worked restlessly for us. Many nights when we were children, my sister and I would join my parents at their catering gigs, sitting in a corner in the kitchen while reading a book or completing our homework. I learned at a young age how to apply myself.

I never had someone question my integrity, and I felt a passionate response to his constant doubt. After years of standing by and watching my parents from afar, I understood the value of hard work. I tried to prove my worth to Gartner by purchasing groceries and contributing to rent. I even bought us passes to the parks and haunt, giving us options for casual date nights.

I kept alive the tradition of frequenting the horror-filled, late-night event at the mountainous studios park, close in proximity to the apartment on Wilcox Place. Gartner remained unenthused during the entirety of the event.
Some nights I sacrificed my evening for him. I would read his body language, since he easily gave away how he felt in the moment with his movements. He moved slowly once he entered our apartment, taking his time and slumping through the remaining hours of daylight. My energy would deplete itself as I absorbed his apparent lethargy. I played it off as if I was the one who was tired, and suggested we stay home instead. Other nights when I attempted to go solo for the night, he would find a way to accompany me, so I let it be.

In an ideal world Gartner would share similar interests with me, but I never wanted him to feel forced into frequenting the parks just because his partner enjoyed them. I felt bad in a way, and part of me wondered if I was unable to be the partner he needed, again. Selfishly I hoped he would just change his mind and come around to it.

A few days after Bondi's birthday, we flew to Florida to babysit for my sister and mom while they went to a concert in

Miami. This time Gartner needed little to no convincing to accompany me on the trip.

We spent the evening of our arrival babysitting my nephew, Wes, while my mother and sister were at the concert further South towards Miami. We took Wes to a playground close to the Airbnb my mom had rented before nightfall. I watched as Gartner and Wes ran around the playground together and thought that maybe we could have a kid of our own one day. We could hire a surrogate and grow our family. I was nervous about having a child, but Gartner told me when we first started dating that he wanted a family. The idea of having a kid with Gartner frightened me less, somehow.

My mom and sister returned from their show around midnight. Gartner and I fell asleep intertwined with one another, curled up into each other's arms as if we were the other's security blanket, protecting one another in our sleep.

The next day we took the Brightline back to Orlando, napping lazily against one another in our assigned seats as the train carried us to the station. Once we arrived back in Orlando my father picked us up from the airport station and we grabbed Puerto-Rican takeout for lunch. Gartner and I spent the remainder of our evening comfortably lounging around my parents' place until we fell asleep.

The following morning, we visited the Animal park and dined at a buffet together with Wes. The afternoon was spent admiring the many animal exhibits together, and I liked to imagine how everything must have looked through his youthful eyes. How incredible it must be for Wes to be creating these memories for the first time; it was a feeling I knew all too well and I hoped he would retain those memories for just as long as I had. I also wished Gartner felt a similar thrill for it all. I knew it was intense, having such a jam-packed weekend across multiple theme parks. Especially for a person like Gartner, who didn't quite understand how big of an impact it played for people born and raised in Orlando. But I wanted him to make the effort, I wanted him to try for me. And I wanted us to have a good time together. I didn't think that was asking too much.

Later that evening, Gartner and I drove to the studios park to meet up with friends for the nightly haunt. We made our way inside the gates and located my longtime friend Chel and her fiancé, Walton. We met after I graduated high school and began my career in the parks. We spent the first half of the night together, until Chel and Walton left a few hours later. I sensed that Gartner was wanting to leave as well, but I wasn't up for it. Then we located KT and Kash once we completed all the houses. The night was surprisingly slow. For an average Floridian, this would be a great sign. That meant you could easily get everything done and wander around the park, taking in all the horror you wanted. But Gartner wasn't your average Floridian, he was a sleepy beach bum from Santa Cruz, California. Two different universes.

Towards the end of the night, I could tell Gartner was struggling to keep up with our pace as a group. I was walking a few feet ahead of him, deep in conversation with KT when I noticed the annoyance displayed across his face. I slowed myself down to check in with him.

"Hey, you, okay?" I asked.

"I am really struggling, my feet really hurt," he replied.

"I'm sorry baby. We should keep up though, the night is almost over and once we're home, I'll rub your feet," I said as I pulled his arm over my shoulder to help him walk faster. I'd gladly carry his weight with no complaint.

I had hoped it would be the night we snapped back in sync with one another. Where he would find a deeper love for the haunt and the parks, where we would bond over the memories made together. I found myself yearning for his declaration of love for the haunt that was my child-like pastime. His declaration would be my validation and make me more at ease with our togetherness. Instead, I got the sense that he wanted to go home. I knew I must have been annoying him as we ran laps around the park.

I tried to arouse some sort of excitement within him but was met with no success. I felt his sour mood seep into my own energy. I knew this would cause an argument and I shamefully wondered if he was exasperating his tiredness to regain my attention from my friends. I tried to push the thought out of my head and focus on the present. I was having a great time there, after all.

For the rest of the night, Gartner staggered behind the group, trudging along behind us remorsefully. I understood it had been a long day for him; we had started at the animal park with my family earlier in the day. I wished a part of him tried to hide his annoyance, or at the very least, find a way to not let it affect the energy within the group. I felt like this was the sort of social awareness thing people would have caught on at this point in life, knowing when to maintain a pleasant demeanor at the very least to keep up the overall morale.

When we finally left later that night, Gartner said to me as we drove back to my parents' house: "I hope you realize how lucky you are to have me as your boyfriend because I do not think many would have stayed with you tonight, they would have gone home."

"I am sorry your feet hurt that bad baby, I promised I would rub them for you when we got home," I emphasized.

"You kept leaving me," he said, his words quick and painful, like a punch to the gut.

"I wasn't leaving you. I was hanging out with my friends who I had not seen in months, I missed them," I responded, hoping he could understand.

"I told you my feet hurt, and you did not stay with me. You really hurt my feelings when you did that," he said, needing to emphasize that I was in the wrong once again.

I gawked, unaware how to continue the conversation. I decided apologizing would probably be best.
"I am sorry, I didn't recognize you were in that much pa-" I started.
"I told you my feet were hurting, and you just left me," he said over me, cutting me off.

"I am sorry," I said again, emphasizing each word. "I didn't realize the pain was that bad, I just wanted to talk to my friends. I haven't seen KT in so long... I was just having fun." I was slightly annoyed at myself for the way my voice dropped at the end, as if I truly had done something wrong. As if I had something to be guilty for.

"Next time I expect you to stay with me," he said, ending the conversation.

\*\*\*

I continued to struggle to adjust to life in Los Angeles. The resort had quickly turned into a toxic environment when I had hoped it would be the opposite. I was reminded of my past. When I was in the sixth grade, they didn't have enough tables and benches to accommodate the number of students filling the lunchroom. Those who weren't lucky enough to find a spot - usually those not well liked or had little to no friends - found themselves in the few alternative spots. Either on the concrete floor, locked away in bathroom stalls, or hiding in a classroom of a particular teacher.

The first time I found myself on that concrete floor, I stared up at my peers who appeared to not notice me. I felt invisible. I became uncomfortable in the skin I was born in. It felt like a similar situation again at the resort. I spent my shifts there reserved, suppressing the part of me I was hired to express. I only found comfort in my drives back to the apartment on Wilcox Place.

On the drive from Hollywood to Anaheim, the sights were limited beyond the warehouses and distant mountain peaks. There wasn't anything notable to admire other than the suburban concrete mixes beyond the LA county line. But once you reached the Interchange from the 5 to the 101, the scenery changed and became my favorite part of the drive. The road curved downhill along the side of the mountain, bending into where the city was nestled.

Most nights when I arrived home to the apartment on Wilcox place, I was spent. I trudged my way up the stairs and heaved myself onto the bed with Gartner. The troubles from the resort would bounce around in my head. A few of my coworkers refused to acknowledge my existence. It could be due to some sort of karmic retribution I was forced to endure for something I did in the past. I accepted my fate, not feeling I had the energy to do anything about it. Besides, I knew I didn't have to work there if I didn't want to.

I confessed my feelings to Gartner. I felt isolated and disconnected from the city. I found it difficult to befriend anyone I worked with at the resort other than two girls: Jai and Adi. I was fortunate and lucky enough to befriend them both, but it had never been hard for me to develop friendships before.

***

In early October, Gartner purchased tickets to see Orville Peck at the Palladium on a whim of spontaneity the night before the show, one of his personality traits I adored. The concert was postponed and moved to Halloween week. It should have been a festive week. I worked the day of the show at the resort. I had hoped to nap beforehand, but Gartner prevented me from resting.

It was eight in the evening, and Gartner walked ahead of me by twenty feet. Normally I would be the one leading. Out of the blue he began speedwalking away from me. I had never seen him walk so fast.

He turned around to look back at me, stopped, and proceeded to wait for me in a dramatic manner. He wore an agitated expression on his face, and I wondered what had upset him today. Once I caught up to him, he asked me why I was walking slow.

"I am not walking slowly," I said, "You are running away from me, and quite honestly, I'm wondering what is up with you?"

"Nothing," he said shortly. He strode off from me again, and I attempted to keep up with his pace.

His demeanor was irritable. I could tell something had been off with him from the moment I called him when I was leaving work earlier. His tone of voice was unenthused and dry. I asked him if he was upset, but he ignored the question.

He avoided eye contact with me. He stared off in any direction but my own gaze. Something shifted within me as we began to bicker in the crowd over his attitude. I realized people were watching, eavesdropping in on our argument. What were we arguing about again? I wondered if this had spiraled into something I never wanted it to be. Everything I said irritated him. My voice felt diminished. Where was my voice? I became hyper aware of my surroundings. Why was he so angry at me? Did he hate me? My sense of time and space seemed to have gotten away from me. It felt like all we did was argue.

I did not want to make it worse, but I couldn't stand next to him any longer while the air around him wreaked hatred towards me. I could feel his angry energy radiating off him like a furnace in the winter.

I broke away from him as I excused myself to the bathroom. I walked up the flight of stairs onto the second floor where the toilets were located. I had always wanted to see a show at the Hollywood Palladium, and years later there I was. I mentally checked off the box on my bucket list, then realized the experience was being tainted while I fought with who I had hoped was the love of my life. Not exactly what I had pictured for my first show at the Palladium. And then there I was, avoiding Gartner in the last private stall.

Oddly enough, I was far too comfortable in a bathroom stall. I spent my life in bathroom stalls with the immense stomach pain from my spherocytosis. I could stay where I was for the remainder of the night if I wanted. In the end I knew I would walk out of the stall and head downstairs to find Gartner in the crowd; I just didn't know when.

I sat on the toilet seat, contemplating calling my sister or mom to explain the argument between me and Gartner, but then I stopped myself out of shameful fear. I did not want to give the impression that the relationship had failed, because I did not want it to fail. Gartner asked my mother, father, and sister for permission to marry me. Then he moved me and my animals across the country to live with him. That had to equate being in love. The relationship would work, it had to, because the love was real. I sighed. The restroom was busy, with people flowing in and out of the stall next to me. I found peace in the simplicity of those occupying the bathroom around me. I thought I could have stayed here all night, avoiding my problems in the last stall.

I had been sitting there for at least fifteen minutes when Gartner texted me: "Where are you?"

I realized I couldn't lie to him. I texted him back: "bathroom" before I had time to think through my next move. His black boots appeared at the base of the stall door. The door rattled as he began to bang on the door.

"Come on, let's leave," he said in an annoyed tone of voice.

I exited the bathroom stall and left quickly, actively avoiding eye contact with anyone who witnessed Gartner banging on the door as he yelled at me to leave.

He seemed to ignore me as I explained how embarrassed I felt. I told him how rude it was to storm into the bathroom and bang on the door like he did.

"Would you have stayed in that bathroom stall all night had I not asked where you were?" he asked me.

I had thought about it. I would not have stayed confined in the bathroom. I would have ran out of the Palladium and taken off somewhere to be alone, just me and the city of angels.

"No... I was about to come out," I lied blatantly. I hadn't planned when I would leave yet. It also didn't seem helpful at the moment to tell him this.

Somehow, I convinced Gartner to remain at the show. It would be better than going home to sit in the apartment in silence. As much as I wanted to run away at that moment and find a spot to be by myself, part of me thought Gartner would detest the idea. Maybe I should have done it anyway.

We stood in the left corner of the general admission crowd, over by some support columns. Gartner refused to get near me throughout the night. He and I watched each other out of the corner of our eyes. I wanted to reach for him and tell him how much I loved him and how much I hated to see him upset with me. I hated that we were fighting, but I could tell by his demeanor that there was no way to fix the current state of his mind. There was simply no remedy to solve our problems in the immediate moment.

Halfway through the show, I saw a path of tears stained across his face and realized he had been crying. He was careful to not let me catch too many glimpses of his ocean blue eyes as they released his emotions. I assumed it was because he was crying from the show.

After we returned home, I fell asleep on the couch with Ghost curled against my legs. I found myself staring out at the black night sky and asked the universe what I did to deserve this. In my previous relationships, neither me nor my partners had ever slept separately after an argument. I felt embarrassed falling asleep on Gartner's couch, feeling decreasingly comfortable in the apartment on Wilcox Place.

Jude fell asleep on the bed curled up against the back of Gartner's legs. Zu and La were spread out around the apartment on blankets, keeping a watchful eye over Ghost and me. I wondered if they could feel the tension between us. I assumed they understood from our unusual sleeping arrangements. The kitty sisters had continued to fight with Jude every so often, although we had started to notice the beginning signs of their adjustment to one another.

The next day I had a phone call with my mom, and I confessed in lesser detail about my argument with Gartner and our current predicament. My mother told me that I should be patient with him, and that both of us were experiencing a transformative life experience by living together for the first time. I understood the advice my mother offered, but I wasn't sure if it was what I needed to hear. In the moment I wished she would tell me he was being a dumb mother fucker. Deep within my personal fear, I worried that my family did not want me to come home, and that was why my mother hadn't offered returning home as a solution. I eventually worked through the self-doubt in my head. I knew my family always had my back.

I had planned to spend the remainder of the holiday weekend at the Studios Park for the last night of the haunt.

Since we had not gone as much as I had wanted to throughout the season, we agreed to go for Halloween night.

During the final night of the event, we walked through my personal favorite chainsaw wielding house. As we navigated the dimly lit maze, a performer recognized the Twenty-One Pilots symbol on my hat and pointed it out, displaying the symbol back to me with their hands.

I associated the moment with my home, an interaction that would organically happen back in Orlando. For a moment, it felt as though the veil had thinned and I existed in both Los Angeles and Orlando at once. It felt like a secure reminder that maybe I was where I was supposed to be. Los Angeles felt like home, and this was my new home. My seeds had grown roots, and I felt established within the city, and I suddenly felt at peace. A sense of calm washed over me. I knew I would adjust to the West Coast life. I felt optimistically hopeful for my future, spotting the golden lining in the sunset.

## Winter on 66

I began to feel more homesick than ever as we approached the holidays. We spent our weekends tending to household chores at the Laundry Pop on Sunset. Other days we'd go to one of the hotels at the resort and explore their details further, as an official local. There were hidden gems to be found when you had the time to look.

On days when we weren't exploring the various holiday offerings throughout the parks, Gartner and I were at work.

The days went by slowly, and the money was as dry as the brunt of late fall claimed the city. Gartner convinced me to stay in Los Angeles for Thanksgiving, and I vowed to cook a full spread for our holiday supper.

One night Gartner and I were in a passionate embrace on the bed and shared a kiss. His mouth moved in awkward patterns, and I tried to ignore the uncomfortable feeling as I maneuvered my tongue to match his own. Suddenly he stopped and pulled back from me. He stared into my eyes, somewhat grinning.

"What?" I asked.

"You know what I have noticed?" His grin continued to spread across his face.

"What?"

"You don't like to make out," he said matter-of-factly.

The unexpected comment shocked me internally and I felt myself freeze up. I was not sure how to respond. I found this odd for him to proudly state and felt myself succumb to self-consciousness. Had that wretched November day from my past affected every level of intimacy within me? I wondered if Gartner forgot what I told him of my past. His tone suggested that he had revealed some estranged secret of mine. As if he outwardly expressed his findings in hopes that it would embarrass me.

"What makes you say that?" I asked him after a moment of deep thought.

"Because we never make out, and I was just thinking about it as we were trying to do it now."

"So, because I have not made out with you recently, you assume I do not like to do it? Is that not an odd thing for you to claim? I never said I didn't enjoy it."

"But you never make out with me," he pushed again.

I considered my options, which would be to confess to Gartner that his kissing skills needed improvement, or accept what he claimed as truth to not cause an argument. I chose the latter, which was unfortunately not the first time I let a man invent his own truth, and forced me to accept it. I had no intention to upset him but if I was honest, he would have been upset.

"If that is what you think, but I disagree," I said instead. I would not accept a lie-covered truth.

Maybe I should have been honest with Gartner and told him I did not find him to be an experienced kisser. Sometimes his kisses felt clunky and forced, but I couldn't have cared less - I still loved him even if he could not kiss the way I wished he could.

*** 

My time at the resort in Anaheim would come to an end sooner than expected. We aimed to make the most out of my free admission and one day Gartner, Pink, and I visited the parks together. The sun was bright. It felt good in the late fall air. The parks were adorned and decorated with rich forest greens, deep garnet red, and royal gold for the holidays.

We entered the original park and passed through the brim, where we were greeted by the well-known resort band that curated performances within the park. Pink spent her formative years in band in high school before she moved on to color guard in her college years. We stopped to admire the performers.

I felt a sense of calm wash over me, the same that happened frequently when I was inside the park grounds. I was at peace listening to the trumpet and drums colliding together to make cheerful sounds. It captured the essence of the main street we were on.

I glanced over at Pink and noticed her wiping her tearful eyes. She turned to me and caught my eye before she started to laugh, and I followed suit with her.
"This is beautiful," she said.

"Yeah, it is," I said back. I grabbed her hand and held it while we continued to watch the band perform.

A moment worth a thousand words, and it was hard for either of us to describe. A seagull flapped their wings overhead and flew above us in the cloudless blue sky. I smelled candy and cinnamon wafting through the air. The trees rustled as the beginning of a windy day creeped through. I took a breath and examined my limbs, feeling closer to the ether of life than I had felt in recent times. We watched the performance until the band ended, proceeded by a bow and them exiting backstage.

The moment was unique and seemed to prove a point that the park was for everyone. I cherished this feeling of elation and relished in the gratitude that took over Pink's expression. The moment transcended the physical bonds of the every-day experience, and it encapsulated a magic specifically unique to a child-like wonder, often sought after the more we aged.

***

On Thanksgiving Day I woke up at six am and put the turkey in the oven. I stayed up until one am the previous day prepping the bird. It was my first time cooking my own personal turkey, and I was determined to end up with a tasty carvery.

I took Ghost on a walk while the food was in the oven. The city was quiet. I often read articles online about the emptiness of Los Angeles during peak holidays, and the revelation of how many non-native Angelenos inhabited the city did not shock me. But the quiet shocked me, the peaceful stillness in an otherwise overstimulating city. The morning was crisp and cool. I wore a hoodie and sweatpants along with my favorite cow slippers that Rissa gifted me during her wedding.

In the distance, the sun crested over the mountaintops to the east of the city, and I wished the Jasmine bloom was in effect. I would have given anything to smell the pungent flowers at that moment. I realized I have always been a man meant to live in the warmer months.

It turned out that I crafted a meaningful Thanksgiving feast. Pink came over, followed by my coworker from The Market and his boyfriend. The Turkey was cooked to perfection, and I was beyond proud of myself. I FaceTimed my mom and showed off the bird, wishing she was there to witness it herself. All in all, it was a good day.

You might have never noticed Gartner was present. He left me alone while I prepared and cooked the bountiful feast, I was a much better cook than him. After the meal was served, I felt myself containing the awkwardness by engaging in conversation with the others present in the room. Gartner remained mostly quiet throughout the remainder of the dinner.

After the holiday we returned to our routine schedule. I worked early mornings before the sun rose at the resort in Anaheim. When I drove home, I would stop at the dispensary or grab something for dinner along the way to break up the long traffic-ridden drive home.

Some nights after I made it back to the apartment on Wilcox, I pulled a double at The Market down the street. When I first moved to Los Angeles, Gartner would drop me off and pick me up after a late shift, but eventually I began to walk alone. Thankfully I grew accustomed to the walk. Before I moved to California, Gartner told me he was worried I would treat living in Los Angeles as a vacation, yet I believed I had proven him wrong. I was a hard worker. I knew that about myself.

I would walk into The Market through the sliding front door from Santa Monica Boulevard. The piercing, dry air swooped in just enough behind me before the door slid shut. The grocery store was compact and built underneath an overpriced apartment complex.

During the summertime huge flies circled overhead near the juice bar, over to the right of the entrance. I spent the start of my shift swatting at the bugs with an electric fly swat.

The store was overpriced, and my coworkers and I were overworked and understaffed. When I first moved to Los Angeles, I had hoped for a healthier job market out west than back east. There were far more job postings available in Los Angeles compared to back in Orlando. Plus, jobs in Orlando had seemed less favorable.

I expected the culture to be different, more welcoming and inviting in Los Angeles. Except I found that was not always the reality. I quickly realized that most of the people I regularly interacted with in the store were transplants. Even though Gartner was a native Californian, he had somehow been duped into moving to the transplant neighborhood of Los Angeles. I wasn't sure if I would have picked this as the neighborhood to live in if it would have been me. Some transplants are drawn into a place for the wrong reasons. I wondered if those around us were less thoughtful of their intentions than Gartner and I. Or maybe it was just me, and Gartner fit in just fine. I was the oddball.

After I punched my employee ID into the timeclock to begin my closing shift, I took my place at the registers. The night was a constant flow of people. Some nights I would operate the counter alone. My manager would step in to assist when the line began to back up into the aisles. I was supposed to call over the P.A. system, but I never called. I figured if people needed their groceries they would wait, and I would rather clock out early anyways.

On my break I would sit outside, facing the cars as they drove past on Santa Monica Boulevard. I'd look west towards the coast. Sometimes I pretended I could see the glint of the ocean off in the distance. If I did not want to sit on my break, I would take a walk around the building until I could find a side street with a view of the Hollywood sign or the Griffith Observatory nestled amongst the mountains. I would never get used to mountains. I still felt robbed of mountains growing up in a flat state like Florida.

During the jasmine bloom and warmer nights, I walked down the street to find the nearest bushel and breathed in their heavenly scent, ingesting the sweet, flowery smell through my nostrils. I thought of it as healing myself.

At the end of my shift in the dark cold night, I started my walk back east to the apartment. Gartner had sworn to always pick me up if it was dark outside when I clocked out of work, but he had stopped doing it for over a month.

"I am tired, I do not feel like driving," he would say, after I had just been up from four in the morning till eleven at night. I would arrive home to apartment three Wilcox Place and find him awake, lounging in bed comfortably and playing video games.

*December 2024*
*(One month prior to January 3rd, 2025)*

My shift at work that night was long, slow, and painfully cold. The coastal desert winters were too brisk for my bones. I was not built for the cold weather; I learned this quickly in the few years I lived in Denver. I carried a hoodie in my car even in the Florida summer because businesses keep their air conditioning exceedingly low, making you think you were in the arctic, despite it being sweltering hot outside. So no, I was not one that enjoyed being cold.

I sat on the edge of the checkout counter, peering out over the store and the décor that jumped out at me. Sharp reds accented with indistinct grays. I was sure there was a psychological science behind the color choice, but I found the pallet horrendously ugly. I waited for the manager to finish their closing duties for the night. Once the tasks were complete, we walked together out of the store with a security guard.

Once outside, the air hit me and sent a small shiver down my body. I rustled up the last of my warmth to savor for my seven-minute walk home. Gartner was not picking me up from work again.

I spun in circles past the Builder's First Source shipping yard while singing Punish by Ethel Cain. The artist's newest single was released the first of November. Since it came out, I kept the song on repeat, unable to stop it from playing in my dreams while I slept at night.

The sky was a milky gray, with the marine layer colliding with the clouds in the sky. It shadowed the skyscrapers, snaking through the valleys to the other side of the Hollywood hills.

Nighttime in LA was beautiful. I took a detour and veered left down a side street so I could loop and listen to Punish once more. I continued spinning and singing in tune with the pitch. I had that overwhelming feeling again, the sense of longing for something I wasn't quite sure I could identify.

The thought of leaving Gartner suddenly occurred to me. Then I thought about when I could, and the answer did not necessarily excite me. I wondered if I moved with him just so I could live in Los Angeles. But of course, that was never true. But maybe if it had been true, it would make it easier to accept a bittersweet end to the love I so badly wanted to work.

I sang the chorus out loud without fear of being heard. Strangers yelled every day in the streets of Los Angeles and typically no one listened. Why should tonight be any different?

I………… am…………..... pun…ished….. by love…………
I………… am…………..... pun…ished….. by love…………

As the song concluded I turned the key to the apartment on Wilcox Place and opened the door. The lights were on and Gartner was awake, waiting for me in bed.
"I could hear you singing," he said to me.
So, someone was listening, I thought.
"And so, what?"
"Nothing, but you know, I saw you detouring around the apartment," he continued.
"I just wanted to walk a little more," I said, trying not to feel or sound guilty just for extending an already short walk.
"You, okay?" he asked me.
And I felt bad for lying when I said that I was okay, but I also feared causing a fight. Throughout the month we argued over whether Gartner would join me for Christmas in Orlando. I was once again reminded of our argument over traveling to Orlando in July, and again to New York in August.

For once Gartner showed no signs of irritation as he agreed to attend the Studios Park Passholder night with me, though he was not particularly enthused. I wondered if he had agreed to soften the blow of his travel rejection.

The cold air and surroundings reminded me of my home, and I took note of everything I saw. It was clear that the theme parks brought me great comfort; I liked the idea that I could almost be in Orlando if I tried hard enough. I liked that there were similarities that made it feel as if I had never left the sunshine state.

The park was decorated for the holidays. In the center promenade sat a large, crooked Christmas tree contorting and stretching towards the sky. The tree was a replica of the beloved Dr. Seuss classic.

In the background, a steep cliff dropped off to reveal a stunning California backdrop. I snapped back to reality that I was not in Orlando, but was still in Studio City, California. I overlooked the San Fernando Valley toward North Hollywood and turned my gaze towards the east as I spotted the Warner Brothers studio and beyond that, the city of Burbank. I turned my head to the West and beyond where Simi Valley and Calabasas sat nestled.

California was gorgeous. Throughout the valley, lights twinkled and glimmered as people shuffled throughout their day in the city. I thought of what it must be like to have grown up here as a child from their perspective, staring up at Studios Park atop the mountain. If you were in a two-story house across interstate 5 you could see directly into the park.

One thing California lacked was adequate privacy. Not because it was Los Angeles and the city was overstuffed and overdeveloped, but because the mountains provided a vantage point I had not experienced in Florida. As much as mountains could conceal, contain, and hide you away, they could also expose you and create a targeted viewing point.

The night felt childlike, I had yet to experience the holidays in the studios park. After many previous years of experiencing the resort in Anaheim's holiday overlay it was a breath of fresh air. I hoped Gartner could understand the underlying value of the night for me; the importance it would fill my heart with. I felt my connection to Gartner over the night deepen, we indulged in fifty milligrams of edibles before we entered the park.

Our eyes were red with fascination. We watched the holiday show in the main plaza, where the large, crooked Christmas Tree ignited before our eyes. I held Gartner's hand during the performance and the warmth from my heart directly warmed my heart.

The remainder of our evening was spent in yule-bliss, again I felt a sense of ease and naive hope. We could make it if we tried. There was a sincerity to who we were together. Two-halves of a coin trying to face each other at the same time.

*** 

My last day of work at the resort approached rapidly. I had decided to leave before the Christmas holiday, they had refused my time off and I knew I valued my family time in Orlando more than I valued the job and rather than be fired for calling out too many times consecutively, I'd leave on my own time respectfully. The company hosted a special employee only shopping event on the promenade that was made to resemble a picturesque American central street. The structures, sidewalks, and lampposts were all stylized off small-town America in the early years of the nation's development.

The buildings resembled 1800 to 1900 architecture. The atmosphere felt authentic and provided a comforting warmth. The simplicity, yet originality of the street design added to its overall effect. There were smells of pastries and decadent goods wafting from the corner street towards the train station that capped off the entrance and exit to the park.

It was difficult not to feel an emotional response to the experience. It stripped away the outside world and cultivated a light-hearted culture that kept the nightmares from outside of the park gates from infiltrating. It was pure bliss wrapped up in its purest form.

Once the parks had closed that night and were clear of guests, Adi and Jai met me inside. It appeared we were one of the few employees who decided to attend the event. We took our time walking through the brick street. It was a cold, winter night in southern California.

The fog cast what looked like a thick, wet blanket over the sky that melted into the earth below it, striking my skin with a piercing cold.

Other than our group, only a handful of people rustled around the cold with us, too foggy to make out who was working and who was shopping. In a way, it felt like we were the only people there.

If we had been in Florida for the event, it would be overcrowded with employees who were lucky enough to be off the clock for the night. The culture difference between the East and West Coast parks was vastly different. The heart was not quite the same.

Somewhere on the East Coast, my home remained quiet and mildly cold. I wondered if my mom could feel me tugging on her heartstrings all the way from LA.

I typically detested the foggy weather in Southern California. However, that night it felt hauntingly beautiful. I took Adi home after we finished shopping with Jai. It was well past midnight, and the highway was covered in a blanket of fog as thick as wool ahead of me. My headlights added little to no guiding light. Lights glinted from homes and skyscrapers that guided me home as I drove the familiar path on the highway. I felt a sense of peace and felt calm. Sadness was present, but it was welcomed like an old friend, comforting me as I accepted that not all bad weather was actual bad weather.

After I dropped Adi off, I took my time cruising back up the 91. The trees in the town of Cerritos were tall and loomed over the roads. I was always fascinated by how different parts of southern California could look compared to each other. If you told me we were in Florida, I would believe you.

The fog cleared up just as I drove through the 5/101 interchange. The city skyline shined brightly against the dark Los Angeles sky, illuminating the way as if a burning eternal flame. The hills rolled into mountains in the background. In the distance the Hollywood sign sat layered against the hills that surround it.

Gartner had decided to remain in Los Angeles for Christmas. Instead of arguing with him before the trip, I agreed to let him stay home if he traveled with me during the season's pre-holiday week so we could celebrate with my family.

During our holiday vacation in Orlando, we attended the resort's version of the Studio Park for an afterhours event with my family. Gartner was quiet and unenthusiastic throughout the night. He kept his hood pulled up over his head, complimented by a pair of sunglasses that covered his eyes. It felt like he was trying to disappear and avoid making any effort, with me or my family. I gritted my teeth and tried to focus on making the most of the time I had with them instead.

He later inferred that he had not felt well for the duration of the trip, blaming it on a cold he claimed he got after being forced to ride the bus to work when I borrowed his car to drive myself to work in Anaheim. I said nothing. The trip was lackluster, and I thought perhaps we should have just stayed in LA. Maybe Gartner deciding to remain at our apartment for the holidays instead of joining me in Orlando was an unforeseen gift from the universe.

The next morning, Gartner remained asleep in bed while I grabbed breakfast with my junior year high school teacher. It had been a few years since I had seen her. She asked me about Gartner, and I found myself confessing to her that things felt tough, but he had been supportive and extremely loving towards me.

"He encourages me to write," I said.

"That's good," she responded.

"Yeah, but I don't feel inspired. We're engaged but I am worried."

"What are you worried about?"

"I am not sure," I said, which was honest. I wasn't sure where the problem lied.

"Just remember, love is not enough," she said. I tried to let her words sit with me and was grateful to still have this person and her wisdom in my life.

On the last day of holiday vacation, my Aunt Isa hosted a family gathering. Aunt Isa asked Gartner what he wanted food-wise as he was the special guest, and he chose bar-b-que. Her island counter was lined with various smoked meats, potato salad, baked beans and cornbread, and decadent southern sweets.

We presented gifts to one another. I gifted my aunts and cousins Christmas bulbs from the resort. I customized one of the bulbs for my Aunt Don to display her last name. She had always been a huge supporter of me. In return she gifted Gartner and me a crystalized brick with an etched picture of us we had taken just a couple weeks prior, placed deep within the crystal frame.

Later, once we had returned home and began packing our suitcases for the flight back to California the next day, Gartner told me his favorite family member of mine was my Aunt Don. Apparently, the gift she gave us had resonated within his heart.

On the flight home I suffered from insane sinus pressure, which worsened as the flight progressed. Luckily the middle seat remained empty. I was hunched over towards Gartner in the window seat, holding onto his leg and shaking vigorously. I tried to calm myself by remembering that the plane should start its descent into LA at any moment, and that my head would soon be able to relax from the atmospheric pressure.

The flight attendants periodically checked on my wellbeing. One of the attendants brought me a can of ginger ale as a comforting gesture. Gartner rubbed my back and the tilt of my neck as he tried to comfort me.

I was thankful to have him. His touch brought me comfort. If I was alone, I would have been petrified. One of the flight attendants stopped by again and complimented Gartner on his attentiveness.

"You are a great boyfriend," the attendant said to him, then turned towards me and said, "You've got yourself a good one." She proceeded on her way then, continuing towards the cockpit up the aisle.

Once the attendant walked away, Gartner said to me: "You see, even they know how lucky you are," he paused before he continued: "I am a good boyfriend, and you are lucky because no other guys would do this for you. No other guy is like me."

He said this so confidently. I felt too nauseous from the headache to tell him he was irritating me.

Gartner stayed at our apartment on Wilcox Place for Christmas. His birthday was two days after New Year's Day: January 3rd. When I first met Gartner, he told me his birthday was January 1st. Later he would reveal to me his real birth date was the 3rd, claiming he often lied because he felt his birthday was overlooked growing up due to the excitement from the back-to-back holidays wearing off. My mom was also born shortly after New Years Day and once told me the same sentiment.

When I landed back in Orlando for Christmas, KT picked me up from the airport. She drove us downtown to meet up with Kash for drinks. We stopped for food along the way and smoked a joint together.

She asked me how California had been. I was honest with her when I told her I was struggling with assimilating into the environment and found the cultural differences on the West Coast challenging compared to the East Coast. I admitted that I believed these differences affected my ability to make friends, and that it had been easier to adjust in Denver than it was in LA. I could feel myself trying to adjust, though. Recently my job at The Market had started to grow on me, and while I was upset to leave the resort, I suspected it would help my mental state and maybe give me the push I needed to find a different job closer to Hollywood that would challenge me creatively.

"What about Gartner?" she asked me.

I sighed and stared out the window at the night sky and oak lined streets that were bare from the winter blues.

"I do not know," I answered quietly. "Part of me feels like I annoy him every day, like there is nothing I can do to satisfy him. Can I be honest?"

I looked in her direction and locked eyes. KT was stunningly beautiful, my most recent queer friend that I had grown close with. Her eyes were a soft green that appeared almost translucent. She's got a slightly crooked smile that adds a unique charm to her elegance, reassuring her eccentric personality.

"Safe with me," she said.

"Our sex had not been good." It felt good to finally admit it out loud.

"Oh, that is not good, that's always a sign," she responded.

"Not that it's not good," I said backtracking, "I do not want to sound mean, I just- you know for me sex can be difficult due to my past. I feel like that has been affecting me deeply with Gartner. The issue is that I feel like he does not care about my level of comfortability. And it has unfortunately turned me off."

"What do you mean?" she asked me.

"That sounds harsher than I meant to... I am trying to say that when I lost my virginity it was not exactly grandeur... it was... well, it does not matter actually," I said, shaking the memories from my head.

"I need a lot of comfort and a lot of lubrication. Most of the time my body is sensitive and reactive. I can't control it. I just tighten up... and he does not like to use lube. It has been... not always the most comfortable...." I continued, trailing off and shifting my gaze from her, slightly embarrassed.

"Relationships are difficult and that's exactly why I am not in one any more... I understand what you are saying, and you have obviously told him what happened to you, so it begs the question of why he acts like he is unaware of the issue, or just ignores your reasonable requests," she said thoughtfully.

The realities continued to grow more complicated to combat, with the riddles of our relationship becoming more difficult to decipher. Each age I turned seemed to present a newfound challenge, a new lesson to learn.

After a few beers downtown, KT dropped me off at my parents' place and I let myself inside. My bedroom is the first door on the right down the hallway. The inside of my childhood bedroom was now lined with a crib and stuffed animals belonging to my nephew. My parents had converted the room for their grandbaby. I thought about him and the warmth I knew I would feel when I saw him the following day.

The thoughts relaxed me as I laid my head to my pillow and fell asleep.

I was tired, so I spent my days and nights lounging around my childhood home. I refused to leave the house except for food and to drive around the neighborhood every so often. I felt out of place, the same sinking feeling I felt at Rissa's wedding. It felt icky and uncomfortable to be back in my home. I thought being home for the holidays would curb my depression. I thought I simply needed to be in the comfort of my hometown, but as time ticked by, I had the notion that the Time Bandit had stolen all the time allotted to make Orlando my home. My home was in Los Angeles now, amongst Gartner, my friends, Palisades beach, and De Longpre Avenue. If you can identify specifics and favorites over generalities, it must mean you've established a home.

When I lived in Denver, I never felt as if it was my home. A manager for a restaurant who frequented my job in the city asked me one day: "Do you feel like you are on vacation?"

"In a way, yes," I said to her.

"Then this isn't your home yet," she said, shrugging her shoulders as if it was that simple. In a way, I understood her point.

Every few hours while I was home, I would receive a text message from Gartner that gave me the impression that he was also in a depressive slump, starting the moment, he dropped me off at LAX. I woke up from a nap to vibrations from my phone as Gartner rang me. I answered. When he spoke, his voice was monotone.

"Man, I am so bored..." he sighed and I remained silent, hoping he would continue speaking before I had to break the silence.

"I have felt really lonely from the moment I dropped you off at the airport," he continued, that sad edge to his voice again. "I wanted to say that you were right, and I should have flown to Florida with you for the holidays."

I was shocked that he admitted to me what I knew all along, but I was more annoyed that he decided to admit it entirely too late.

I liked being home. However just like in California, clouds had rolled in through the state of Florida and a dreary winter persisted. Luckily, no rain fell from them. It was a dry winter - perhaps I brought the arid climate from California with me. The weather cast a dull ambiance over the holidays. Gray clouds hovered and shaded the hibernating trees, and sharp grass waited for spring rains so they could blossom and thrive again. The grass would eventually grow at a rapid rate and take over the landscape that likely wasn't for another few months, though.

The Christmas holiday passed lazily and unenthused, just as the past year had been. I found myself wishing then that I could stay in Florida. I was too comforted by my home state, despite looking forward to my return to Los Angeles. I had felt myself adjusting and atoning to life in the city of angels. I hoped I could adapt more and reconcile for the past few months and really begin to establish myself. I was determined.

While I was away, I had time to reflect on the last few months of living in the city. I thought perhaps I had to endure a harsh fall and cold winter to blossom in the spring and summer. Maybe the new year would turn around, and before I knew it, I would be thriving in LA. Maybe I would no longer have this longing sense of wanting to retreat home.

I thought of the routines that Gartner and I developed, and my growing familiarity with the life we created together. It had worked its way into my comfort zone, and I started to develop favorite eateries and customary traditions that made sense for a Los Angeles lifestyle. I was ready to return to what I started to build with him.

I flew back to California the day before New Year's Eve. Gartner picked me up from the airport when I landed that night. It was a bone chilling evening in Los Angeles. When we arrived home, I asked Garner with glee if we should open our Christmas presents. I put forth a lot of heart into the presents I had bought him. I excitedly told my coworker Jai one day about all the presents I planned to buy him, and she confirmed that my intentions were romantic and pure. I loved gift giving, and I could no longer wait to present them to him. I couldn't wait to see his reaction, and of course a part of me was excited to see what he had gotten me in return.

Instead of agreeing to open the presents the night I returned home, he insisted we sleep and open them the next morning after we awoke. I didn't want to argue, but it seemed ill-spirited. It had already been some time since Christmas day. I would have thought he would be excited to have our own mini-Christmas celebration together; however, he told me once that before because his family was Jewish, they did not partake in an abundance of gift giving. He said he would need to adjust to these differences but still seemed overwhelmingly unamused to me. I chose to ignore the ill feeling in my gut and go to bed like he suggested. I was too tired to play a guessing game with him.

The next morning, I poured myself a steaming cup of coffee, excited and ready to open presents. In the few months that led up to Christmas, I had contemplated what to give Gartner. He had sent me a list of items he wanted, with most of them being out of my budget. The grandest of the gifts I bought him was a PlayStation 5. It was also expensive, but I was able to purchase it on payment plan. I had given it to him before I had left for Orlando, so he had something to do while I was away. I expressed my excitement and sought second opinions from my friends and family regarding the other gift options, like a Botanical Lego set and a few heartfelt surprises.

The first gift he opened, albeit not his forte, was a box of mystery pins from the time we had spent feverishly running around different stores in the resort to hunt for a specific pin in a set. He turned the box over in his hand as he unwrapped it, his facial expression unyielding. He frowned and set the box down.

"Looks like you bought that as a present for yourself," he said finally, without much emotion.

I feel the chords connected to my heart snap. It felt like such a harsh thing to say, especially as soon as he opened it. As if he couldn't connect the dots of why this was meaningful, and what it could and should have meant for the both of us. My enthusiasm was slipping and it had hardly been five minutes. I was now worried about the rest of the gifts I got him. I found myself dreading seeing his reaction over anything.

I felt my mind dull as it glazed over. I left the physical realm of my consciousness as Gartner unwrapped the Lego box and raised his eyebrow at me:

"Why did you buy me this?" he asked in an almost condescending tone, tossing it over to the side.

My stomach rolled over itself, nausea building in what should have been such a memorable morning. I didn't have it in me to tell him that I bought the Lego set because he loved plants, and because I thought he liked spending quality time with me. I figured we could have spent a day building the Lego plants as decoration for the apartment, and that it would be a heartfelt memory together.

"You really hyped up your gifts," he started, with ice in his voice. "And so far, I am unimpressed. Your most impressive gift is the PlayStation."

I felt a deep remorse building inside me. I realized I would never be able to do enough for him. I've always expressed a significant portion of my love through gift giving, so much so that sometimes I refused to give an unthoughtful gift if I was not satisfied with what I found.

I had loved gifting presents since I was in grade school. My mother had taught me how to appropriately wrap Christmas presents when I was in the fifth grade. It was a skill I was proud of, and something that filled me with joy anytime I had the responsibility of finding the right gift for a friend or family member, whether it was for Christmas or a birthday.

Deep within me, I felt the start of a cry creeping up to the surface. I suppressed it back down into the pit of my stomach. I felt stupid as I opened Gartner's gifts for me, saying thank you after each one because I refused to be so rude towards another person, especially when they spent their time and money picking out something just for me. It seemed like Gartner did not understand that himself. Truthfully, I found some of his presents unimpressive, but I would never tell him that. Because I loved him, and it felt extremely cruel to do such a thing to a person you loved on Christmas.

## Little Tampico

The night of New Years was tiresome and aggravating. With each boom from the fireworks outside, Ghost shook uncontrollably. Gartner and I argued over closing the windows to help muffle the loud noises from outside to soothe the anxiousness of my dog. I hardly slept that night as Ghost continued to shake the bed. It overwhelmed me and I worried for his sense of comfort. Gartner didn't seem as bothered.

The morning after, we remained in bed as Gartner and I played video games on the PlayStation 5, passing a joint back and forth to one another. I couldn't deny that I felt myself fading when I was back in Florida over the holidays, and Gartner was irritable from constantly seeking validation while I was away. I thought it showed clearly from his reactions to my presents. I unfortunately felt disconnected from him, at the time of year when you were meant to feel closest to loved ones. I wondered if he recognized how he had hurt me. I had begun to accept that I had held on to parts of Gartner that had been an illusion of merriment.

He developed personality traits that were fueled by the excitement of when we first met. He was motivated by lustful energy, powered by its intoxicating fumes from the moment we met. He loved the idea of me, but I was not quite sure he understood how to unconditionally love me, or anyone he had ever loved before.

My mother once told me she would never be able to abandon my sister or me. She had carried us within her womb for nine months. We were a part of her, and she would never be without us. I understood that kind of devotion can only be forged through the intimate bond of motherhood. I wondered if Gartner's mother had felt the same about him. If she still loved him enough to continue emailing him, while occasionally sending him money. I believed she must feel the same. Did Gartner not inherit that trait from his mother? I wished he could see past my tendencies that so often seemed to annoy him. I wish he showed more signs of being capable of loving unconditionally. Because lately, everything felt conditional with him.

Later, New Year's Day, Gartner and I drove to Laundry Pop on Sunset across the 101, not far from our apartment. I still liked that about him, how he included me in his weekly routines, bringing me into his little world. We always took up multiple units. He insisted on his routine, despite the cost of each cycle at the laundromat being expensive.

I had once asked Gartner if there was a laundry room at Wilcox Place, and he swore that it was too old and shoddy. Then one day as I came home from work, I witnessed someone hauling their laundry from around the corner in the courtyard. I looked around and spotted a fully capable machine and laundromat set up. I confronted him about it, but he shrugged it off instead. I had no desire to argue back or try to change his mind. I thought I could help and offered to wash our delicates and bedsheets in the complex's unit but again, he told me it was a bust and convinced me not to.

While we waited for our laundry to finish, we talked about his birthday. It was coming up in a few days, and we previously discussed driving north to Santa Cruz, but he was indecisive.

"I think we should go to your hometown for your birthday," I suggested again. "You've talked about it a lot lately, and I think it would be good for you. Maybe even healing." I wanted to be the encouraging partner for him.

"Yeah, you might be right," he responded, slightly surprising me. "I would love to show you where I grew up, it's so beautiful - I think you would love it. Plus, we can visit Rissa while we are up there."

He told me his original plan had been to propose to me in Santa Cruz. I knew he wanted to show me around his hometown like I had shown him around Orlando when he visited me.

Showing your partner where you're from was intimate and revealing. You learned more about them, the environment they were raised in, and it allowed you to place yourself into their own perspective. I knew he wanted to show me the part of him that Santa Cruz had created.

I believed we were both true lovers. That our hearts beat at the same rhythm. We had devotion deep within us, the type that filled us to the brim with self-fulfillment to show those we loved most our foundations we had built.

Yet Gartner was still indecisive. As we continued to talk about his birthday trip, he switched destinations from camping in the Sequoia National Forest to driving down to San Diego and using our 3-in-1 city ticket my mom had given to us as a Christmas gift. The Gartner switched up completely, settling on remaining in Los Angeles and enjoying a staycation instead.

Once Gartner decided we would just stay in Los Angeles I went to bed, exhausted and ready for a full night of sleep. Ghost would finally be able to sleep peacefully after the firework debacle from the night before.

The following day was January 2nd. I was shaken awake by Gartner. Dim gray light peeked through the windows and pierced my sleep-filled eyes. I deduced that it was early morning. I had only slept for five or six hours. Gartner was beaming at me; I had not seen him this happy in weeks. I couldn't deny that I was shocked to see him in such a good mood.

"I booked a hotel in Santa Cruz after you fell asleep last night," he said excitedly, rushing to get the words out. "I want to leave in an hour because we have to drive the Pacific Coast Highway up north." His energy was palpable, bouncing all over the place. Again, I was just shocked to not see him glum and moping.

"Okay..." I said groggily, rubbing my eyes awake. "Can you make me some coffee please?"

"It is my birthday month, and you want me to make coffee?" he asked in a shocked voice.

"I thought you don't allow birthday months," I snapped back, more snidely than I had intended it to sound. I hoped he wouldn't notice. I couldn't help but be annoyed, though, after all the crap he gave me during August.

"Try not to take too long to get ready," he said instead, walking away.

I sighed and rolled myself out of bed. My feet were shocked as they landed on the cold, wooden floor of the apartment. The winter continued to be brisk, with the cold air trapped by the clouds as they hovered over the city in the early morning, weather reports suggested a warming front would push the cold out of the city and bring forth the warmer SoCal weather. I wished Gartner had woken me up in the middle of the night to tell me news, instead. I felt blindsided and rushed, along with being overly tired from the lack of adequate sleep. I obviously neglected to pack the day before due to his indecisiveness, but wishing I had done the opposite. Now I feel short on time.

My brain was hardly proactive as I shoved random pieces of clothing and shoes into a bag. I asked him what our itinerary in Santa Cruz would be, with him only revealing minor details. I wasn't sure if it was because he wanted it to be a surprise or if it was a lack of planning on his part. He mentioned visiting the famous boardwalk and Wharf. He said he also wanted to drive through the various small towns he had grown up and around before his parents had inherited their house in Capitola.

I hoped I packed all the necessary clothes. I felt nauseous as always, and the caffeine from the coffee was not helping. It took me a little over an hour to finish packing, gather Ghost, and slide into the passenger seat of Gartner's silver Camry to begin the drive north to Santa Cruz.

We stopped for food at In-n-Out in Ventura after an hour of driving along the Pacific Coast Highway. I asked him to stop earlier so I could grab some snacks, but he refused. He claimed he didn't want to spend excessive money that he assumed he would be required to pay for my snacks. This irritated me, because I had my own money to pay for myself. I simply wanted food to help ease my nauseous stomach, which he was aware of.

I decided to not argue with him, because somehow, I felt as though he would turn it into something bigger than it should be. After he criticized my Christmas gifts, I started to wonder if I had ever actually caused any of our previous arguments. I started to recognize that he often saw himself in the right, and me in the wrong. No matter what the truth really was. Being the one to avoid conflict, I often allowed myself to take the brunt of fault to avoid things escalating. Now I grew tired of it.

The drive curved along the rocky shoreline of California that bridged the coastal gap between the southern and northern parts of the state. My nausea worsened as we continued to swerve along the cliff side, continuously curving to the left and right. I tried to focus on my breathing. I tried to focus on the idea that this would be a good trip for us. I tried to remind myself that I loved this man, that I wanted to be here with him. Still, the nausea continued.

We arrived in Santa Cruz after the sun had set. We unloaded our belongings into the hotel room and then took Ghost on a lengthy walk around the grounds. After feeling settled, Gartner led me on a guided tour in the direction of the boardwalk. He took me down different alleyways and walking paths throughout the small beach town. I was amazed by the walkability of the otherwise small town. In Florida, the local beach towns I was accustomed to were not easily walkable or accessible. This was a nice change. We were able to walk from our hotel to the beach in fifteen minutes.

He guided me to train tracks that crossed over the water, long forgotten and unused. The tracks acted as the local shortcut and teen hang out spot. I found myself wondering what it must have been like to grow up here. I pictured a younger Gartner, sitting on the tracks and dangling his feet over the ledge where the San Lorenzo River met the mighty Pacific Ocean. In the distance, Sea lions were clustered together on rocks that pierced out of the foamy sea, sleeping lazily.

In the dark of night, the foam was easy to make out as it splashed and frizzled against the rocks. We watched in a peaceful silence as the waves crashed onto them. The stars reflected against the glassy surface of the ocean and if you were to look far enough west, it almost appeared as if the sky and sea were one.

We stood on the abandoned train track overlooking his hometown. The wooden support beams beneath our feet, keeping the tracks suspended in mid-air, were still in decent condition. There were some gaps that had appeared over time, where chunks of the supports had fallen to a watery grave.

Gartner hopped over one of the gaps in the tracks and extended his hand out to me. He knew I had a fear of heights, and I had already made a comment about how high up we were when we had started to cross. I trusted him and took his hand. I hopped and landed in his arms with a thud. Safe and protected.

We sparked a joint, with the wind blowing faintly across the sky and through my hair. The moisture in the air penetrated deep into my bones. I shivered. The sky was a dark black that could only be observed in winter. He pulled me into an embrace and kissed my forehead.

"Deeper than the ocean," he started.

"Higher than the sky," I voiced back.

"Bigger than the universe," Gartner repeated my favorite lines.

"And so much more" he finished with a whisper in my ear.

I kissed him hard in return.

We stayed up late into the night, with it almost being three in the morning when we made it back to the hotel room. Gartner set an alarm for 7 am. I groaned and asked if we could sleep in, but it was no use, it was his birthday tomorrow, so his 7 am command would be followed.

The exhaustion pulled at my mind, tempting my consciousness into sleep. Just as I was about to fall asleep, Gartner was on top of me. He kissed me and pulled me into him. I wanted to love him passionately, but my brain lacked the capacity to physically engage with him at the time.

I asked Gartner if we could hold off from sex for the night, truly just wanting to fall asleep in each other's arms. He responded to my question with a quizzical expression on his face. It made me feel guilty. I knew it was his birthday, and I knew I should try to do what would make him happy. But it also didn't feel right to agree to intimacy when I wasn't mentally or physically prepared for it. I obliged anyway, trying to keep myself awake for him. Instead, I found myself escaping from my own mind, ascending to the ceiling. I felt myself chained there, abstract in a way that was neither here nor there.

My mind went fuzzy, and I felt nothing. I was face down in the bed and my neck was crammed to the side. I stared at the clock on the nightstand, just wishing for it to be over. It felt awful that I could feel this way while Gartner was pleased. It wasn't Gartner's fault that I felt this way. I thought I was unable to express my fear to him, because I was worried he would take it personally. I also felt terrible for myself and the inability to feel an intense connection with Gartner at the moment. I wondered if he could sense I was elsewhere, metaphysically. I don't think he could, but if he had then maybe things would have turned out differently.

I sighed and gripped the bedsheets in my hands, twisting them in my fist as he finished. I laid there naked and exposed, feeling discombobulated. I closed my eyes and cursed the man who caused me to feel this way about intimacy before I fell asleep. I wondered if there would ever be a time that I was up for intimacy in the way I'd heard it was meant to be experienced. Of course I wanted pleasure and closeness. But at that moment all I wanted was sleep, and to push the uncomfortable moment and thoughts as far out of my head as possible.

The next morning, I wore the shame on myself. It resembled bruises on my body, only visible to myself. I feared my scars would tear open and bleed on Gartner. I worried this could be the end. He was blissfully unaware that I blacked out during intimacy with him the previous night. The logistics changed, the answers intensified, and the resolve became increasingly complicated.

"Happy birthday my love," I said to him after I conditioned myself. There was a part of me unraveling underneath my skin. I wanted Gartner to have an amazing birthday, and I didn't have the time to fight the war in my mind.

"Thank you handsome, I have a lot I want to do today so let's get moving and get breakfast!" he said excitedly. He truly had no idea.

We ate buffet food from the hotel breakfast. I felt more nauseous than I had in the past few days and tried to focus on getting down some of my breakfast. I took a few bites of oatmeal and realized it was one of the times where my stomach did nothing to help me further. No matter the easy-to-digest foods I consumed, I felt ill and uneasy.

I hoped I could get a nap during the day. Gartner asked me to take a shower with him after breakfast and I reluctantly joined him, wishing desperately that I could have a moment to myself. I felt raw and exposed from the night before. I needed a second alone, so I could ease my mind and focus on Gartner. Flashbacks from my past had infiltrated my mind, replaying my darkest memories on a vicious loop. Yet with it being Gartner's birthday, it felt like that wasn't going to happen.

It was another cold and wet day. Rain moved through the bay in misty bands that seeped through the town and across the coast. I suggested we take our time with sightseeing because of the rainy weather. The reports said the chances of rain would lessen in the afternoon.

Gartner insisted on starting the tour of his hometown in the morning, though. He wanted to begin with showcasing the house he grew up in, on the foothill of a mountain in Corralitos. Again, I felt like I had to agree with him and just go with it. I tried to stuff down my overwhelming emotions and put on a brave face. The day was meant to be fun, after all.

From the moment we arrived in Santa Cruz I found his behavior odd. I wondered if he was experiencing some sort of manic episode caused by the anxiety he felt returning to his original home for the first time in years. I wondered if my sixth sense could pick up his emotional frequency.

Gartner parked his car in the front driveway of his childhood home. I could not fathom the idea of pulling up to a house you no longer lived at and sitting directly outside of it. In Florida that could result in you getting screamed at by its occupants, if not pointed a gun at. Then I realized we were in California, and not everything is the same. I still found the practice strange, nonetheless.

The house wasn't what I had imagined. It was at the end of a dirt road, with four other houses scattered around in a square. Around them was cement gravel that completed the unmaintained road. I could almost imagine Gartner making his way through the meadows to the east from the bus stop in town late at night. To feel lonely in the shadows of the mountains, feeling pale in the moonlight. I felt a tug at my heartstrings and wondered if I was picking up on Gartner's emotional depths.

We briefly stopped at a nearby community park afterwards, letting Ghost run around freely. It had been a few weeks since we let him run around off leash in a lush, open field. I felt better out in the fresh air. It helped to not be confined in a vehicle while shifting through winding roads. Suddenly I was thankful to have grown up in flat Florida, but maybe growing up in California would have conditioned my body to motion sickness. I still felt nauseous from my spherocytosis, and the motion sickness only made it worse.

After the park we stopped by a stand-alone, locally run marketplace in town. We roamed the aisles of the small market. In the back of the store, I found homemade beef jerky displayed at the deli counter. I summoned Gartner over and we picked out a peppery blend to take with us for a snack. The clerk behind the counter took a few minutes to study Gartner. "Do you remember me, Gartner?" he asked.

At first, Gartner just stared blankly back, unsure of who stood before him.

"It's me, man, Ryder," the man at the deli said. I recalled hearing the name from one of the stories Gartner told me from his childhood. They had grown up together.

Ryder continued to glance in my direction. I was about to introduce myself when Gartner spoke up and said: "This is Robert, my husband."

I was taken back but tried to conceal it from my face.

"Nice to meet you," the words came out of my mouth mechanically, but my mind asked itself why Gartner would say we were married.

In the few times I tried to plan the wedding with him, I felt defeated by the end of the conversation. The cost was pricey and every idea I had was over Gartner's budget. I would have rather spent money on the wedding versus a three-thousand-dollar ring, but that was not up to me. He expected me to return to him what he had done for me on principle. I never cared about the monetary value though; I just wanted his love.

I then reverted to feeling guilty about the fact that I would have never spent that much money on a ring if it were my choice. Sometimes I felt Gartner wanted to flaunt his wealth. That did not appeal to me. I felt like I had just been flaunted to Ryder at the convenience store in a similar way.

I tried to brush it off. I had no time to react as Gartner and Ryder conversed with one another. My mind wandered during their brief catch up. I found it hard to excuse myself and stood awkwardly by. At the mention of a husband, Ryder's face showed a small lapse in expression as he attempted to hide the initial shock from his face.

Outside of the store, I was still in disbelief.

"I can't believe you told him I was your husband," I said as we walked across the dirt road to where the car was parked.

"Yeah!" Gartner exclaimed excitedly, with his face beaming. His eyes had a unique shine to them I had never seen before. His smile took up half of his face: "Did you see his face? He was so shocked!" He laughed then in a manic way, and I realized we were on opposite ends of the reaction spectrum.

"It threw me off. I did not expect you to say that" I continued, wanting to understand his reasoning behind the odd behavior. "But he seemed nice. I know you mentioned him to

me before." Despite my confusion, I wanted to steer clear of aggravating him. He shocked me and he had no idea.
"We will never see him again anyway," Gartner said then, shrugging his shoulders.

"But you know that will probably get back to your parents though, right? Do you care?" I wondered if he had considered this.
"No," he said simply.
"I need another coffee," I said instead, changing the subject.

After the market we drove by his elementary school at the top of a large hill. From there we stopped at a coffee shop nestled into the side of Soquel Drive. The shop felt homey. There were trees surrounding the collection of businesses, with a creek running through the area bordering the small plaza.

I was surprised by the amount of gravel roads that existed within such short proximity to the highways around the area. The difference between California's urban to rural gradient jarred me at times, always giving me an entirely different impression of the state.

Gartner led us to The Forest of Nisene Marks State Park next. The rain moved through the area and muddied up the grounds. I realized in my rush to pack that I forgot my hiking boots. I grumbled about it, which irritated Gartner.

I tried to make up for it in the shoes I had, but the grounds were ridiculously muddy, and it was difficult to keep up. A steady rain cloud paraded over the state park, dousing the area in a constant rain. We trudged through the rain for fifteen minutes before I couldn't enjoy myself anymore. I wished I had brought my boots. I asked if we could come back later when it was no longer raining but instead of responding, Gartner stormed off back to his car. The whole way he was cursing me under his breath.

I knew he was frustrated with me. He wished I had the ability to wing it and not worry so much. I considered his opinion for a moment and accepted that I had been bratty over it. I insisted we come back the next day on our way home. The park was beautiful even in the rain, and I was sure it would be better in the sun when we could fully explore it.

After the short-lived soggy hike, Gartner caravaned us in the direction of his parents' current home. The town we drove through to get there was small and snaked through winding streets. I still felt nauseous from all the motion. It also probably had something to do with how odd this whole scenario was, given his lack of contact with his parents.

Gartner turned into the driveway of his parents' home in Capitola. My anxiety spiked for him. I wondered where his parents were? At any moment they could have easily approached the car, and then what? I almost wondered if Gartner wished his parents would walk out of their house and find us parked in their driveway. Part of me understood why he was too stubborn to make the first move to rekindle their relationships. I knew he thought about it every day.

"What happens if your parents come out and walk up to us?" I couldn't help myself from asking. If anything, I assumed we needed a game plan.

"They won't come out here," he said. I wondered how he could be so confident.

"Would you talk to them if they did?" I asked.

"I dunno," he responded quietly.

The tension felt tight and constricting within the car. The air inside the vehicle was sharp and stale. My head ached. I wondered if Gartner felt the same. I had enough anxiety for the both of us, and I wondered if he too was operating on fumes. Neither of us slept well.

I tried to imagine how he felt at that moment. I studied his breathing, his chest rising and setting rapidly. He had to be nervous. Or was this all for show? A mere spectacle? What would happen if his parents walked out here? Would he introduce me as his husband to them? I had the ring on my finger, so it would be believable. I considered removing the band for a moment but shook the thought from my head.

He pointed to the Star of David flag hanging from their porch.

"Told you I was Jewish," he said in a half-joking way.

As if I had never believed him when he told me before. I never thought it was important information, as I was Catholic by baptism but never practiced the ideology. I found it never set right with me. I had assumed the same for Gartner, but maybe it had meant something to him. I probed him about the subject.

"I never doubted you, but is it important to you? Being Jewish?" I was trying to seize the moment of vulnerability we found ourselves in to learn more about who he was. If it were to happen anywhere, the front of his parent's home seemed like a good enough placement.

"No, I just don't think you believe me sometimes," he said, indifferent.

The ignorance was harboring too boldly. And just like that, the moment had passed. His parents weren't coming out to make amends, nor was he making any effort to go up to their door. Most of all, he continued to avoid giving me any real sense of who he was. I feared I would never be able to penetrate the guarded wall built around his heart.

He turned the engine over and pulled out of the driveway.

\*\*\*

Gartner steered us west towards the coast and parked his car in a public lot. We walked to the edge of the seashore. I chose to not bring up the awkward moment in his parents' driveway. If his parents were terrible people, why on earth would he park his car idly outside of their house, unannounced?

I tried to shake the thoughts circling my mind and focus on the otters splashing around in the stormy ocean just fifty yards out. I loved that in both Florida and California; you could always spot playful wildlife around you. It gave a lively feeling to both states, constantly surrounded by life.

We returned to the hotel in the late afternoon. We showered and changed into warm clothes for dinner. Gartner planned to take me to visit the wharf and eat at a restaurant he frequented when he was younger. We started our walk in the direction of the pier.

I was starved, considering I hardly ate breakfast that morning and had kept myself nourished off a single piece of jerky from the market.

It turned out that the restaurant Gartner wanted to take me to had been forced to close a week prior, after a massive swell moved through the coast and overtook the pier. The water caused the pier to collapse, making the restaurant inaccessible. It was an instant downer to the evening.

Gartner cried for several minutes due to the unforeseen change of plans. He stated he was out of a backup plan, with his head down and upbeat energy clearly gone.
"I am sorry..." he said sullenly, and somehow, I felt guilty.

"It's okay... I am sorry the restaurant is closed, but I am hungry," I tried to get him to focus on our next move. "Is there anywhere else to eat around here?"

"I don't know, I haven't been here in a long time so I don't know what is around... but I can wait to eat till later when we go to Little Tampico," he replied, refusing to make eye contact with me.

I was hangry and overly exasperated with myself and the entire day. I grouchily complained to Gartner. I wished he would have planned better. He reminded me that he had checked to make sure the restaurant was open, and according to Apple Maps it had been. Clearly the internet had not updated the closure yet. We bickered with each other. I accepted my fate and recognized that my hunger would fully take over my expressions and mood.

Gartner suggested chicken fingers and fries from one of the vendors at the boardwalk and I continued to grow irrationally irritated. My hanger overtook all rational thinking, and I huffed out a complaint which irritated Gartner further. I apologized then, with Gartner leaving me frustrated on a bench as he purchased the food from the boardwalk vendor.

We ate them together on the bench facing the indigo sea, a silent forgiveness mutually agreed upon over the meal as we watched sea lions swim beyond the break of the ocean.

After my hanger was subdued, we purchased ride tickets for the boardwalk and walked towards the Giant Dipper, a historic wooden rollercoaster boasted in the early years of American beach culture of the 1920s.

The coaster was surprisingly powerful. The mechanisms of the model tickled my inner coaster-nerd, and my inner child was restored for a moment. The on-ride photo displayed Gartner with his hand up, almost as if he was on the back of a bull wrangling it for fun. On the other side of Gartner was myself, gripping his free arm with my own. My mouth was wide open as the image captured me mid-scream. Despite the previous arguing, I enjoyed seeing the picture of us - like it captured us as the happy couple I imagined us to be. In a way the boardwalk seemed lacking, and I wondered what it was like during the peak of summer.

We scooped the car up from the hotel after getting back from the boardwalk and headed to the Mexican spot Gartner frequented with his family. My stomach was on the fritz after feeling nauseous for so long. Plus the intensity of the Giant Dipper only cursed the icky feeling further. I attempted to order grilled chicken from the kids' menu but was rejected due to the age restriction policy. Instead, I settled on a shredded chicken burrito.

The table across from us began to sing happy birthday to someone at their table. Gartner beamed at me from the other side of the table and asked me to sing him Happy Birthday.

Instead of singing him the damn song right then and there, I told him I would sing to him later in the evening. At the moment I hadn't considered what Gartner must have felt at the time. I should have just sung him happy birthday. Gartner deserved so much more from me that day. I fucked up. Just because I was nauseous and hangry, I couldn't sing him happy birthday. Sometimes we sabotage our own lives.

An unseeable force set forth the beginning of our end. An inconceivable set of circumstances that led us to that moment in time. I was blind to how combustible we both were in the moment and ignited the spark that would soon lead to destruction.

I wanted to get Gartner a birthday cake, but after spending the entirety of the past week together, I had not aligned my time to sneak off from him and purchase him a cake and candles. I silently acknowledged the comparisons between both of our birthdays. How the expectations of our plans spoiled quickly.

I believed in fixed points in our timeline. Moments in our life we are unable to stop, unable to control. A fixed reality point. A lesson to learn. Maybe I was actively living through a fixed point in time controlled by the Time Bandit. I could see the end; but I clung to the last sign of life that remained. I did not want the end to come. I rode the high from Gartner for months. Yet the crash was imminent.

The rest of dinner went by in an uneventful daze. Back at the hotel, Gartner took a light nap and although I was dead tired, I was kept awake by my anxiety over the day. The hike, the nausea, the weather, the closed pier, the unhappy birthday song… it was a disaster that I hoped I could make up for. I bought us tickets for a late night showing of Nosferatu at the movie theater downtown earlier in the day, so I figured maybe we could recover there. I hoped we could rekindle more of the day.

When Gartner woke up, I reminded him we were meant to meet up with Rissa for brunch the next day. He threw his hands up, exasperated as he said: "Why did you tell her we were coming up here?"
I blinked at the question, not sure why he was asking.

"You told me to tell her we were coming up, that had always been the plan?" I said, confused with his frustration.
"No, that was you," he said, clearly forgetting his own words from before.

"No Gartner, you had suggested it.," I reminded him, annoyed at his sudden forgetfulness. "You came up with everything for this trip from the beginning, and I remember being shocked at you mentioning we should see Rissa anyway."

"You always tell everyone where we are going and invite too many people," he responded instead, shaking his head at me. "What if I just want it to be me and you?"

"Then it can be just me and you!" I said back, my voice rising with disbelief in his sudden change of mindset. I had already messaged Rissa about meeting up, so I was internally thinking of how I could come up with some excuse, just because my fiancé never wanted to be around my friends. "Also, I am unsure who 'everyone' is? Rissa is one person. I know for a fact that you like her, so I don't understand why you are acting this way about eating breakfast with her? We just spent the entirety of the last week together, just the two of us. So, it is clearly not about the alone time. Can you please tell me what your problem is?"

"It is always about what you want," he snarled back. "We can eat with her, it'll be fine."

I sighed, wondering how we got into another argument over visiting a friend. I wondered when Gartner decided he no longer liked Rissa. Again, I was ashamed for immediately thinking of ways to get out of the brunch with her so I could keep my own sanity.

Gartner and I distracted ourselves from arguing as we watched the new episode of RuPaul's Drag Race. After the show ended, we walked ten minutes downtown for the movie in an uncomfortable silence.

The movie dragged on, and while I found the composition and editing intriguing, the plot and story was not as appealing to me as I hoped it would be. I knew Gartner would find plot holes to complain about afterwards. Gartner disliked every movie I had ever picked for us to watch.

After the movie, Gartner led me to his past hideout spot as a teenager, where he would conceal himself for hours with his ex-boyfriend. He plopped himself down in the corner of a small courtyard with a cluster of trees and fountain in the middle. He pulled me closer to him and kissed me. His mouth warmed my own in the cold winter air.

I had taken Gartner to a place I frequented with an ex once. He made a comment after, expressing his discontent as if it were an insult for me to take him there. The irony was not lost on me that he was doing the exact same thing to me that he himself had once complained about. I briefly wondered if it was intentional.

We walked back to the hotel after sharing a few bittersweet moments in the courtyard. My hands had started to go numb from the cold. I could tell Gartner longed for bits of his past that he no longer had traces to. I wondered if he thought about his exes and where they would be in real time.

We spent most of the walk in silence. We were exhausted, both physically and emotionally, even if Gartner did not want to admit it. I fell asleep quickly, forgetting to sing happy birthday to him. Another fuck up of mine. The next morning, I woke with the shame of forgetfulness. I felt like Gartner and I had unwillingly entered a competition to see who could fuck up whose birthday worse.

I hoped I could make up for the previous day. The sun peaked through the curtains and the weather appeared to be more comfortable. Gartner pushed himself out of bed and started to pack our suitcase. He listed off the locations he intended to show me before we drove home to Los Angeles. I reminded him that Rissa had planned to drive down so we could eat together.

"I do not understand why you have to tell everyone when we go somewhere," he started the same argument over once more.

The morning fog holding my brain captive was slowly wearing off, and this time I had no intention of arguing with him. I considered my options.

"Do you want me to tell her never mind?" I offered, trying to appease him. "I am confused why you are upset about seeing her."
I could tell he was irritated by his demeanor.

"Because I want it to be just us, yet all you do is invite people," he snapped back.

"You never said that before yesterday, and you had originally suggested we visit her when we came up here anyway when we started to plan your birthday trip a month ago," I reminded him.

"That was then though," Gartner responded defiantly.

"You did not ask again, you just assumed it was okay still." I couldn't wrap my head around his reasoning.

"I had told you before we began driving up here, and we talked about it just yesterday?" Was he having memory issues? Or just being difficult after deciding to change his mind? "I do not understand the big deal; it's not like you do not like her?"

"I wish you had not told everyone what we are doing," he repeated.

"I told one person, but you know what - it's fine. I will tell her not to come down," I said exasperated. I messaged Rissa that Gartner was not feeling well and to not drive down.

"Great, now she is going to hate me," he said as if it was my fault. "You should have let her come still."

"You are the one who said you wanted to be alone, and I am trying not to upset you, Gartner, so what is the problem?" I felt like screaming.

"She probably thinks I am an asshole now," he said under his breath, pacing around the hotel room.
In my head I acknowledged that she probably did but decided to keep it to myself.

"You have no idea what I said to her! I told her you weren't feeling well, so it is not that big of a deal, Gartner." I felt like we were going around in such a pointless circle. It was getting us nowhere. I couldn't believe the day had just started.

"I wish you never did," he snarled.

"What is up with you, Gartner? You are being annoyingly difficult this morning, and I am over it," I huffed.

"Me?" he questioned wildly. "YOU are the one who has been a big baby this entire trip. You have complained about everything."

"I am sorry for doing anything that upset you yesterday, that truly wasn't my intention," I tried to reason with him, once again feeling guilt from the previous day's events. "I have not been feeling well but I've been trying my best. I am sorry, I do acknowledge I was hangry and grumpy yesterday. That was not your fault, so I am sorry."

"It wasn't just yesterday or the past few days," Gartner said back. "For months now you have been miserable, and I have not enjoyed it. Everything has set you off."

I could feel my temper boiling and I tried to subdue it the best I could. "I am not miserable, Gartner," I said sternly. I began to feel crazy, as if Gartner had forced his way into my mind.

It was true that in the past few weeks I had felt better. After the week with my parents, I felt refreshed. Part of me understood myself better, and the nature of my feelings better. I realized I outgrew Orlando, and while away from Los Angeles I fantasized about my life back in the city. I felt determined to return to the life I had built and shape it into a more focused reality. I would prevail. I always had. Maybe Los Angeles could become a long-term home. And I wanted to do all that with Gartner. However, I began to suspect that he did not.

"I am not miserable," I repeated, more forceful this time. "I spent the holidays with my family in Orlando, and after being on vacation for two weeks, work at the Market has started to feel manageable... You are showing me around your hometown, I saw a red wood tree for the first time... there is nothing for me to be miserable about," I said confidently. "Well then maybe you are just hangry, so you should go eat because you are being a brat," was Gartner's response.

"No, I was nauseous and did not feel well, just like I have the last few days. It's because you have not allowed me to get proper sleep like I have been asking for. I am not going to let you guilt trip me into thinking I have been miserable when I have not - maybe I fucked up some things yesterday, and I am sorry for that. Like I said, it was not intentional, but I have not woken up every day actively trying to ruin your day." Could he not see anything from my point of view?

"Yes, you have," he said, doubling down on his commitment to me constantly being in the wrong. "You really do not see it, but you are terrible to deal with. I've told you before and I'll tell you again: you are so lucky to be dating me."

"Okay, Gartner, I was not going to argue with you today," I responded quickly and with lack of emotion. I was so over this. I felt myself going numb to it all. "Again, I am sorry for anything that I have done to upset you. I really don't enjoy you implying that I appear miserable every day, because that is not how I feel at all."

"You have been, and you have been so rude about everything. You are ungrateful and a brat," he said simply. Nothing I said or did would make this better, it seemed.

I was reminded of his response to the gifts I had given him. Funny how he was blind to how bratty he had acted then.

"You fail to realize how much you upset me after you opened nearly all of my presents and verbally disliked them," I started, feeling the need to get this off my chest. I couldn't just let him stand there and make me feel like shit while not taking any accountability himself. "I spent a lot of time picking out those gifts for you. You just sat there ripping them to shreds and I should have said something to you... but I decided not to because I love you and I wanted to give you the benefit of the doubt. Maybe you reacted that way because you had unexpected anxiety about coming back here to your hometown." I hoped the vulnerability in my admission would cause him to understand me.

"You have been miserable, and even your mom confirmed it for me- she agreed with me," he said defiantly. He was clearly not going to acknowledge anything I just said.

"Do not ever try to use my mother against me like that," I snapped, letting the anger rise to the surface. "Don't ever try to put words into her mouth, I know she has never said that to you," I said coldly.

He remained silent for a beat as he furiously folded his clothes and placed them into the suitcase.

"So now what?" He said after a while, breaking the silence. I struggled to find my voice.

"I have no idea, but I have been ready to move on," I tried, still attempting to be the peacemaker. "I have not wanted to fight with you at all today."

"Well, you are in the wrong," he said.

"Look, clearly you think you are in the right and clearly I do not think I am in the wrong," I felt like I was in a debate with a toddler at this point. "I already apologized for yesterday and anything else I've apparently done that has upset you, because that was not my intention. I am not here to be mean to you, Gartner. I am here because I love you and want to be with you."

"I don't accept your apology, because you are wrong," he said in a matter-of-fact way. It seemed his cruelness had no bounds.

"Well, what are we going to do then? If we are unable to move on? I can't do anything for you other than apologize. If you can't accept the apology and move on, then what is our next option? To break up? Because I do not want to-"

"Did you just break up with me?" Gartner cut me off before I could finish the sentence.

"No, Gartner, I was trying to point how foolish this is-"

"I told you to never utter that phrase to me again. I told you if you ever threatened to break up with me that I would leave you and you would never see me again," he shouted the words at me, spitting out of his mouth like venom.

"Gartner, I did not say we should break up," I yelled, trying to prevent myself from either rolling my eyes at his ridiculousness or starting to cry. "I was just asking what our options were if you are not going to work with me and move on!"

"I am taking Ghost for a walk," he said, which instantly aggravated me because Ghost was my dog.

"No," I said as I got out of bed and threw on my clothes. "I am taking my dog on a walk, and I am going to call my mom. You figure out whatever it is you need to figure out, but I am not playing this game with you." I left the room with Ghost without looking back, letting the door slam behind me.

## The End of the Beginning
## (January 4ᵗʰ, 2025)

In hindsight, I knew it was over when we drove through Cliffside. The windows were down. Sza's "Another Life" played loudly over the speakers of his silver Toyota Camry. The sun started to peak through the gloomy clouds across the bay.

I think that was what I disliked most about California's weather. The clouds, the fog, the rain, and the mist that hung over and hovered above the cities. It made me feel like boys like me belonged to the rain. I longed for the sun.
Gartner had the windows down despite it being wet out. The Pacific Ocean crashed along the cliff's shores. I could feel the crisp air tinged with salt nip at my hands, and I knew Ghost was cold in the backseat.

The sun peeked through the clouds in small gaps. When it finally streaked through just enough, it warmed my limbs. The stormy weather was finally clearing. Gartner had the volume up to the max. He played sad songs on a loop, as if he had searched the word for fitting playlists. Finally, I repeated what I said to him the day before:

"We should go to the park we went to yesterday, I'm sure it will be much better weather and not as muddy. Maybe we can make up for yesterday."

Gartner agreed, though he wouldn't meet my gaze or look in my direction. When we arrived at the park most of the clouds had cleared. The few that remained drifted by quickly out of sight. For once the clouds moved fast in California.

The forest was damp with vibrant shades of green reflecting off the flora and fauna that could only be observed after a fresh rainstorm left the brush feeling replenished.

Ghost loved hiking. He was small and compact, with a surprisingly good grip and decent vertical leap. His favorite activity was to sprint with all his might, and he was fast. If dog racing was legal, I would have submitted him simply because I knew he liked running so much.

Gartner and Ghost were ahead of me by fifty feet. Ghost ran back and forth between us, sprinting in between the gap in our strides. He loved Gartner so he stayed close by to him, but every so often he would run back to check on me. Sometimes he would lay down in the middle of the pathway until I got close enough for him to declare his resting period was over. Then he would take off again.

As much as Gartner kept his distance, I tried to chase him, hoping to close the distance between us. I still had hope we could see it through. I thought that him agreeing to the hike was a good sign, a step in the right direction. I thought it meant we were about to embark on a new path, a lighter one than the one we'd been teetering across these last few months.

There was an overlook to the river far below us. I observed sunbeams cutting through in long rectangular shapes, their paths dictated by the tall trees. I took out my phone to capture a photo. I loved sun beams, the way they illuminated the specific areas they encountered. Again, my heart clung onto the piece of beauty like it was a sign from the heavens that things would soon be alright.

Gartner kept his distance from me the whole time we walked. I decided to let him, thinking that space would be good for us. To reflect on what we wanted, which I assumed was each other. I was unaware at the time but as the seconds ticked by, I lost him increasingly. I was oblivious to how much I had hurt him earlier. I was of course aware of how he had hurt me, but I think the difference was in which one of us wanted to try, and who was already prepared to let go. After an hour of hiking, we made it back to his car and began the drive home to dry, dusty Los Angeles.

After the second consecutive binge of sad music, we decided to stream the first episode of season 17 of Drag Race on his phone for the remainder of the journey. The episode came out on his birthday, just the night before. I had messaged my mom earlier to tell her about the argument we had. I confessed how Gartner had told me it was over. I also expressed that this was not what I wanted, that I thought the words were merely said during the heat of the moment. My mom texted me back, giving advice on how she felt we should handle our feelings:

> As I sit here and think, this comes to mind. I have seen a positive change in you since being with Gartner, and I think both of you need to realize that you don't always have to agree or get along. But if you care for each other, it's important to work at the relationship........ that is it.

I read the message out loud to tell Gartner what my mom had said, but he offered no response. I took it as a sign of the end. I felt my hopes and heart deflate. He had stopped caring. He was not willing to give me anything. Not even his thoughts on the matter. I should have known from the beginning how quickly he could shut down and shut people out. I just wished it wasn't at my expense.

The highway cut through a valley, where rich earth churned up on either side of us as we passed part of America's Heartland. We passed by the growing crops meant to feed the country. Every so often the plowed earth morphed into apple groves that ran far beyond my eyesight.

I noticed a black bird perched on a branch and then spotted another. One after the other, multiple birds of the same species were perched every twenty feet from each other, high up on a tree branch. They looked like hawks but instead of the fawny gold feathers I saw back home in Florida, these had feathers that were jet black with tinges of silver, gray, and white. I deduced they were falcons.

I found a fascination with birds. As much as bird people are described as quirky, I realized I am just as odd - if not more so - and therefore I too was a bird person. What was there to not like about birds? They were admirable. They had fascinating cultures to them. Some species needed to remain together, like chickens in a flock or penguins who mated for life. Other birds sang pretty songs. I found that there was a lot more to like about birds than there was to dislike. I admired the falcons, just like I would have admired the hawks back in Florida. Different birds, different states, but with the same enjoyment. For some reason that brought me great comfort at that moment.

The sky was a ripe blue, with no clouds in sight across the valley. I was sure the falcons were preparing for a bountiful hunt as the sun set over the western mountains to my right. I looked back at Gartner, staring at the features of his profile as he drove. I wanted to remember him.

I realized from my most recent relationship that I needed to pay attention to the details more, to try and take a picture to store within my memory. Lock the picture of this person I had loved so deeply in a vault that only I had access to. Just for me.

His eyes met mine then, displaying the purest shade of sea blue. His eyes resembled the aftereffect of waves colliding, returning to brilliant blue from a foamy white. I needed to capture the moment. His eyes were gorgeous. They sparkled at you, like the sun's reflection against the glassy surface of the ocean. Gartner was aware of the power his eyes held over me. Before, after he said something slick in an attempt at acting cute, he would often make an audible noise that sounded like a cartoon going, "Dink!"

His eyes were not the only part of him to sparkle, his teeth had a similar shine to them, too. He knew that as well. I think he knew a lot more than he ever let on. One thing I had always been right about was how incredibly close we were in personality. Two halves of the same coin.

I messaged Princess, Bondi, and Pink, since they were my security blanket. I needed their support. Pink was in Philadelphia for the new year, so I asked Bondi to pick me up after we were back in town. I figured Gartner and I would need some space after an emotionally exhausting day. I thought we needed the space. My mom told me it was not a good idea, but what was a good idea at this point? We had been stuck with one another since I arrived back in Los Angeles a week ago. At this point, I thought we had spent too much time together.

When we arrived at the apartment on Wilcox Place, it didn't take long before Bondi showed up to get me in her beat-up, white Chevy. Florida girls and their beat-up white vehicles. Before then, Gartner and I said little to nothing to each other. There was nothing to talk about, and he had clearly not been present since that morning. He hadn't met my gaze since I took the mental portrait of him in the car, a few hours prior. I knew this was going to be a slow burn to the death of us.

When I left the apartment to meet Bondi he told me to not come home late, which was another way for him to limit me. The more I thought about his words, the more it made no logical sense considering the following day was Sunday. Neither of us worked the next day, and we had just spent several hours in silence after arguing all morning. What was there to rush back for?

Bondi looked at me with her big doe eyes, any icy shade of blue that made you feel like someone was invested in you. The type of eyes to make you feel like someone loved you. Those eyes held weight, meaning, and value. I did not manage to cry, though. Try as I might, and I wanted to, badly. "Well, what happened?" she said.

I repeated the story in a partially dazed summary. I was already tired of repeating my tale of sadness, and I had only repeated it once so far to my mother, and even that was a brief conversation. Saying it out loud just made it all too real, like once it was out of my internal thoughts and out into the world it became a reality that we were most likely going to break up.

I told Bondi about our drive up north to Santa Cruz, and how it started out good but then I got sick, and it all went downhill from there. I told her how some inconveniences were out of our control. I also told her that I had been hangry and grumpy at some point. Then I told her about how I forgot to sing him happy birthday, which I felt terrible about. As I revisited the events I realized we were both at fault. I wished I could go back in time, but of course the Time Bandit would never allow it. All he was ever good for was moving me forward, preventing me from staying in a moment.

In hindsight, I told her I believed everything had been building up to the moment of breaking. Despite how I had tried my best to maintain it, our relationship felt destined to fail for some time now. I told her how Gartner had clearly given up. I also told her about his response to my mother's message, which she agreed was rude of him to disregard such a thoughtful message from her. I felt grateful to have a friend in that moment, someone to listen and confide in. I felt like I had been trapped inside my own inner monologue for the last week when I was just with Gartner. Constantly second guessing whether I was in the wrong all the time or if it was a two-sided issue. In a lot of ways, I felt validated.

Once we were safely inside Bondi's apartment, the girls streamed a sequel to a scary movie about a contagious smile. I had not seen the first, and I hardly watched its counterpart as it played on the television in front of me. My mind was still elsewhere.

I ordered myself fast food, as I had not eaten since that morning. I decided not to tell Bondi or Princess about Gartner's request for me not to be out late. I knew it sounded weird and controlling. I did not want them to form an opinion. There was a part of me that was still hopeful that things would work out, and I didn't want my closest friends to disapprove of Gartner completely if I was to still be with him. Part of me felt a weird guilt at not expressing everything to my closest friends in LA, but the forever romantic in me just wanted things to work with Gartner. I decided that I would order an uber to go back to my apartment around midnight, since Bondi's place was only 15 minutes away.

At 11:40 PM I told Bondi and Princess that I would call an uber home, but they shut me down.
"No-no do not be silly," Bondi said, shaking her head at the idea. "I will take you home when the movie is over."
I didn't want to be rude, so I said: "Sure okay, how much longer is left in the movie?"

Bondi shook the apple remote and revealed the length of the movie and its play time. According to the counter on the right side of the screen, the movie had forty minutes left. I would arrive home around 12:40 AM. Not terrible, I thought. It seemed doable. Perfectly acceptable. There was no need for Gartner to get upset.

After the movie ended, Bondi drove me home. I didn't want to tell her I was nervous about returning to the apartment on Wilcox Place. I also didn't want to confess what Gartner had told me about not being home late. If I told Bondi and Princess that he told me to come home early, they would be annoyed with him. They would surely tell me he was being controlling, which maybe wasn't that outlandish of a thing to think.

I never really thought about how controlling he could be. I didn't want to contribute to any negative thoughts towards him. I started to think how he had not bought me flowers or chocolates recently, but it had also been sometime since we showered together, and I rubbed him clean with a loofa. Maybe we both fell out of love with each other. Like we had simply become roommates, navigating around each other while playing the role of a partner. Minus the little things, the intimate details that seemed to really count. It hurt to think about walking away, to leave him and my life in Los Angeles. I had just started to adjust to life there and just started to enjoy the idea of making the city a big part of my future.

At the moment, staying in LA would not be an option, especially after Bondi and I discussed it. She did not suggest moving in and splitting rent with her, even as a temporary situation. I wasn't sure if it was because of my cats and dog, or if she just did not think of it. I tried not to let it hurt my feelings, but I was unfortunately sensitive. It felt like there was a sense of urgency with the matter, so if she were going to offer her place up it would have already happened. Or maybe she too was hopeful for a rekindling between Gartner and me.

I could already feel Gartner's annoyed presence beyond the door of apartment 3 as I turned the key to unlock the front door. His negative energy radiated off him, casting out from his mind and escaping his body to manipulate the air I breathed in. I felt abnormally sensitive. I knew this wouldn't be good.

As I stepped inside the apartment, Gartner acted as if I had woken him up and peered lazily at the stove clock directly opposite of him. The time was 12:47 am. I suspected he had not fallen asleep before I came home.
"It is one in the morning, and I asked you not to come home late," was his choice of greeting.

I was instantly annoyed, and it set me off. I decide to be honest with my feelings for once, to no longer bite down on the words that so longed to be expressed. Not for his benefit. Not when he could so easily say things to intentionally put me down.

"First off, it is not 1 am. I wanted to come home earlier, but Bondi and Princess had put on a movie and when I said I would call an Uber, they insisted I wait until it was over so I could save money and have Bondi drive me back. Honestly, I did not want to tell them about your request to have me come back early, because to be frank with you it is weird, and I did not think you wanna come off as the weird, controlling asshole." I let out a relieved breath, proud of myself for saying what needed to be said.

He remained silent and still for a moment. Then he flipped back over and went to sleep. He made a point to sprawl out across the bed, leaving little to no room. It was obvious I was not allowed to sleep with him. I gritted my teeth.

I went to sit on the couch with my laptop, streaming Sex and the City to feel a sense of comfort in this increasingly uncomfortable space. I eventually fell asleep. Of course, I did not sleep well. I awoke only thirty minutes later. I could hear Gartner tossing and turning in the bed, and I knew he had the same feelings as me. We both wanted to fall asleep together. We craved the intimacy we had lit between us like an eternal flame.

No words were necessary for what happened next. I crawled into bed with him; I couldn't help it. He moved closer to the edge of his side of the bed in response, refusing to move his head in my direction. He held out against the magnetic urge for physical touch. We had already had our last cuddle together despite me being aware of it at the time. The Time Bandit had slipped in and messed with my life yet again. I had spent my last night being held by Gartner in Santa Cruz, right after dissociating from our intimacy. The night we got back to LA was probably the last time I would ever sleep next to him, the thought came in my head as I laid there, craving his touch. At least the Time Bandit let me be conscious of that. Or was it crueler to be aware of the end, to sense it and face it head on? It all felt horrible, it all felt like too much.

Neither of us slept that night. Even with everything that had happened between us in such a short amount of time, Gartner still wanted to do our routine laundry run. He drove us over to the laundromat and we did our typical chore of washing and drying our clothes. I tricked myself into thinking that things were normal, that this was a sign things would return to normalcy. The only reason the delusion was eluded was because he still refused to look at me at all. I missed feeling his eyes on me. I felt as if I had disappeared. I sat in our silence, trying to focus on just being near him. It was a twisted trick, being close physically but feeling thousands of miles apart, both mentally and emotionally.

When we returned to the apartment on Wilcox Place, Gartner finally said those final, crushing words: "I do not think we work well together anymore, and we should break up."

There was no longer any shock, for I had known this was coming after the last few days. It did not make the blow hurt any less. He argued with one another anyways. Neither of us yelled; both of our voices were kept sturdy and at an appropriate volume. He eventually told me he would allow me to spend as long as I needed in the apartment until I had enough money to move out on my own. This felt impossible, to remain in the space that was ours and yet act like strangers.

I stepped outside to call my mother and confirm our end. She seemed to absorb my own denial. I accepted my fate easily, as if I had been prepared for it. I guess I had been, in a way. Learning about Gartner's relationships, or lack thereof, his capability to cut everyone out including his own family - it was only a matter of time before I was added to his 'no contact' list.

I went outside with Ghost in tow; I needed his closeness and comfort. The air was dry and the sun was out, with the cold seemingly pushing itself out of the city. The remainder of winter was unseasonably warm. I returned to the apartment then, determined to talk over with Gartner what life would be like if we continued coexisting together until I could move out. It helped to focus on next moves rather than think about the emotional reality of it all.

"So, you will have to be okay with how I live my life personally and the jobs that I take on," I said to him as I entered the apartment. "If I need to take a job you wouldn't want me to, I am going to. You have to accept that, especially if we are no longer together."

My transparency only led to Gartner's irreversible explosion. To him, he found that I disrespected him. He wouldn't allow me to regain full control over my life, even if we weren't together. He stormed out of the apartment in a huff, only to return several minutes later. He had a calm resolve on his face, the opposite of the scowl he wore just moments ago.

"I booked you a one-way rental car back to Florida. You leave Friday," he said before heading back towards the door.

I was unable to form a response. Gartner then grabbed his keys from the holder on the side of the door, turned the handle, and gave me one final look before leaving the apartment. I stood there; jaw dropped in disbelief. My time in LA was over; it had been decided.

Ghost and I arrived at Bondi's apartment a few hours later. Princess waited for me, sprawled across the L-shaped couch in Bondi's living room.

"I just woke up from a nap," she said sleepily. "Have you guys seen this weather alert?"

"Yeah, I was watching the news today while I was packing, something about a windstorm? Whatever that is," I

234

said halfheartedly. It did feel nice to discuss something other than my life falling apart in a matter of minutes.

Bondi quickly changed into her work clothes and shouted to us that she was leaving as she walked out the door. After the door closed the silence overstayed its welcome. Princess filled me in on the latest friend group drama, giving me a decent distraction. It seemed all of us were actively living through a crisis revolving around ex-lovers.

I had not been around for any of the fun as of late. I was too wrapped up in Gartner and making my life work, adjusting to Los Angeles. I had fallen out of touch with my friends, and out of touch with myself. I wondered if my friends had talked about me amongst themselves, how I had drifted away from them. I suspected my friends might've noticed Gartner's indifference towards them and my hobbies. The fabrics of who I was, of what defined me. They were perceptive. After all, they knew me better than anyone else.

In vain, I hoped my friends had talked about it. It would show that they cared about me, and I wanted someone to care about me. To care was to love. I hoped they loved me just as much as I loved them. I was in a vulnerable state, thinking I had nothing without Gartner. I knew this wasn't true, though. But my fear internalized the thought in my head. Maybe the Time Bandit was testing me, maybe controlling more than just time.

I kept my responses to a minimum. Princess continued to rant, now wanting to discuss Bondi's obscene choices, her erratic behavior that I felt was not necessarily abnormal from Bondi anymore. I wondered how long we could continue to ignore the tough question: What if Bondi needed help that we couldn't provide? A devastating question to ask amongst friends. We so often preached to one another about facing the harder facets of life, to be transparent with one another. But so far even for myself, I had yet to speak my mind on what was keeping me up at night.

"I am starving," I said. The days blurred together, and I realized I had hardly eaten.

I ordered food from Uber Eats. After waiting for the meal to arrive, I realized I had sent it to Gartner's address at the apartment on Wilcox Place. I texted him, reluctantly, because I didn't have the money to order myself another meal. It was already late, and I was low on money. Now I was all too aware that I had to travel back across the country to Florida in a matter of days. I suddenly felt nauseous again.

Gartner agreed to bring my food, to my surprise. The wind howled viciously as he pulled up outside of Bondi's to drop it off. I thought the wind wasn't supposed to pick up until the following day, but apparently the Santa Ana winds had arrived early, and the gusts were strong.

His eyes were dark and stormy, no longer shining like the beautiful blue I knew they were. There was still a beauty to them, even wet after he had clearly been crying.
"Thanks," I said when I had the bag in my hands.

"I didn't want you to be hungry," he replied without making eye contact. "I know you haven't eaten."
"Be careful with all this weather," I said back.
No response.

I watched his silver Toyota Camry pull away from Russell Avenue. I let myself back inside and ate the food in silence. Princess didn't ask me how it went, she already knew. She had developed a good sense of reading the emotions on my face. She was more intelligent, observant, and empathetic than most gave her credit for, and maybe I did not give her enough credit myself when we were younger.

"Damn," I said, looking out the window. "The winds outside are crazy; I thought this windstorm was supposed to start tomorrow morning? And now it says we're on a fire watch?"

"I know, I can hear a gust going by outside every few minutes," Princess said. She didn't seem too worried, so I tried to calm the nervousness in my bones.

After I scarfed down my food, I took Ghost on a walk around the neighborhood. I wanted to get it out of the way before the weather worsened. We had been lazy couch potatoes since we left the apartment on Wilcox Place, and I knew we both needed to move our legs. When we got back, I fell asleep on the couch next to the Princess, with Ghost curled up between us. It was the last time I would get adequate sleep for the next few days.

January 7th, 2025

      I woke up the next morning to the news broadcasting a story about a fire that had started in the Palisades around 10:30 am. I checked the clock, it was now 11:30 am. Damn, only an hour, I thought. The wind was so chaotically strong that when I took Ghost out for a morning walk, I was forced to shade my eyes from the dust that carried through the air by its powerful gusts. I kept the walk short, wanting to get us both back inside to safety.

      Once back inside the apartment, I told Princess I had texted Gartner that I would stay at Bondi's until the wind had died down. I would pack the rest of my belongings at Wilcox Place once the weird weather passed. I was both relieved and pained at the thought that I would not see Gartner again until then. The circumstances were not easy to deal with. I suspected Gartner would not be there when I arrived to pack the rest of my belongings and pick up the cats. At the time, I had to leave them. I knew it was only temporary, though.

      "The winds are strong out there, it's kind of a weird ambiance outside," I said to Princess after a moment of silence.

      "Apparently the Palisades fire is spreading quickly," she responded, her eyes locked on the TV screen.

      "I'm ordering coffee if anyone wants one," Bondi said as she emerged from her bedroom.

"Me, just a drip, medium, please," I said.

      "This fire is tripping me up," Bondi said, taking place on the couch to get a glimpse of the constant news cycle.

"We were just talking about that," Princess chimed in.

      "I really do not want to work today," Bondi said. She started typing into her phone, likely asking if one of her coworkers would take her shift.

"You think they'll stay open if things get any worse?" I asked. "Pink comes home tonight too, are you meant to pick her up?"

"I texted my bosses already and I guess it's work as usual, and yes," Bondi responded, clearly upset at the prospect of still needing to go into work. "But I am worried about her not making it home. What if her flight is cancelled? It says we can experience up to 100 mile per hour gusts in some of the metro areas tonight."

I figured we would deal with what came our way. Bondi slipped outside with her dog, Kida, returning with the coffee that had been delivered during her walk.

"Bro, I do not like this weather," Bondi reiterated, visibly shaken up. "It's hot, and still windy. I thought the wind was supposed to stop during the day?"

"I thought the same when I walked Ghost, but it is pretty bad," I said back.

"Well, that settles it, I am not going outside then," Princess answered in a determined voice.

"Have you talked to Gartner?" Bondi asked, looking at me.

"No, not since I texted him earlier this morning and told him I would be coming by tomorrow instead of today to finish packing," I replied.
"When Chad and I broke up, he was just like that," Bondi said.

I knew she was doing her best to comfort me, and I appreciated that. I felt overwhelmed. I had my mind focused on getting to Florida, knowing it was already coming up so soon. But on the bright side, I knew I would feel better the moment I breathed in the thick, swampy air.

As she left for work around four pm, Bondi told us she would return home around midnight with Pink. I ordered myself take out from the only Puerto Rican restaurant I had found in the Valley that was up to par with my standard. I ordered chicken empanadas, pernil, tostones, and arroz con gandules. I was in dire need of comfort food.

The Eaton Fire in Pasadena became breaking news right as I ordered my take-out. Multiple brush fires had sparked around the metro area, and first responders battled against large flames fire off the eastern side of interstate five in the valley.

The news reported that another intense windstorm would push its way through the Los Angeles area that night. The collective fear across the city had grown over the ability to utilize helicopters to drop water across the active burning with the continued high gusts.

My food arrived by 7:05 pm and I ran out to meet the courier. I handed him a fist full of cash I had scrounged up, thanking him for driving in the conditions and quickly retreated inside.

The fire in the Palisades continued to rage on, intensely spreading at an unbelievably fast rate of five football fields per minute. The fire exploded in force from 10 to 200 acres in just thirty minutes. Everyone was in disbelief. It was only getting worse.

I plopped down on the couch next to Princess and began unboxing the food. Out of nowhere, there was a large gust of wind followed by a loud pop. The lights inside the apartment faded and then went out completely. Princess and I locked eyes with one another in the powerless apartment.

"Ain't no fucking way that just happened!" Princess said aloud, mimicking my own thoughts.

Princess laughed and shrugged and then pulled out her laptop. She placed her laptop on the coffee table in front of us and played a movie while we ate in the dark living room. When the movie was over and our stomachs were full, I got up and opened the front door to the apartment. There was a second screen behind the main door, allowing us to get a glimpse of the outside world. The constant whistle of winds and large gusts created a natural fan for the apartment. At least it kept the inside chilled. I convinced Princess to leave the door open while we waited for Bondi and Princess to come home later that evening.

We watched outside as the wind whipped through the small corridor between Bondi's apartment complex and the stucco house next door. As the night shrouded the city, the Santa Ana winds worsened as they combined with a storm coming in from the Pacific Northwest that had pushed its way south. They collided together, with the hot and heavy air sitting over the metro area. It created the perfect conditions for what the news would refer to as a Hurricane of Fire the following night.

I took Ghost on a walk as nightfall drew in. I knew he needed to go out, and I wanted to get it over with fast. We walked past the soundstage of the well-known television drama series, Grey's Anatomy. It was a hot set that sat directly behind Bondi's apartment. I had seen characters from my favorite childhood TV show walk from that soundstage to their dressing rooms. My phone vibrated. followed by an alert tone as I received a notice from Los Angeles County implementing a curfew and shelter order in place.

I knew the actors and actresses were headed to change out of their wardrobe and return to the nightmarish scene outside of the studio, into their grim realities they could not act their way out of.

Pink texted us photos then, from her flight's perspective of the fires raging below on the ground. After years of living in the hurricane epicenter of the world, I had never experienced such devastation at a rapid rate. I thought it must have been easier to rebuild a home that had been flooded, versus burnt to the ground. The images were haunting: bright orange and red flames danced, combined, and devoured the now-scorched earth.

Large black plumes of smoke jetted out above the sky. The wind captured the billowy smoke in the atmosphere and whisked it across the night sky. It tainted the stars, moon, and mountains as the smoke floated past. The lights from houses that had yet to burn out or had simply forgotten to be switched off juxtaposed the blacked-out neighborhoods without power. It created a sharp contrast in the livelihood being disrupted.

My adrenaline was high. I couldn't sleep. Pink and Bondi arrived home around midnight. I felt relieved that all four of us were under one roof. Sometimes I had my doubts about our friendship. Sometimes I thought those doubts were warranted and that was because we were humans who are imperfect. In those moments where we act less than, we are not always good people. But I believed in multiple chances, and I saw the good in those I loved. More often than not, they continued to show good over bad.

That day, however, I had no doubt in my mind. That day I loved my friends more, just as I always had and always would. The four of us sat on Bondi's couch, Ghost nuzzled next to Princess who he had taken a liking to. Kida stood guard at the front door, watching leaves wiz by as they were pushed from the Santa Ana Winds.

We scoured the internet for news on the fires engulfing the city and found gut-wrenching stories. Helicopters were grounded with the inability to drop large vats of water across the burning earth. The heavy winds affected everything. Then smaller brush fires sprouted up across the county and valley. It seemed like it would never end.

People fled their homes while first responders stood idly by with little to no resources. California prisoners were then recruited as firemen, to serve the very people who incarcerated them. Fire crews from the Northern California bay area and the Vegas desert were requested as back up for the uncontained wildfires.

The city started to face a very real possibility of losing the battle. Some battles were already being lost, as historic neighborhoods continued to burn. Pink wanted us to stay awake, but I couldn't keep my eyes open any more. My adrenaline from the evening had worn off. I felt exhausted and depressed at reality. It was bad enough how the last few days had gone. Now it felt like the whole world was ending.

***

When my eyes opened the next day, the sky was a shade of yellow as if the sun had started to round the curvature of the earth. As the first light touched the sky, it filled with light so quickly that if you were to blink, you would miss the turning point from jet black night to sun-golden dawn.

I checked my phone and found a plethora of text messages from friends and family who had seen national headlines of the devastating fires, checking in on my well-being. It was eleven in the morning but from the light outside I thought it could have been much earlier. When I arose from the blow-up mattress in the spare room and peered out the window beyond the blinds, I saw that the shroud of smoke from the Palisades fire had fully engulfed the sky.

A large, brown-gray billowy smog flowed from the fires burning out west and crossed the city, blanketing the sun. When I stepped outside to walk Ghost, the heat felt even more intense than on the hottest day in the central deserts of America. The combination of ash and smoke created a magnifying scope effect, and I felt as if I was a tiny ant who fell prey to a bully with a magnifying glass.

Luckily the wind died down enough for helicopters to drop water deposits over the fires. I watched them fly overhead above the city, delivering resources before taking off towards the Hollywood Reservoir to collect another vat of water.

When I walked back in the door of the apartment, Bondi, Pink, and Princess were all huddled on the couch together over Bondi's phone.

"I am ordering coffee; you want your usual?" Bondi asked me.

"Yeah, for sure, thanks," I said, still somewhat distracted by the scene outside. "The copters are flying all around out there, and it is so hot."

"These fires are getting too close for comfort at this point," Bondi said back. "That fire out in Eaton could easily hop over into Glendale, and that's just banging on the doorstep of the neighborhood at that point."

"They do not have any containment," Pink said solemnly.

After a moment of processing in silence, I said I needed to go to my old apartment on Wilcox so I could pack the rest of my belongings up and collect my kitties. It had made sense at the time to leave them behind, since I needed a new carrier for them after the original carrier I moved them in broke. I had asked my sister to order one to Bondi's house since I was low on money.

"So, he's really just sending you back like that?" Pink asked, seemingly shocked by Gartner's harsh reaction to the breakup he committed to.

"Yeah, he just booked me a rental car like that," I said, staring down at my feet. "Now I'm attempting to get the car earlier because I was supposed to leave on Friday..."
"That is so crazy," Pink said.
"You should not leave," Princess chimed in.

"What would I even do? I'm not making money here currently," I said. "I have no way to stay or survive."

I dumbed down my job and my life for Gartner when I moved cross country. He was the one that said he didn't want me to serve or bartend. For some reason I had obliged, knowing I was missing out on potential gigs and tip money. When the coffee arrived, we all went out together to walk the dogs and check in on the surrounding areas in the aftermath. The streets were lined with tenants presiding on Russell Ave, just milling around, talking to one another about the current events and checking in on each other's wellbeing.

One of Bondi's neighbors handed us each a mask to wear. The air had grown thick with ash as the two major fires spewed smoke into the bowl-like shape of the city. Bits of ash drifted down from the sky as if it were specks of snow. It landed on cars and pavement, and anything that was exposed outside. Occasionally a fleck landed in my hair, death clinging to the living.

Pink dropped me off at Wilcox Place after the walk. When I walked in the door, I found it was empty. Gartner was not inside. He had left before I arrived. He told me he would not be there, but I secretly hoped he was lying. In just a matter of days, he had become unrecognizable to me.

I saw past his current façade, though. Or maybe he let his guard down just long enough for me to see it. He resembled an unhealed child, one that still pined for his family's approval. Now as a grown man he was unable to accept that anyone could love him. He couldn't fathom someone putting forth effort to be there for him. At the slightest inconvenience he was ready to call it quits, to shut me out from him completely and hide from the hurt he was too afraid to feel if he let it go any further. I understood it, but I found it cowardly. He was going to let go of true love due to his unresolved trauma and fears. It would just end up hurting us both in the end. And maybe that's what was always meant to be, with the Time Bandit bound to laws unknown to man. Although deemed necessary by his trickery, sometimes they were inexcusably cruel.

I scanned the studio apartment, the hardwood floors. I looked at my green, red, and yellow-patterned boho carpet that had a tear in it from when Ghost chewed it as a puppy when I had just gotten him. It looked like it belonged there. At one point, so did I. But everything was over now, disintegrating before my eyes.

There was a space on the TV stand where the PlayStation 5 I bought him for Christmas had once sat. It seemed that he took it with him, afraid that I would take it back out of spite. I inspected the closet and found he had taken some of his own clothing out of fear that I would take them. Some of my crystals were missing, so presumably Gartner assumed some of mine were his. Or maybe in his eyes, he was allowed to claim things while I was not. I was not about to argue with him over it. I accepted my defeat once again. At this point I knew that if I suffered any further casualties, it would not change anything for me.

I packed sporadically, throwing various items into my suitcases so I could carry them home easily. I walked to the cupboard in the small, box-shaped hallway that led to the bathroom and reached up to search the top shelf as I felt for my passport. After searching for my own passport, I realized that Gartner had taken his passport. I assumed he must have taken mine with it, after being located next to my own.

I was irritated with him for thinking I would take anything that was not my own. I dialed his phone number, hoping he would answer my call since he had already taken to pretending that I did not exist.

"Yes," Gartner said curtly over the line.

"Hey, I think you took my passport by accident," I said.

"I do not have your passport," he responded with resolve in his voice. "I have no clue where you put it, so I do not know why you think I would have it."

"I put my passport where you put your passport, on the top shelf of the cupboard in the hallway," I said, reminding him. "When you grabbed your passport, you probably grabbed mine by accident. Why would I put my passport anywhere else other than next to where yours was located? You are the one who suggested I put it there, so we could keep important documents together."

"I will look and call you back," he said gruffly before clicking to end the call.

After a minute my phone vibrated, and it was Gartner's name displayed on the screen. I answered. His voice was shaky and high pitched like when I knew he was anxious:

"Hey, I am sorry about that, but you are right. I grabbed your passport by accident; do you want me to bring it back to you?"

"Yes please," I said, and another click ended the call. I couldn't imagine why he would think I wouldn't want him to bring it to me.

After I packed my belongings into boxes, Gartner returned and let himself into the apartment to return my passport. I had just loaded the kitties into their carrier that arrived just in time before Pink dropped me off. It was a double decker carrier, so each cat would have their own space stacked one on top of the other. I couldn't thank my sister enough for helping me out with it.

Gartner's cat, Jude, perched herself next to my cats in the carrier. Jude looked at them through the mesh that kept them separated. Gartner's face welled up as he began to cry. "This is really sad to watch," he sobbed. To think, at one point he wanted me to get rid of my cats.

I felt the weight of our love hang in the air, turning decayed and stenching it like the smell of rotten eggs. Our love had rotted out.

The scene was sad. We watched as Jude purred and rubbed against the outer shell of the carrier, up against the mesh. They had all become friends over time. Cats love to socialize in large numbers, since they are pack animals. I wondered if they were sharing goodbyes with one another, wishing each other well. They must have known we were leaving. Animals were much more intuitive than humans.

My heart hurt. I could feel it breaking again. I didn't know how much was left to split apart. I was longing to tell him how much he meant to me. I loved him, even still. I desperately wanted to kiss him. I was worried we had already shared our last kiss. I tried to stare into his eyes, but he negated his gaze. His ocean blue eyes were now lost to my reality. I did not know how I could console him, let alone myself. And yet I had no words, my voice was caught in my throat. The dry air outside had rubbed my inner vocal cords raw.

I was unable to remedy the hurt I caused him, even if that had not been my intention. I never thought he would be the one to pull the trigger. To think it all ended for me at the same speed the fires devoured the coastal desert, just outside the walls of the apartment on Wilcox Place.

I felt selfish for feeling as devastated over the end of our relationship with all the anguish that transpired in the fires taking place. I knew there were other tragedies aside from my personal heartache. I harbored shame internally, unable to separate the amounting sense of sadness welling up inside. I felt confused and defeated. I remained in the same clothes I wore the day we left Santa Cruz. I was too stunned to focus my attention on multiple tasks. Plus, the rest of my clothes were now squished into suitcases.

After I finished packing, Gartner and I both decided it was best for me to leave my boxes behind until we were able to pick up the rental car. It didn't make sense to do it any sooner with the active shelter-in-place ordinance from the city. I contacted the rental company again to try and get the car sooner, but they were unable to get me a rental earlier than Friday. That was three days away.

Bondi picked me up instead of Pink, waiting for me in her car downstairs. Gartner didn't follow me down. I sighed as I got in the front seat of Bondi's car after I loaded the kitties into the backseat.

Her car was a mess, but it was always a mess. We sat in silence on the way back to her apartment. There was not much to say. Bondi did not want to say the wrong thing to me either, which I understood. I tried to take the moment of silence just to breathe.

Pink wanted us to go to her apartment because the power was on, but I had no desire to leave Bondi's apartment, even if there was no power. Disrupting my safe space was not ideal for me at the moment, even if I was familiar with Pink's apartment. I was tired and I couldn't keep moving from place to place.

Fortunately, when we walked through the front door of Bondi's apartment, we found that the power had been fixed while we were away. So, we hunkered down in Bondi's apartment.

I was beginning to feel a semblance of calm when our phones received an alert for the Sunset Fire located in the Hollywood Hills near Sunset Plaza, just a few short miles from the apartment on Wilcox Place. The apartment on Wilcox Place is only two short blocks down from the last evacuation zone, barely making the cut off. I felt our hearts collectively shatter.

Bondi turned on her TV, tuning into the news. We witnessed another nightmare event unfold before our eyes. A devastating scene of tourists and locals were shown fleeing hotels, theaters, homes, and stores, all running east down Hollywood Blvd. Heaps of cars were gridlocked, preventing their own salvation.

The evacuation order extended to the Chinese and El Capitan theaters, a chunk of the Walk of Fame, and the Roosevelt Hotel. Hollywood Boulevard was shown live as masses of people walked with their suitcases and bags to flee per the evacuation order.

I texted Gartner. I was concerned for his well-being. He was stubborn and headstrong, though. He told me he had his belongings packed and was ready to evacuate if needed. We argued with one another over whether he should leave then, but he refused. I couldn't find it in myself to push further.

'If something happens and Jude is left alone - I want you to take her' he texted me then.

'Don't wait until it's too late. If the fire on Sunset spreads it will happen quickly' I texted back.

'I don't know where to go and Jude is all I have now' he wrote back.

'You can come with us if you need to'

'No, I am not leaving until I have to' he texted back.

I felt irritated and emotionally drained. I needed the night to end. I knew I would not sleep well that night while worrying about Gartner and Jude's safety. I could tell the breakup was taking an emotional toll on him, and I hated that he was alone while the fires ravaged the outside world surrounding us.

Princess and Pink drove over to Bondi's apartment. We held a group meeting and agreed to pack our main belongings into Bondi and Pink's car and drive further into Los Angeles, away from the fires. The plan was to go to Echo Park, where Princess' brother and friends gathered in their apartment. There was no time to think of anything else, so we left.

The streets were empty. Every so often an escape vehicle pulled out of a nearby house or apartment complex. Families, friend groups, pets, and loved ones were all fleeing out of fear of the unknown. The winds had become forceful again, the ash and dust illuminated as it swirled through the air under the streetlights.

Ghost and Kida were in the back of Bondi's car. Kida was better in a car than Ghost. I was in the front seat as Bondi drove us east towards Echo Park. My cats were in Pink's car and Princess rode in her passenger seat. We set out into the dust-filled night.

I began to cry as we rounded a corner on Beverly. Bondi reached over and grabbed my hand. I turned to her with tears streaming down my face.

"Sorry for crying, I do not know why I am," I said, trying to play it off.

"Because this is scary, and it is okay to cry," Bondi said as she choked down her own tears. "I have lived in LA for seven years, and I've been in that apartment for five of them. Where are we supposed to go if it gets worse?"

The silence that hung in the air was as thick as the smoke and ash suffocating the sky above us. We finally made it to the next safe house. The apartment was a large loft styled two-bedroom. It had both an upstairs and downstairs. Three other people had evacuated from their homes, seeking shelter with us. The news was streaming on the television in the living room. The broadcast showed the farms in the Palisades releasing their livestock and horses out into the wild. Farmers hoped the horses could outrun and escape from the flames ripping away at their homes. It was devastating to see. I couldn't imagine how scared the animals must be, even with their heightened instincts. I hoped they would be alright.

All there was to do for those stuck and waiting inside was to drink and idly watch as homes and lives disintegrated before their eyes. I wondered again what was worse, hurricanes or fires? This felt worse than any hurricane I had endured before.

Embers from the Sunset fire were carried by the powerful winds cutting through the city, like a sharp knife breaking the surface of human skin. The embers landed on the exterior of a house and within fifteen minutes the four-story structured home was burnt to the ground.

I began to feel overwhelmed with my own reality. I could feel myself having a mini breakdown due to the discomfort. I was the exact opposite of calm and comfortable. I was thousands of miles away from my family, I had three animals and a single bag of luggage to my name, with the rest of my life strung about the apartment on Wilcox Place. Multiple fires burned intensely around the city, holding us all hostage. At any moment, the city could burn completely. The fragility of life set in me and I felt my breathing intensify.

I hoped to conceal my anxiety from the others in the house because I didn't want them to see me overreacting, but I felt like I couldn't control my emotions.

There was a dog someone had brought with them that appeared sickly. I didn't want Ghost to catch anything and began to stress over the thought of them being sick. I moved with Ghost to the office room at the front of the loft apartment and laid down on the hard floor. I brought Ghost into my embrace. I tried to recover my breath. I imagined that I was back in Florida. I could almost imagine hearing a woodpecker in the distance, and that it was a nice fall day.

I remained on the floor even after I heard footsteps, and voices wondering where I had gone. One of the voices belonged to Bondi. I heard her walk down the hallway in search of me and Ghost. I kept my eyes closed but felt her peering at me from around the corner before hearing the click from the turn of her heel. It told me she had located me and turned around to return to the others in the living room.

I wondered if my friends could tell I was mentally unfit. For a natural disaster, from a breakup, maybe from life itself. I began to cry heavily into Ghost as he nuzzled into my cheeks. He licked the salty tears as if it could heal me.

I had left my life in Orlando, claiming there was nothing there for me. I chose for my life to exist in the Hollywood foothills. I thought the western sunshine was meant for a swampy man like me. I liked who I was in Los Angeles.

Closer to midnight, first responders were finally able to knock down the sunset fire. The flames were halted from spreading any further and the process of containment began. Princess, Bondi, Pink, and I gathered our belongings and drove the cars back to Bondi's apartment in Los Feliz. I was able to pick up my rental car a day earlier than expected. I was set to leave the next day, Thursday. I just needed to get through the rest of the night.

Once we were inside, I let myself into the second bedroom and set up the air mattress
Bondi kept for anyone who ever needed it. I laid down on the mattress and felt the weight of the day cave in on myself. I began to cry again.

I thought of Gartner in bed with Jude just a few miles away from where I was. I was just glad they were okay and out of harm's way. Once I was back in Florida, I knew I would need to hibernate. I fell asleep quickly at the thought of being back in the swamp. Of being far away from all my problems in Los Angeles. Running away didn't seem so bad at the moment.

***

When the sun rose the next morning, it perturbed through the mixture of ash, smoke, and smog in the air. It casted an eerie light over the greater Los Angeles area. Gartner agreed to pick me up and drove us to the enterprise rental car in Silverlake. My rental was a large Jeep Wrangler, white, and lightly dusted with ash from the fires surrounding the city.

I drove back to the apartment on Wilcox Place. I knew it would be my last time there. Gartner helped me carry the few boxes and suitcases down to the Jeep. Once the last of the boxes were loaded into the vehicle, I followed him back up into the apartment and took a final look around.

I faced Gartner and examined him. He was shirtless and breathing heavy. He stood at a distance from me. I could tell he was as nervous as I was.

"I'm going to get my own dog," he said, breaking the silence.

"You should, I think that would be good for you," I said, and meant it.

I was unsure what else to say then. I tried to imagine Gartner a few months from now, alone with a dog he adopted and Jude. But what kind of dog would he get? Maybe a Boxer. Or maybe he wouldn't adopt one at all. I wondered if Ghost would miss Gartner. I pushed the thought out of the depths of my mind. I could already feel him slipping away, and he was standing right in front of me.

"Please tell me when you get home," he said, his voice softer than I'd heard in a while.

"Please respond if I do," I said with desperation in my voice.

"I am sorry this didn't work out," he said then, his voice tinged with sadness.
"I really tried," I responded.

He leaned forward and gave me a final sweaty hug goodbye. Then he sent me out the door. Just like that, it was over. I was at a loss for words again. My reality was happening far too quickly for me to process it. Time had been stolen from me. I mentally left the present timeline, trying to set my sights on the period in the future when I would be far away from the heartache. I needed to be alone. I could recover if I got time to myself, time to process everything.

When I arrived back at Bondi's apartment, I organized the remainder of my items scattered around her place. I organized the boxes and suitcases strategically in the backseat to make it comfortable for both Ghost and the kitties while we drove across the country.

Out of all my pets, only one of the cats could withstand car rides. She would climb around and leisurely explore the vehicle. She was the definition of a curious cat. I once thought I lost her after she had gone missing in the vehicle on a previous road trip, only for her to reveal herself from an unknown hiding spot hours later. This was after I spent most of the drive in a state of panic that I lost her.

I dilly dallied throughout the remainder of daylight, nervous and unsure of what the future held for me. I thought about the job market back home, and my inability to get a single interview before I had left to move to California. I mentally prepared myself for rejection upon my return. I tried to be hopeful that I had reaped my karma. I figured enough bad had been thrust upon me to where I must be able to receive some good karma instead. I just needed to cross the Florida state border.

I killed time loading the rest of my boxes, clothes, and suitcases strung around Bondi's apartment into the Jeep. I could feel myself subconsciously prolonging the departure. This could be my last time in Bondi's apartment for what could be months. Maybe even longer. I wondered if I had done enough with my time while I lived in Los Angeles. I hoped I did, though I could not say I felt satisfied leaving.

I sat down on the couch opposite of Bondi, Pink, and Princess and their friend Sav who sat next to her. I stared blankly at the TV that was streaming yet another throwback early 2000s music video. Princess had been on a 2000s kick lately.

"Whatcha thinking about?" Sav asked me.

I blinked rapidly as I returned from my thoughts:

"That I am ready to be thirty. I'm so over these past few years of my late twenties," I said. I couldn't hide the bitter edge in my tone.

Sav was freshly twenty-one, naive to living in Los Angeles after just shy of a year. Explorative, open minded, and optimistic. He was fresh and revitalizing. I thought to myself that if he had already befriended someone like Princess, he would do well for himself living out in LA.

"Why is that? I feel like I am gonna love my twenties," he said with excitement.

"There are a lot of big changes, and it is not that I necessarily am sensitive to change - I just think the changes themselves present a deeper conundrum. Every time I am on the cusp of an answer, a new problem is presented," I rested my head in my hand. I had no idea how I was meant to do a cross-country road trip with my current mental state.

"Yeah, this shit is for the dogs," Bondi said, causing me to give a half of a chuckle.

"Yeah, I would say I have dealt with a lot of shit that I just did not want to deal with," Princess chimed in. "It's been dramatic, but I have found that I really enjoy my peace and learned how to identify those who obstruct my peace, and how to avoid it. I think it has gotten easier for me over time, though."

"I would not say it has gotten easier to navigate life, if that's what you mean," I responded., "However, I think it has gotten easier to say yes or no to things."

"I like the way you said that Princess said, nodding her head thoughtfully. "I would agree with you, and I know what will serve me and what will not."

"I think there are some pivotal moments in your late twenties, and you must figure some shit out," I said to Sav. "There are also some harsh realities you'll have to face, and they happen one after another. I felt like from twenty-six up to thirty it's kind of nonstop. And these are the fixed points in your timeline."

"So, should we take a shot then? To eternal youth?" Sav asked mischievously.

Bondi, Pink, Princess, and Sav all took shots of tequila and continued streaming old R&B and hip-hop videos on YouTube. I gathered up the rest of my belongings, knowing the time had come to go. Once the car was fully packed, I returned to the apartment and looked around the group. They asked me not to leave. I don't want to, but I needed to. I needed to get the fuck out of Los Angeles, and I needed to get the fuck out of California. The state line to Arizona was my current finish line.

Once I was across the state border, I knew I would be reborn. It would be easier from then on. I felt I couldn't stay another night there. For my mental health, I needed to be anywhere that was closer to Florida. I don't want them to know how badly I needed to be alone, especially after the last few days. I didn't want them to think I wasn't in need of their support; because of course I was. But I needed quiet. And I needed space from everything and everyone.

The rental was fully packed. I grabbed the kitties and Ghost and loaded them into the back of the Jeep. I took my last steps inside the apartment, finding my friends streaming the Laffy Taffy music video while they took shots and danced together in the living room.

I didn't want to interrupt their fun but finally had to say: "Alright, I gotta go." I checked the clock on the wall, and it already read 9 pm.

My friends looked at me with sad eyes, and I knew my eyes reflected their own sentiment. We felt one with each other, and our emotions ran deep. Our bond expanded all the atoms that made up our anatomy and the tangible world around us. We remained in silence for a moment.

"I just want to say," my voice cracked as I started. "You all have been incredible to me these past few days. Truly, thank you for dealing with me and all of this," I gestured my arms around to emphasize the size of the 'this' I was referring to.

"You all have shown me that you are my true friends, and I love you all deeply. Thank you for everything."

At the end of my speech Bondi, Pink, and Princess were all surrounding me in a large embrace. I could see Pink's eyes as they welled up with tears.

I could feel myself crying then. My friends were crying, we were crying together.

"I do not want to leave," I said, breathing out sharply. "I know," Bondi said, hugging me again.
"We will all walk you out," Princess said.

I got into the car and that was it. It was time to go.

I left Los Angeles, California, at 9:13pm on a Thursday. It was January 9th, 2025. I began my long drive back to Orlando, Florida. I watched my friends wave goodbye to me as I drove east on Russell Avenue, tears streaming down all our faces until I could no longer see their silhouettes in the rearview mirror.

I needed gas before I began my drive to Arizona for the night. My goal was to make it out of the burning state of California, and I felt safety in the Saguaros beckoning me. Arizona was a safe space for me. I had sought refuge in the desert state more than once.

The Los Angeles streets were quiet, an ominous orange glow encompassing the city from the flames that continued to burn. Ash had started to fall more steadily since the morning. The rental car had a thin layer of speckled gray across its white paint.

I filled the tank at a Sinclair before hopping onto Interstate 5, driving South to Interstate 10 East. Once I was on the highway it wasn't until I reached Riverside that I encountered traffic that felt like I was part of the herd fleeing from the chaos behind us.

I stopped again at a gas station in Palm Springs, with heavy traffic and a damned Tumbleweed that hit the front of the rental. The wind was just as strong traversing the Coachella Valley as it was in central Los Angeles. Large masses of sticks smashed into the car ferociously, with the crunch beneath the force of the vehicle echoing through my ears. I felt myself shudder and found myself sobbing again, needing to collect myself and at the same time, needing to fill up my tank. If I could manage to fill up then, I'd have at least half a tank in the morning to drive on.

The wind was strong as I filled the tank of the Jeep. For a moment I thought I would fall asleep where I was, but I knew I had to make it to Arizona. I would feel better if I made this goal- at least that's what I told myself.

Once back on the interstate, I found myself trapped within a mess of traffic. CalDot had shut down one of the two lanes on the interstate highways leaving Palm Springs. What should have been a two-hour drive nearly doubled to four. I was exhausted but I was close to peace at last.

## *Wilcox Place*

At the end of it all, I would never hate Gartner. I would never wish him poorly, but I would also never wish him well. I would simply never speak ill of him to anyone. I merely wished to never speak about him again beyond the words contained within these hollowed pages. I spent a year falling in love with someone who dismantled everything we built in a single weekend of deathly flames.

And what did I get in return? I restarted my life, twice. Precious time had come and gone. I would not say it was wasted, but I knew it was time I was unable to gain back. The Time Bandit knew what they were doing. I missed a year of my nephew growing up. Him learning to speak new words was lost to me.

I had started to adjust to life in Los Angeles, and I had felt myself relaxing into that era of my life. Returning to Florida was daunting. I would be embarrassed from the collapse of my relationship and overwhelmed by the ever-changing expansion of my home, and I hated to admit that. Gone were the days of overgrown woods and orange groves. The marshlands I grew up to know and love turned into modern apartments, all resembling each other and boasting the same amenities as the competitor across the street.

I found myself drifting in and out of thoughts as I continued driving along Interstate 10. Ahead of me, I could see the state line of the Arizona border. I made it across at 2:37 am pacific time. I pulled over immediately at the nearest exit and stopped at the closest gas station to park the Jeep in an overnight lot. I closed my eyes and rested.

I made mistakes on Gartner's birthday that I wish I had not, but I apologized for them. Though I was not sure if the apology was ever fully received. I did not book a one-way rental car, after all. Gartner did.

When I left Gartner that day, he gave me a sweaty hug goodbye and told me I would never hear from him again. My heart sank to the depths of despair, but he never noticed. I tried to think positive as the warm light from the rising sun hit my eyes when I awoke the following morning.

As I moved through the early hours and scooped a black coffee, two hashbrowns, and an orange juice from a McDonalds next to the parking lot I had found refuge in, I noticed I had developed a dusty cough, a parting gift from the fires. They would make sure I remembered their wispy grasps that the flames had taken a hold of my life. The heat was unforgiving and relentless, consuming everything in its path and leaving a reminder, some more grim than others.

Just as much as I wished to check my phone to find a missed call from Gartner, I prayed I wouldn't. Maybe this was where we were meant to leave our love, like the wick of a candle melted through and unable to reignite. For a moment, I wished I had gotten a baggie to make it home in less time, but I shook the thought from my head as I felt several shifts occur within me.

I checked the girls' locations as I continued driving home to make sure they were okay. Their location avatars remained huddled together at Bondi's apartment in Los Feliz. I accepted this as a good sign.

As the sun began to set on my second day driving home Princess and Pink called me, avoiding asking any questions about Gartner but instead talking to me about mundane topics. Before they ended the call, they told me that they loved me and to continue driving safely. I appreciated them immensely. Each mile that put me closer to Florida and further from California cracked my heart more, torn between a home I knew in a past life and a home I had just started to create. I had no time to say goodbye to the life I knew, no time to relish in the moment of all that I had built.

I found avoiding the content pertaining to the fires was in my best interest, as I couldn't bear to be hurt any further by the sorrows of those I couldn't immediately soothe.

The winter weather outside was at its peak. The temperatures were brisk and as it hit nightfall the temperature dropped to a brittle freeze. I stopped for gas again in New Mexico.

I was wearing the same clothes I had worn the days before and as the air hit my exposed legs, I realized how uncomfortably cold it was outside. My body ignored the shock, still numb to everything. I continued to pump gas. I wondered how long a numbness like this could last. I continued to cough from the ash and dust clinging to my lungs from days spent under the plume of smoke and ash.

As the mountains faded behind me and the terrain began to alter in appearance, I rationalized the change in my head. I attempted to coerce myself into thinking it would be good for me. I let myself believe nothing was meant to be. I thought of my junior year English teacher who I had breakfast with when I was back in Orlando:

"Love is not enough," she had said. I always considered her wise, so I clung onto these words like a lifeline.

I wondered if that was the sign, then. For my destiny to come by my ancestors, sent through the other side of the vail. Love was not enough. Our relationship was born out of the desire of the same goal: to be in love. I had hoped our love was real. But if it was, then how did we meet our end? I accepted that I would never hear from him again. I would never hear his laugh. I would never stare into those ocean blue eyes as they smiled back at me.

At nearly three in the morning I arrived in Ft. Stockton, Texas. I reserved a room at the Fairfield Inn, the only Marriott Hotel in a hundred-mile radius.

Once I had snuck my animals into the hotel room through a heaping camouflage of blankets and pillows, I moved my body into the shower and let the hot water wash over me. I sat myself on the floor and tried to imagine that the water could wash away the past two days, along with the ash and dirt that still clung to my hair and body.

The sound of the running water soothed me, and I let out a deep breath. It felt like the first in days. I could finally feel a sense of peace by myself. The worst was behind me. What was done was done, and now I could focus on moving on. I finished washing up, wishing I could take longer but aware that I was under a time crunch. I had to wake up at six the following morning to make the drive to Mississippi. I was planning to stay at Hutch's place. The drive was nearly fifteen hours, but I knew I had to make it.

Before I fell asleep, I changed my alarm to eight in the morning, realizing I would be way too tired, and that I should take full advantage of the comfort of sleeping in a bed. I managed to get Ghost and the kitties out of the room the following morning, dodging the hotel staff as they tended to their duties around the premises. The biome outside was an ugly desert, with rocks and dust and small trees that were dormant for winter. They all sat scarcely around the barren stop-over town. I was ready to be somewhere else.

I considered I was making decent time once I made it to San Antonio and felt a sense of relief wash over me when the cities began to resemble the familiarity of southern architecture. Almost like something you would find in Florida. My eyes burned from all the crying I had endured, and it felt like my face was stained a permanent shade of red. Bags had formed underneath my eyes from the lack of sleep, but at least I had a shower the night before and wore fresh clothes, free from the smell of wildfires.

I reached Hutch's house just after midnight and found her waiting for me on top of her outside staircase near the front door. The homes along the beach in the gulf states were built on stilts with wooden staircases leading up to the front doors. It was meant for protection against the natural forces of water during hurricanes or flooding. I made it out of the car and over to her, giving her a long, grateful hug. I breathed in the coastal air and felt immensely better to be with one of my oldest friends and closer to the East Coast.

She led me to my room and instructed me to get to sleep. She would be gone in the morning but had promised to bring me back breakfast. She told me her sister Jules had been visiting from college and was asleep in the room opposite where I was. She would be there in the morning when I woke up. I was excited to see her after several years.

Hutch turned on the television in the room before she left to stream my favorite show: Sex and the City. I smiled at her for the kind gesture, and before she left she gave me one last hug, followed by a kiss on the cheek. Then she exited the room and closed the door behind her. I knew I was lucky to have friends all over the country who would look out for me. I also knew I would do the same for them, finding comfort in knowing I conceived small safe spaces throughout the states.

Somehow, I knew I would feel better. My deep state of hurt had already softened when I saw Hutch's large brown eyes and wide smile waiting for me on her doorstep. No questions asked. No judgements were given, only love and adoration. I may not have the love I craved the most, but I had something better: the love I deserved from those who cared for me, all of me, every last bit of me, every atom that encompassed my flesh-encased skeleton.

California would always be a home for me, I knew that. I built a life for myself in the walls of the city of angels. I had favorite restaurants. I knew which grocery store carried the best stock. I knew which roads to take if highways were jammed with traffic. I had friends who lived from Silver Lake to Cerritos to Riverside to Anaheim to San Jose. The love of my life might not exist in California, but there were plenty of others who loved me in the city. No matter if Gartner and I were no longer together, there would always be a sense of belonging I had there.

I cried and coughed myself to sleep, remembering all that I could of the life I had built with him. I wondered when I would make it back to Los Angeles, or when I would be able to paint my love letter for all the city had taught me, and for what Gartner had shown me.

The following morning, I remained frozen in the warmth of Hutch's guest bed. My kitties and Ghost had surrounded themselves around me, protecting me the entire night. I wondered if they knew where we had spent the night - and where we were headed after. I wondered if they would be comforted by the familiar greenery of Florida shrubbery.

Once I summoned the strength and courage to show myself in the public quarters of the house, I found Jules seated on the living room couch watching television.

Once she caught sight of me, she beamed at me from her sprawled position from the couch. The last time I had seen her, she was just at the start of high school. She was in university now. I was reminded of the Time Bandit yet again, knowing the years had flown by too quickly for me to grasp.

"It's nice to see you," she said, bringing me to the present moment. "When Hutch told me you were coming in on your way home, I delayed my drive back up to school for the night so I could see you!" she said with glee.

"That's so sweet, it's nice to see you too! I missed you and your sister," I said.

I wondered if Hutch had told her why I had driven home so suddenly but suspected she had kept it to herself - our bond had formed itself off a no-repeating-information clause. We stuck to it.

I might not be home in Florida yet, but I was in the next best thing in Pascagoula, Mississippi. I was safe here, kept coddled in the warmth of Jules' and Hutche's love.

Hutch returned shortly after I awoke with breakfast. I packed the small backpack I brought up with me the night before and began to load my animals back into the rental after we shared egg and sausage sandwiches with one another. I wished I could have stayed longer, but I desperately needed to be in a place where I could stabilize myself in the comfort of my own personal solace.

As I loaded the rest of the vehicle with my belongings and made for my exit, we found Hutch's boyfriend, Chandler, and his father, Rick, talking in the driveway next to my vehicle. Chandler introduced me to Rick and informed him of my drive from California to Florida. Their interests were piqued by the fires that ravaged the state, while I was desperate to forget them. I found myself stifling another cough as I was asked about my experience. I found myself stuttering to answer for a few seconds before Hutch interjected and saved me from answering myself.

"That's why he left - he had a lot going on and the fires were the tipping point," she said. Simple and to the point, while leaving little to be speculated on. The answer was there, non-descriptive.

"We found some sticks embedded into the grille of your rental and removed them for you," Chandler said to me, which I recognized as a gesture of kindness.
I laughed and said, "Thanks. That was from a big ass tumbleweed that flew in front of me as I was fleeing the city

driving through Palm Springs. I left it there as a traumatic reminder, I guess."

The group laughed at my honest and vulnerable confession, and I laughed with them. There would come a time when this would be a distant memory, and I wondered how I would interpret it fifty years from now.

I said heartfelt goodbyes and hugged Hutch for an undefinable amount of time, where even the Time Bandit couldn't steal the moment from us.

As I drove away from Hutch and Chandler's home, I found myself crying again. I allowed myself to feel every emotion I could feel. I let myself imagine another life, where Gartner and I returned to Los Angeles and lived out our lives together. Then my thoughts would spiral from fear and the shock from the reality of it all, with our ending continuing to be bitter and bleak. I wondered if my daydreaming was a message from beyond the vail, confirming what I had already known to be true - that we were never meant to last.

What we had was not perfect, but not everything in life that held significance was bound to be perfect. Our time together was our own, something the Time Bandit could never take away from me. Our story was one that was meant to be told, with the memories condensed into a narrative of adoration. The good and the bad, every facet of our devotion on display. Etched on paper. We will always have the story of Wilcox Place.

"...Yeah, you've changed
But did I ever know you?
Or did I hold you
Facing away from me
The air in your room never moves
Live and die by TV no one's watching
Do you hate me?
When this is over
Maybe then we'll get some sleep
I've been picking names for our children
You've been wondering how you're gonna feed them
Love is not enough in this world
But I still believe in Nebraska dreaming
'Cause I'd rather die
Then be anything but your girl
I never meant to hurt you
But somehow, I knew I would
Will it be like this forever?
I'd reach into your body
And fix you if I could
Will I feel like this forever? (Forever, forever, forever?)
Are you angry?
Do you hate me?
And darling, time may forgive me
But I won't..."

- Ethel Cain: Waco, Texas

## Thank You:

Thank you to my friends and family who supported me throughout the years of my life leading up to this moment. To my parents, my sister, my aunts, and cousins who have supported me - even if they have not always been able to understand my point of view fully. To my friends, thank you for supporting me in this journey, and thank you for filling me with love. I am eternally grateful.

Thank you to my chocolate family and my managers who not only encouraged me to write but turned a blind eye when I would be typing away on my iPad in the back when I had downtime.

Thank you to B, who gave me their highly logical opinion on some very important information.

And to my dear friend, Karissa, thank you for adopting the role as my editor-in-chief, thank you for your dedication not only as my friend but as a supporter of my writing, to help me perfect my craft. You have been so pivotal to the successful publication I am so eternally grateful. Thank you for encouraging my growth. You have been amazing in every sense of the word.

## About the Author:

G.P. Anthony was born and raised in Orlando, FL. He has lived in Denver, Colorado and Los Angeles, California. He draws inspiration from his life. He has been an avid writer his entire life and 'Wilcox Place' is his debut publication.

Authors Note:

Wilcox Place was written out of love and desperation to remember. I wrote the novel over the course of one year; I used Microsoft Word to write the novel and Google Docs to edit the novel with my editor Karissa. I designed the cover including the front, back, and spine on Adobe InDesign and Adobe Illustrator.

www.ingramcontent.com/pod-product-compliance
Lightning Source LLC
Chambersburg PA
CBHW022033240626
47154CB00007B/2380